Pictures of Us

Pictures of Us

todd alexander

HODDER

HODDER AUSTRALIA

Published in Australia and New Zealand in 2006
by Hodder Australia
(An imprint of Hachette Livre Australia Pty Limited)
Level 17, 207 Kent Street, Sydney NSW 2000
Website: www.hachette.com.au

National Library of Australia
Cataloguing-in-Publication data

Alexander, Todd.
  Pictures of us : a novel.

  ISBN 0 7336 2029 9.

  I. Title.

A823.4

Text design and typesetting in 11.5/17.5 pt Sabon by Bookhouse, Sydney
Printed in Australia by Griffin Press, Adelaide
Cover design by Ellie Exarchos
Cover image by Getty Images

Hachette Livre Australia's policy is to use papers
that are natural, renewable and recyclable products
and made from wood grown in sustainable forests.
The logging and manufacturing processes are expected
to conform to the environmental regulations
of the country of origin.

For Judy and Peter –
the best parents a boy
could hope to have.

Maggie

'You have to be strong, Maggie. Just stay strong.'

Maggie was shocked to hear such a cliché and stared at her friend in disbelief. She thought it was a stupid thing to say to someone whose husband might be dying. Strong? Strong? She felt like arguing, why do I have to stay strong? But outbursts of that type were so unlike Margaret Apperton – she was a well-spoken woman who kept her emotions to herself. Why did no one know what to say in moments such as these?

The table had turned completely silent and no one could look her in the eyes. Their lunches lay untouched in the warm sunlight. It was almost as if *she* was the one who'd been hurt. Please, someone say something, she thought. I can handle anything but this silence.

She rose slowly from the table, the feet of her chair making a high-pitched scraping sound. Two or three of her friends made a half-hearted move to follow, but Maggie left them behind as she walked numbly from the restaurant.

The lunch had begun so beautifully with a bright blue sky, the harbour's emerald green glimmering with the glare from the sun and seagulls riding high on invisible currents of air. Once a month she and five friends took the train to Sydney and spent the afternoon in a nice restaurant, drinking wine and chatting about their lives. Maggie started the club after spending two years of retirement bored and lonely, placing an advert in her local paper seeking a ladies' luncheon club. It'd been so out of character that she feared what her children would have thought, had they known she was being so bold.

'I just need some company while your father is at work,' she would have defended herself weakly.

The first lunch was overly formal – six complete strangers meeting for the first time, asking polite questions about each other's lives and answering with reserve. Maggie thought about cancelling the club after its forced debut; at fifty-seven she felt it was too late for new starts. Then Kathy called her the next day to say thanks and to help organise another lunch. Kathy's enthusiasm had overwhelmed Maggie and she had felt trapped into going again. It had, after all, been her idea.

Maggie woke at six as usual, the morning birdcalls serving as her alarm. She got up, went to the toilet and let the dog in. It was Patrick's dog really – a frumpy but lovable mongrel called Leroy. He followed Maggie everywhere unless Patrick came home, then it was as if Maggie didn't exist. In the mornings the dog was docile and affectionate, following her from room to room and standing at her feet as she cooked Marcus' breakfast.

While the eggs were crackling away, she made herself some herbal tea and toast with marmalade. Together, she and Leroy looked out at the Broadwater as two pelicans circled in to land. She could almost hear what the dog was thinking – if I could jump that bloody fence I'd get amongst ya's – and, as if sharing the joke, he turned to look at her and licked his lips. She threw him the crusts of her toast, marvelled at his peculiar ability to smile, and went back to the stove to turn the eggs.

Marcus was still snoring when she went into the spare room to wake him. They only ever shared the same bed if they had company, because his snoring was so pervasive it kept her awake and made her irritable. She stared a moment at his exposed foot, its heel rough and scaly, the toes oversized and hairy.

'Breakfast.'

He half grunted and came to instantly. 'I was dreaming about plane crashes again,' he mumbled. 'Can't seem to shake it.' This was one of his recurring dreams, along with the one where he lost his teeth, rotted out with decay. He read that dreaming about losing teeth was a sign of sexual frustration but hadn't managed to find out about crashing planes.

'Breakfast is on the table,' she repeated, not wishing to enter into today's analysis.

Leroy came in and began licking between Marcus' toes. 'Hey, fella.' He smiled and patted the bed. 'Come jump up here.' With tail wagging, Leroy jumped onto the bed and landed heavily on Marcus' chest.

'Aw,' he moaned, 'you're getting heavier, old boy.'

3

'Marcus, you don't want to be late for work,' Maggie urged him to get up.

'I'll be right,' Marcus said as he continued to rouse Leroy into an energetic frenzy.

So much for him being quiet today, she thought disapprovingly.

Maggie and Marcus owned a restaurant supply company that had begun as an operation from a friend's garage and grown to have a multi-million-dollar turnover. Maggie felt the stress of her office administrator role had steadily increased as the company grew in size and eventually knew it was time to retire. The business looked after them well; they'd come a long way since Marcus was working three jobs to support Maggie and their young children.

When Maggie announced her retirement plans to Marcus he was supportive and encouraging and told her that she deserved to have time to herself, she had been integral to the company's growth so retiring before him could be her reward. She thought that he would find it impossible *not* to join her in retiring, hoping they could rekindle some of the friendship responsible for bringing them together in the first place, but he insisted that he was still healthy enough to keep working and the ninety-minute drive wasn't too taxing. Now, almost seven years later, he was sixty-eight and still working a five-day week to retain absolute control of the business.

Marcus finished eating and went to have a quick shower. Maggie rinsed the breakfast dishes and fed Leroy some raw chicken wings. Leafing through the cable television guide was a habit she was unable to break, but sitting in front of the TV for hours on end was something she refused to indulge in.

'What's on tonight?' Marcus asked.

'Not sure,' she replied, without looking up. 'I'll probably be too tired after our lunch.' The 'our' was used to exclude Marcus and he detected it easily.

'Ah, of course,' he said, smiling in defeat. He pecked her on the cheek and walked out the door, slamming the screen behind him. Every morning the loud bang of the screen made her clench her teeth but she'd long given up reminding him to close it quietly. Maggie didn't look him in the eye to say goodbye, she rarely did.

At eight o'clock she made the twenty-minute walk to Kathy's house and joined the chaos of getting three school-aged children ready. They all called her Maggie, which was a nice compromise between calling her Aunty or Gran (which she found too affectionate). On lunch days Maggie always went to Kathy's in the morning. The excitability of young children provided a welcome change of pace to Marcus' silent shuffling around the house.

The walk to Kathy's was mostly uphill and it bothered Maggie that with each passing year she felt it becoming more difficult. She found herself resting against the boot of a car at various stages to catch her breath, making her feel every one of her sixty-two years.

There was no need to knock on Kathy's door – it was always unlocked, if not ajar, and she had been given an open invitation early in the friendship. As she opened the door,

Emily ran out in front of her, screaming. David, her eight-year-old brother, followed closely.

'Oh dear, hang on a moment,' Maggie stopped them. 'What's going on?'

'David put my Action Man in the toilet!' Emily wailed.

'Did not!' David yelled.

'Did so!'

'Oh, I'm sure he didn't do it on purpose,' Maggie said awkwardly.

'I told you, Emily, Action Man was just looking for his enemies in the pipes.'

Quite ingenious of him, thought Maggie, best to diffuse the situation by playing along with him. 'My son Patrick used to have an Action Man and he was forever sneaking into my drains and toilets. I remember I had to keep all the toilet lids closed and the plugs in all the sinks.'

Emily looked at Maggie inquisitively. 'Really?'

Maggie nodded slowly so Emily smoothed over her sodden Action Man and walked away satisfied.

David chuckled. 'Thanks, Maggie, she was gonna dob on me and Mum would'a lost it.'

Maggie watched as he went back into the house, deciding to leave the comment hanging. Disciplining other people's children wasn't something she did. Maggie wasn't very comfortable with children and had treated her own like adults. She couldn't fathom how their little minds worked and preferred not to risk getting close. She kept herself at a safe distance because she couldn't bear the thought of getting too attached to such fragile beings. She made her way into the kitchen where Kathy was buttering the top slice of a toast stack.

'Hi,' Kathy said. 'You're looking nice.'

Maggie always tried to make an effort on lunch days. The blue dress she wore was quite a snug fit but the colour highlighted her eyes and made the most of her grey hair. 'Thank you,' she blushed, unable to accept compliments easily. 'I think I'm putting on a bit of weight. It's a size sixteen and it seems to be getting tighter each time I wear it.'

'Maybe it's shrinking,' Brett, Kathy's oldest, charmed her.

'Oh, I don't think I can blame it on my washing machine,' Maggie blushed again. Blushing in front of a fourteen year old, for goodness' sake.

'Well, size sixteen is hardly enormous, Maggie,' Kathy said.

'I know, but I remember when I was a size twelve, would you believe?' In fact, she had been a size eight when she had first met Marcus.

'Size twelve! Ha! Imagine being a fourteen through adolescence and ending up a size twenty,' Kathy said, clutching a corner of her oversized dress. Kathy wore her weight in a motherly kind of way. Maggie could see that the children loved cuddling into their mother's bulk; it was one sure way of calming them down.

Maggie's mobile rang in her handbag. Brett chuckled to himself, sniggering at an oldie with a mod con. Marcus had given it to her just last Christmas for emergencies, but it only ever rang when he called to ask her something related to the office systems she'd put in place. She hurried into the living room, which was littered with toys and children's clothing.

'Hello, Maggie speaking,' she said loudly into the small device.

'Of course it's you speaking, it's your phone.'

'Hello, Marcus, what's the matter?'

'Nothing,' he sighed. 'I was wondering if you were okay. You seemed a bit distant this morning. Everything all right?'

Maggie looked at the caller ID display. Was this her husband? He *never* asked her how she was, what she was thinking, why she was sometimes quiet.

'Marcus, I, I . . .' She was simply lost for words.

'Something's wrong, isn't it?'

'No, no!' She felt embarrassed, hoping he wouldn't ask her any more questions. 'I'm surprised by your call, that's all. I was fine this morning, just thinking about lunch, you know how I get. You shouldn't worry about me.'

'I know, but sometimes I can't help it.'

'Well, no need to. I'm fine, but thank you for calling.'

'I was just thinking about you, that's all. I wanted to tell you I hope you have a beautiful lunch today. I . . . I . . . lo–'

'Goodbye,' she said quickly, uncomfortable with this level of emotion. 'I'll see you tonight.'

He hung up.

Maggie was tempted to call him back to make sure there was nothing he was meant to be telling her. Did he really just say those things? For the life of her she couldn't remember the last time he'd ever showed any interest in her life. Maggie frowned and shook her head. Foolish woman! To think that he may have said the L word! She realised hearing three simple words could have had a profound effect on her. I love you. She could have said them to him, she supposed, but it had been so long since she had said them to anyone. Instead, she would surprise him with a nice meal tonight, then she would say, 'I just wanted you to know I appreciate you.'

'Good news, Maggie?' Brett asked as she re-entered the kitchen.

The colour rose again in Maggie's cheeks. Why did children have to be so perceptive? 'No, it was nothing.'

'I bet,' Kathy said. 'You look like a schoolgirl.'

Maggie shook her head again. 'That was my husband – just calling to wish me a beautiful day.'

'Oooh!' the children all chimed at once.

Maggie smiled inwardly, surprised that she should be so affected by Marcus' call. When was the last time she felt needed by anyone? She had wanted to feel it for longer than she could remember.

Maggie started making the kids' lunches while the family sat down to eat breakfast. In all these years she had never sat down to eat a meal with them. Maggie preferred to keep herself busy with the task at hand, any task really. She took their orders for lunch and made sandwiches according to their individual specifications. Thin cheese slices for Emily, three slices of devon for Brett.

Before too long, they had finished their breakfasts and were rushing about getting their bags packed. Maggie liked it least when it was time to say goodbye because Kathy insisted all three of them kiss and hug her. Affection was a confrontation and, in the face of it, she visibly tensed. Brett was first with his teenaged restraint and she could handle that because he disliked the routine almost as much as she did. A taut peck near her ear and a nice pat on the back – easy. David was next, he was more into cuddling than kissing so she could easily plant one on the top of his head as he threw his arms around her. Last, and most dreaded, was Emily, who planted three or four wet kisses on Maggie's lips, hugged her with tiny hands which travelled all over her back and then returned for one or two more kisses. She went through this charade purely for Kathy, as a thank you for the friendship she'd provided all these years.

As Kathy showered, Maggie washed the dishes and tidied the kitchen. When that was done, she busied herself with tidying the lounge room and was even able to make all of the children's beds before Kathy was ready. Maggie knew Kathy wouldn't notice her tidying until later that night.

Maggie usually won their traditional game of Scrabble but Kathy could be lucky with her letters on rare occasions. Today was one of those days. The secret, of course, was using all letters at once. Fifty bonus points could make all the difference.

They'd been playing for around an hour, sipping tea and passing time until they left for the train. Kathy was two points in front of Maggie and had just placed a word worth twelve, 'human'. Maggie looked at her letters for three minutes until out of the blue, the word came to her. IERMOSE. She could intersect with Kathy's 'M' to create 'memories', thereby using all her letters. It was nearing the end of the game, there was no way Kathy could catch her now.

'Memories,' Kathy said, getting up from the table to stretch her legs. 'And fifty points! Quite a fitting word, though. I was just thinking about how our lunches began. How, when I first met you, I knew I'd get along with you. Remember? Emily had just been born; leaving her with my Mum once a month and doing something for myself was heaven for me.'

'Yes, I'm sure it must have been,' Maggie said, not sure of where this was going.

'You know, my mother wasn't much of a grandma to the boys when she was alive. I think she was afraid of kids, worried that she'd come to rely on them for something. When she died, I knew I'd never get over the grief of losing her, knew that I'd always feel like picking up the phone just to have a chat. I also thought that I'd never have anyone anywhere near as special as her. I just want you to know that I'm so glad you're in my life. You've made these past few years so much easier on me – and the kids adore you!'

'Thank you, Kathy,' Maggie said bashfully. 'I'm glad to be with you too.'

'Just so long as you know how special you are to us all,' Kathy said, smiling. 'Even Brett, though he'd never say it.'

'Is there something in the air today?' Maggie said jokingly. 'Everyone I know is telling me how special I am.'

'Well, I hate you for beating me at Scrabble, but aside from that you're okay,' Kathy said, followed by a sly laugh.

They finished their game (Maggie won by thirty-two), and drove to the train. They were met at the station by the other ladies and there was something conspiratorial about the way they were huddled, and the fact that all four of them were there before Maggie and Kathy.

'Well, hello, Mrs Apperton,' Cheryl announced. 'The ladies and I have worked it out. Today marks our fifth anniversary of lunching and we owe it all to you, dear. From all of us, a big thank you for creating the club that brought us all together!' She produced a bottle of sparkling wine from a cooler bag and a beautifully wrapped gift for Maggie. Val started handing out plastic cups.

'I, I . . . I'm totally stunned,' Maggie began, tears welling in her eyes. 'Today has been the most marvellous day. I feel very special and this just takes the cake. Five years is hard to believe! I count all five of you as my closest friends and I thank you for this. Who would have thought after our first awkward lunch we would be here celebrating our fifth anniversary?'

'The even better news,' said Cheryl, her voice raspy after a lifetime of smoking cigarettes, 'is that Val and I pulled off a bit of a jackpot last night. Today's on us, ladies – no questions or arguments. Enjoy yourselves!'

By now they each had a cup of wine and were toasting toward the middle of the group.

Maggie led the cheer, 'To us.'

Before the train arrived, Maggie opened the gift, relishing the moment. She was delighted to find a book signed by one of her favourite authors, some tools for her garden and a small bottle of perfume.

The six of them got quite silly on the journey to Sydney as the train rocked along the track and the bubbly started to take effect. The warm rays of the sun through the window and the alcohol had Maggie feeling particularly giddy.

Val had made a booking for them at a seafood restaurant right on the harbour's doorstep. It was set back from the boardwalk but still provided a lovely view of the Opera House and the coming and going ferries. Although several school excursions walked noisily past their table, Maggie couldn't have been happier with this restaurant. She usually found something appealing on the menu, the service was great and she always got a silent thrill knowing that the place purchased things from Marcus' company. She felt so happy, so lifted by the unexpected events of the morning. Love was something she didn't think about often, something she no longer knew how to express, yet here she was, on a day like any other, but for some reason she felt more loved, more alive, than since she was a young woman.

Lunchtime conversations began around what dish each one of them was thinking of choosing. They all read their menus aloud and discussed what took their fancy. Maggie was a fish lover – light and tasty, she found it perfect for lunch. She felt that red meat only went well with red wine and three or four glasses of red at lunch would have had her under the table. No, white wine was a lunch drink and fish was the perfect accompaniment.

Today she chose grilled barramundi for her main and a potato and fennel soup to begin with. The waiter took their orders and as he left they all began to giggle like schoolgirls. He was handsome in a manufactured way and they suspected he was gay. Of the five of them, Maggie had told only Kathy about Patrick, and that she disapproved of the path he had chosen for his life.

'God, I love this city,' Brigette said.

'You know, I've never really been to another one.' Maggie frowned as she took a bite of her bread roll.

'What?' Cheryl said in astonishment.

'Well, outside Australia, I mean. I was brought up in Melbourne, but that doesn't count.'

'You ought to get Marcus to take you to visit Isabel,' Kathy said.

'No, he'd never take a holiday...only business trips and then he's always gone alone. He once went to France for business and he said it was a complete waste of time, that the French are far too rude. He doesn't believe in expensive trips for leisure.'

'How is Isabel going, Maggie? Have you heard from her?' Cheryl asked.

'Oh yes, she writes these very long letters that come straight from her diary. It's strange, they read like a run-down of her daily itinerary and she shares some very odd situations. I think she writes them for Marcus more than me. They seem to share a special bond...'

'Well...' Cheryl chuckled, 'do tell.'

Maggie noticed that the other conversations around the table had stopped and each of the ladies was focused on her.

'She wrote about an exhibition she saw at the Pompidou.' Goodness, I hope I don't sound pompous, she thought. 'It was called "Masculine and Feminine". In her letter, she wrote there were so many graphic depictions of genitals, or to use Isabel's words, "d's and c's and open a'holes" that she felt like a voyeur and had to run outside for fresh air for fear of throwing up.'

It embarrassed Maggie to even intimate the words that Isabel had written deliberately to shock her.

'She uses words like that to her *mother*?' Val questioned.

'I think it's great that she does,' Cheryl said. 'My kids are that open with me.'

'Unfortunately, that's the irony,' Maggie sighed. 'Isabel isn't at all open with me. In her letters she never asks about what's happening here – it's just "Dear Maggie and Dad", and then she launches into a travelogue of events without saying how she really is, and whether she's seeing anyone . . . all those things a mother likes to know.'

'Well, at least she writes,' Norma said into her glass of wine. She was referring to her own son, a merchant banker living in London.

'You don't hear from Hal at all?'

'Christmas and birthdays,' Norma sighed. 'I suppose that's better than nothing. Tell me, Maggie, has Isabel been over to London lately?'

Maggie would have preferred to be in the conversation that was taking place between Kathy and Brigette. She couldn't help feeling a particular stab of jealousy at the sight of them giggling away while Maggie had to repel Norma's fantasy. She had been insisting Isabel stay for a weekend at her son's cottage in Bath. This had been persisting for close to two years and the only time Maggie ever mentioned it to Isabel, she'd slammed down the phone.

'She seems so busy,' Maggie said to Norma. 'Most of the articles she writes for the magazine are researched on the weekend,' she added a little unconvincingly.

'Horny Hal still after Isabel, is he?' Cheryl cackled from the other end of the table.

The rest of them burst into laughter – they all knew Hal had no interest in Isabel; this match-making was all his mother's idea.

'Oh, sod off, Cheryl!' Norma said, gulping some more wine.

There was more laughter as the handsome waiter delivered their entrees.

'Strangest thing . . .' Kathy whispered in Maggie's ear as the waiter went to retrieve the other three plates from the kitchen, 'I felt a flush through my body at the scent of his cologne.'

'I don't think he'd be interested in your type, somehow dear,' Maggie teased.

'How is Patrick?' Kathy asked.

'What?' Maggie said, realising the connection Kathy had made between her son and the waiter. 'He's fine, he hasn't come to see Leroy for a few weeks but I know he's always busy.'

'So he does tell you what he gets up to?'

'Oh my heavens, no! We don't discuss those things. In fact, all he usually says is in disagreement with something I've said, or to tell me he doesn't like what I'm wearing, my perfume's too strong.'

'You should tell him to wise up, Maggie.'

'I'm used to it now, Kathy. He's Sagittarian, he always speaks his mind and I have learnt to accept that.'

'As long as he doesn't upset you. Now eat up before your soup gets cold.'

'Oh, God,' Kathy moaned as she tucked into her oysters with delight.

'Here's to the Cleopatra machine we won on last night!' Cheryl raised her glass. 'May it continue to provide us with lunches for months to come.'

'And to our anniversary!' Maggie added.

'I have to ask you all,' Brigette said seriously and narrowed her eyes, 'is this outfit too . . . bright?'

There were a few moments of no one knowing what to say.

'That depends on whether I'm wearing my sunglasses or not,' sniggered Cheryl.

'Oh, sod off, Cheryl!' Norma said again and they all giggled.

They took it in turns tasting each other's entrees – with the exception of Kathy who'd consumed her dozen oysters without offering any to the others.

'Chocolate and oysters,' she said dryly, 'you'd be hard-pressed getting me to share them for anything less than sex.'

'I think you're pretty safe around us,' Val joked.

'Ladies,' Kathy said as she motioned for a waitress to bring another bottle of wine. 'You're all mothers – should I worry about my oldest smoking pot?'

Between them they had thirteen children and nine grandchildren.

'How old is he?' Cheryl asked.

'Fourteen,' Kathy said with a shrug. Maggie was disappointed to find out that Brett smoked marijuana but she couldn't condemn him as she suspected her own son of doing the same at his age, and then some.

'Well, I knew that my son was in with the wrong crowd,' Brigette said, her accent making its first strong appearance of the day as she began her third glass of wine, 'but I don't think it was the marijuana smoking I should have been concerned about. Perhaps if I had acknowledged it instead of allowing him to hide his drug taking, he would still be alive today.'

Brigette's only child had died twenty years earlier when he had stolen a car and slammed it into a traffic light as the police pursued him. She never referred to him by name, it was always 'my son'. Come to think of it, Maggie wasn't even sure she knew his name, but she didn't dare ask it.

'Not that I mean to worry you, Kathy,' Brigette continued, 'but if I had my chance again I think I'd demand an open exchange with him. No secrets.'

'Oh, I'm quite glad Patrick and I have secrets,' Maggie said, speaking more to herself than anyone in particular. 'I don't need to know everything he does.'

'My girls told me everything,' Cheryl said. 'I knew every period, every kiss, and each loss of virginity.'

'I just don't want to encourage him,' Kathy said. 'I don't want him to be one of those layabouts with no ambition. I went out with a boy like that once . . . and ended up raising his three children alone.'

'My advice?' Cheryl offered. 'Smoke a joint with him and tell him you understand, but you only want him to do it once a week at most. Always with his friends, and never alone or when they have to drive or are supposed to study or anything.'

'That's outrageous!' Norma shrieked.

'Oh, I don't know,' Maggie turned to Kathy. 'You seem to be doing a great job embracing everything you know about your kids. You show them that you're one of their friends and they respect you for that. It's something I could never do with mine.'

18

'It's never too late, Maggie,' Kathy said. 'I haven't had pot in about ten years,' she added with only a hint of suggestion.

'Why don't you get some for all of us?' Cheryl picked up on the hint.

'Count me out.' Brigette put her wine glass firmly back down on the table.

'You've all lost your minds,' Maggie said with a smile to defuse the situation. 'I'm off to the ladies.'

In the bathroom, she felt a sense of dread. How gut-wrenching that life couldn't continue without her deteriorating. Her future was mapped out and it terrified her that she had no control over how it would end. Though she had finished, she sat on the toilet a few moments longer to regain her composure and steady her rising blood pressure. Maggie eventually made her way to the basin to wash her hands. It was then that she noticed tightness in her forehead, the first sign she was getting drunk. She splashed some cold water on her face and stared at herself in the enormous mirror.

What is it, Maggie? What insanity are you going to let spoil this perfect day? She splashed a little more cold water over her arms and shook away the excess moisture, and her doubts. The main course would be served soon.

As she approached the table, everything softened as though broadcast through a dream. None of the ladies would look at her, consciously avoiding her gaze. Only Kathy made eye contact, her face white with shock. In one hand she held

Maggie's mobile and she slowly rose to hold Maggie's hands in the other.

'Maggie, that was Marcus' work. He's had an accident.'

Maggie began to shake her head. That can't be right. She made her way to her chair and sat down, taking a gulp of wine and a deep breath. The room suddenly turned silent.

'So, what's he gone and done?' Maggie tried to be cheery, though she knew from her friends' faces things must be serious.

Kathy moved her hand up Maggie's arm, as if to warn her of the state of Marcus' condition. 'It happened on the freeway, sweetheart. There was an accident and they've taken him to hospital. They say he's on life support.'

'Where is he?'

'Royal North Shore.'

'I have no idea what to say,' Maggie said awkwardly. 'I suppose I ought to know what to do in this situation but I'm a little lost. I'm sorry for spoiling everyone's lunch. I guess I should go . . .' her voice trailed off.

'You have to be strong, Maggie. Just stay strong.' Norma. It was all Maggie could do to stop herself from wringing her neck.

Maggie got up slowly from the table, her chair scraping against the wooden floor. Then the sounds around her became audible again. The chink of cutlery. The drone of boat engines. Squawking seagulls. The hum of distant traffic and thunder of trains. A plate dropped in the kitchen. Her own heartbeat. It was suddenly hard to breathe – if she didn't move she would faint. She clutched her bag, snatched the blasted phone back from Kathy – who answers somebody else's mobile anyway? – and hurried away from the table, down the stairs and around the side of the sandstone building. She noticed she was on grass and for a brief moment she felt like throwing herself down. Instead, she placed one hand against the cool of the stone. She wasn't sure how long she leaned there fearing she might vomit. Absurdly, she thought I must explain this sensation to Marcus and it took her a few moments to comprehend that there may not be any more conversations to have. She shuffled over to the street and threw out her arm to hail a passing taxi. Her vision was blurry, so the tears had come after all.

The taxi smelled strongly of the driver's sweat, of stale bread, and of a sickly sweet deodoriser. She apologised to the driver, got out and closed the door almost as swiftly as she'd opened it. And then she vomited. A burning, painful rejection of soup and wine, a return to sobriety and reality. Taking a moment to regain her composure, she longed for water but decided she should get to the hospital as quickly as possible, for how could she ever live with herself if her hunt for water was the one thing that kept her from spending Marcus' last moments with him?

It took longer to hail a second taxi and Maggie found it difficult to concentrate on the task. The acid bile coated her tongue and the sunlight made it nearly impossible to gauge whether each passing taxi had its vacant light on. Eventually, she gave up trying to distinguish and stood there on the side of the road feeling foolish with her arm held straight out, hanging with blind hope.

What if he dies? she thought. What if the one constant in her life simply ceased to be? Tears welled in her eyes and her throat burned as she tried half-heartedly to imagine a life without Marcus. Who did she have left aside from Kathy? The simple answer was no one. Patrick couldn't be relied upon for anything and the rift between her and Isabel was now impossibly deep and, even if Maggie wanted to try to bridge it, Isabel was so stubborn that she'd push Maggie even further away at the first sign of an attempted reconciliation. It scared her to think of being alone in the world, to be forced to concede the reason she had not managed to hold on to anyone other than Kathy and these tenuous ties to the four other women who joined her for lunch once a month.

Her arm began to ache but she still stood firm, clutching her bag with the other hand. The reality of death began to wash over her. The commitment to this one event absolutely filled her with dread, how trying it was going to be dealing with this alone, to no longer be needed by anyone. No, she thought, this can't be about my future alone. This was a time to think about Marcus and to turn to a god for the first time in her life, to pray for his safety, beg for his life. Why was she so desperate to keep him? It wasn't as if they were intimate any more, not as though they laughed together or shared private thoughts. But there was just so much she wanted to say, questions she needed answers to, explanations for so many things in their past. Now her past would go untouched, and she'd be forced to continue hiding behind her veneer of aloofness but that was the last thing she wanted now that her life was on a course beyond her control. But what if he wasn't dying? What if the accident wasn't as bad as Kathy made out, what if he was doing fine now and went on living another ten, twenty years? Stop it! She pleaded to the invisible powers of fate, please stop, I don't want to go this way any more.

A cab pulled up just in front of her but she saw the silhouette of someone sitting in the back seat. Perhaps they were getting out? The back door opened and Maggie rushed toward it. Kathy poked her head out of the cab and urged her to get in.

'How on earth?' Maggie began in bewilderment.

'I hailed it from outside the restaurant,' Kathy explained. 'Come on, get in. You didn't think I was gonna let you go alone, did you?'

'But how did you find me?' Maggie asked as she climbed awkwardly into the cab, banging her knee slightly against the metal of the door.

'It was a fluke. I called your mobile, you didn't answer, I figured I'd meet you at the hospital . . . then I saw you with your arm stuck out like a scarecrow.'

'Oh, yes. Right. You called me? I didn't hear.' Maggie closed the door behind her. 'Oh, my phone – I guess I should try to call Patrick and Isabel, let them know what's happened.'

'Would you like me to do it?' Kathy asked as the cab took a sharp turn north.

'It's okay, I think I should try.' Maggie realised she wasn't wearing her seatbelt and fumbled with the strap to get it around her. The strap locked in its holder and she tugged at it sharply several times before taking a deep breath and trying again, slowly. The buckle clicked in place. She paused to take another deep breath. She was now remarkably composed, just having Kathy by her side made things seem manageable.

'He'll be okay, Maggie,' Kathy attempted to soothe her even further. 'Don't alarm the kids just yet, try to stay calm.'

Kathy was right, of course, but something made Maggie's skin crawl at another person telling her how to behave in the situation, *her* situation.

The talkback radio host's voice grated on her, blaring from the speaker behind her ear. The air pressure around their cab held them in a vacuum, each passing car on the bridge pulled them sidewards, making Maggie hold her neck stiff so she wouldn't bang her head against the window. It made her feel dirty to think that thousands of people had sat in this seat. Maggie pulled her mobile from amongst the clutter in her small bag, the one Marcus had bought her for a birthday several years ago. Even as she opened the box she had known it was impractical. Expecting it would be a fruitless exercise, she tried Patrick's mobile first. After three rings it went through to his voicemail, the familiar sound of his 'business' voice telling her that he was unavailable. She decided to leave a brief message, one vague enough to pique his interest but not emotional enough to raise alarm.

'Patrick, it's your mother. Please call me immediately.' The use of 'mother' should be enough to convey some seriousness.

Next she called his office. This time she waited for five rings and with each one she grew more hopeful that he'd pick up and answer in his officious tone. But this too went through to a recorded message. 'Patrick Apperton', he said awkwardly, 'is not available' said a woman.

'Just as I thought,' Maggie said to Kathy, 'there's no answer there either.' Then after the recorded message she said, 'Patrick, it's your mother, you must call me right away. Something's happened –' she left the threat hanging.

Though she knew it was very early morning in Paris, she decided to try Isabel's mobile. Isabel would have a better chance of getting through to Patrick. Not once could Maggie recall either of her children answering her calls. She was forever leaving them messages and waiting anywhere between one and five days for them to call her back in their own sweet time, if they bothered at all. Naturally, no one in the family had taught Maggie how to hide caller ID.

'*Bonjour*,' said Isabel's voice message before continuing in French.

Feeling a little more desperate now, Maggie decided to mention the accident. 'Isabel, it's your mother. Marcus has been in an accident. I need you to call me...please?'

Maggie closed her mobile and turned to Kathy with a smile. 'No luck,' she said bravely, before bursting into tears.

Kathy hugged Maggie's shoulders as she wept. Even in her grief Maggie felt self-conscious as the driver glanced periodically in her direction. What must he be thinking?

They turned into the emergency entrance of the hospital. How sombre and imposing the grey building looked up close – a mecca of death and illness.

Her next conscious thought was of Kipper. Maggie was in the waiting room of emergency and the dog was on the small television screen two metres from the floor. A child sat on a makeshift carpet, his head turned at a sharp angle to see the screen. Maggie couldn't remember exactly how she'd ended up in this room, how they'd paid the taxi driver or how it was decided that emergency was where they needed to be. As she became more conscious, she understood that someone was holding her hand. The chubby fingers were interlocked with hers, and another hand lay resting protectively over both. Maggie turned to see Kathy's solemn face, her eyes full of love and concern.

Kathy had been speaking. 'Don't you think?' she repeated.

'Yes,' Maggie said remotely, taking a risk on what was being discussed. 'Yes, I suppose so.'

'Mrs Apperton?' asked a man dressed in white. He had a tanned, angular face with a distinctive five o'clock shadow. He was probably much older than he looked. 'I'm Doctor O'Sullivan. Please, come this way.'

'I'll be here, sweetheart,' Kathy said softly, slowly letting go of Maggie's hand.

Maggie silently followed the doctor through a maze of dull-coloured corridors. She couldn't remember the last time she'd experienced the cold sterility of a hospital. They came to a small, dark meeting room with two hard chairs facing each other across a plastic-topped table.

'Please, take a seat. Can I get you something to drink?'

'A wa-water,' she stuttered, her throat dry and poisonous.

The doctor poured her a minuscule cup from a water cooler in the corner. He placed it in front of her.

'Not much of a cup,' he said, forcing a smile. 'Let me know if you would like some more.' She swallowed it in one and was desperate for more but wouldn't ask.

'I am sorry that we meet under such ghastly circumstances,' he said honestly. 'Is there anything I can get for you before we begin? Anyone I can call?'

'No, thank you, doctor. I've left messages with our children.' She motioned to a sign on the wall, 'I'll turn my mobile off now, though?'

'Yes, if you don't mind,' he said courteously before getting down to business. 'Your husband suffered a sudden heart attack while driving this morning, Mrs Apperton. The collision would have caused him quite a shock and he suffered a number of cuts and abrasions to the face and hands. I can't be sure whether his initial heart attack was severe but he suffered a series of them, perhaps due to the trauma of the car crash, so there has been quite some damage caused.' Doctor O'Sullivan paused. 'Should I continue, Mrs Apperton?'

'Yes please, doctor,' she answered quietly, feeling the colour drain from her skin.

'The ambulance arrived on the scene and could find no pulse. CPR was commenced and the paramedics managed to revive him but CPR continued for quite some time without your husband's heartbeat returning naturally. Once here, we placed your husband on life support, but it is my professional opinion that he suffered from a considerable lack of oxygen to the brain. We've done the necessary tests and there has been significant brain damage, I'm afraid. The odds of him regaining consciousness are virtually nil. Even if he was to regain consciousness, I doubt he would retain many of his capacities.'

Maggie felt numb. This was so clinical, hard for her to comprehend that Marcus was no longer within his own body.

It felt impossible to refer to him in the past tense. And yet strangely, she felt calm. As though receiving some sentence for a crime she didn't commit – this could all be righted in the future. In a way, the information she received was pointless. Everything would be returned to normal, eventually. Surely this was all just a dream. 'Continue, doctor,' she said blankly.

'You need to decide how long you wish to sustain him on life support. I reiterate that it is my medical opinion that your husband won't regain his mental capacities and if we were to turn off the life support machine he would not survive for very long. Perhaps hours, perhaps minutes. I can tell you, though, he is in no pain, we are taking good care of him. Naturally, there's no hurry in this situation, Mrs Apperton; I don't want you to feel under any pressure. You can take your time to think through your options and, of course, you probably want to discuss them with your family. You should spend some time with Marcus before you decide anything at all. Do you have any questions?'

'No doctor. I understand everything you've said.'

'Mrs Apperton, would you like to see your husband now?' He spoke to her gently but she could detect no hope in his voice.

'Thank you, doctor.'

Maggie followed him through a series of corridors before coming to the doors of intensive care. The smell and atmosphere of hospitals had always quietened her; the stillness, the gathering of strangers in the most intimate of circumstances.

'I'll be outside if you need me for anything, Mrs Apperton. I won't be very far away. Your husband's bed is the last on the left, against the window.'

Maggie pushed through the doors and everywhere she turned she could see medical machines. It finally brought to her the seriousness of the situation. She felt useless now, knowing these events were totally beyond her control.

Walking with her head to the ground, she made her way to the last bed and took a deep breath before raising her eyes to the level of the pillows. Maggie focused intently on the man's face before her, trying desperately to find some semblance of the person she had seen nearly every day for forty years. It wasn't him. My god, she thought, this has all been a hideous mistake. She was about to turn back and explain the mix-up to the doctor but then her eyes caught the name on the clipboard at the end of the bed – 'Apperton' – and just above that, she saw one of Marcus' feet. How could she mistake the dead skin that marked them so?

Maggie walked closer to the bed, staring at this strange face with thick tubes leading into and out of it. His whole body was swollen and she found it hard to believe it was Marcus, but there were his things piled neatly on the bedside table – his watch, his wallet, the mobile phone he had called her from this morning and his wedding ring. This man used to be her husband. Within her she knew Marcus couldn't be saved.

It was no longer the man she knew, just his shell, a vacant body. The wind rushed out of her and she struggled for breath as the tears rolled freely down her cheeks. Though she wanted to, she could not turn her gaze from his face – so at peace, a man whose presence she'd taken for granted for so many years that she had forgotten just how much she relied on him for everyday things. What now, she thought, do I just stand here and wait for something to happen? Do I speak aloud and say goodbye? Out the window she could see silhouettes of office workers going about their daily lives. How potent that life should continue so unashamedly this close to death. She stood, frozen, for ten minutes, unable to sit or move until the doctor's gentle touch on her elbow brought her back to the moment.

Maggie and the doctor walked back to the meeting room in silence as she tried to regain some of her composure. He asked her to sign a set of papers empowering the hospital to effectively end Marcus' life. She'd thought it through and could see no point in sustaining his machinated breaths, delaying the inevitable. What point was there in having Isabel or Patrick see him like this?

'Your husband's personal effects...'

'If you could just send them to me,' she muttered from somewhere deep within. 'Send them next week. Not today, I just couldn't take them with me today.'

'I understand,' he said softly.

What an awful job you have, Maggie thought, what a wonderful man you must be. 'I assume you have my address from my husband's licence, car registration...If that is all...'

'Mrs Apperton, I could prescribe something. If you felt you needed it.'

'Thank you, doctor. Will that be all?' Though she knew she wasn't sounding herself, she also realised that Doctor O'Sullivan would have no 'before' Maggie to compare her to.

'You have my deepest sympathies, Mrs Apperton. With your permission, I would like to call you in a few days.'

'Of course.'

'Your choice of funerary company will arrange for the transportation of Marcus' body. Are there any family members you would like me to contact on your behalf?'

'I will try my children again, if you don't mind. May I borrow your phone, doctor?'

'Of course. I'll leave you alone, you let me know when you're done.'

Maggie dialled her children's mobile numbers and once again she left messages, though this time sounding more desperate. She would turn off Marcus' life support machine and if he could live long enough for his children to see him then that is what fate would decide. She even tried calling the reception at Patrick's work but once she told the girl it was his mother she was given a well-rehearsed excuse.

'His mother? Oh, right!' the girl said and struggled to hide a nervous laugh. 'I'm sorry, he's not available. Can I take a message?'

It was all Maggie could do to stop from screaming at this poor dumb girl. 'Yes, you may take a message actually. Please tell him his father is dying. He should get to Royal North Shore immediately.'

'Oh my God, I'm, like, so sorry –'

'Yes, well... Please, I just beg you to track him down.'

Maggie knew she wouldn't be able to do it alone, so she asked the doctor to find Kathy.

Sitting on two plastic seats next to Marcus' bed, they waited in silence for the doctor to come and do the deed. Maggie sat staring straight ahead, gazing into the office block. How many of those workers had lost their husbands or their fathers? Behind her, Maggie could hear a mother crying quietly as she held her tiny child's hand. An old man on the other side of the room was breathing so heavily that it sounded like each breath was causing him immense pain. A nurse came and conspicuously closed the curtain around Marcus' bed. Maggie held Kathy's hand in her right and Marcus' in her left when the doctor came. It was as simple as flicking a switch. The slow rhythmic beats of his heart as reproduced on the monitor offered a sublime hope but almost immediately, the beeps began to slow. They grew further apart and Maggie couldn't help but count the seconds between them. One second, two, three . . . The beeps were replaced by a constant tone. A flatline, isn't that what they called it?

The doctor nodded slowly to announce that Marcus was dead, and turned off the other machines. He said simply, 'He's gone.'

Maggie sat for a few minutes, unsure of what to say or do. Tears rolled freely down her cheeks and her limbs began to shake. This moment would change things, of that she was sure. This moment would scar her, not only for its immediacy, but for its long-running repercussions. She got up slowly from the plastic chair and went towards her husband's swollen face. She felt older than her years, somehow more helpless than she'd been just minutes before.

'I'm sorry,' she whispered to her dead husband, a man who was responsible for so much of who she had become. Maggie kissed him briefly on the forehead and moved to whisper in his ear, 'I'm so sorry.'

Maggie preferred that Kathy didn't see her like this so she walked calmly through intensive care and took a right turn. She lost her way in the unending corridors and took refuge in the first toilet she came to. She went into a cubicle, locked the door behind her, sat on the toilet seat, and began to sob uncontrollably. Her whole body shook as she wept, tears dropping onto her dress, mucus dripping from her nose. She had not cried like this for many years, she had not been as free with her emotions at any other moment. When she thought of this morning's kiss, of Marcus' phone call, she comprehended how out of character it had been for him. Had he sensed something?

Sudden heart attack? How ludicrous! Marcus' mother had died of heart disease, so had two of his brothers. How could he have been so ignorant, so complacent? How could she not have been prepared for this moment, or done more to prevent it? And she hadn't even looked at him this morning. Stupid woman, taking it all for granted. No wonder this . . . No wonder.

The mobile phone trilled in her handbag. Through her tears, she saw that it was Kathy. She answered but couldn't talk through her sobs.

'Maggie, it's me. Where are you?'

'I . . . I'm . . .' She was sobbing hysterically.

'Where are you?' Kathy repeated. 'You've been gone forever, let me come to you. Are you –?'

'In a toilet somewhere in this ridiculous building. Come?' How helpless she felt.

A few minutes later, she heard Kathy's voice in the toilets. Maggie cautiously got to her feet and unlocked the cubicle door. The two women hugged, crying together, the scent of Kathy's perfume and the warmth of her arms was calming.

'What am I going to do, Kathy? What on earth am I going to do now?'

Kathy sighed. Looking into her tear-streaked face, she said simply, 'No one knows what to do when this happens, Maggie.'

'Stupid Marcus,' Maggie said. 'I was going to go first. He was supposed to nurse me through.'

Kathy hugged her again. 'I'm here for you, sweetheart. Every step of the way.' She put her arm gently behind Maggie's back and guided her to the exit. The afternoon sun was blinding.

'However you found me, thank you.' Maggie wiped away her tears. 'I didn't know how I was ever going to get off that toilet.'

'I've called my neighbour, she'll get the kids for me. I think there's a bar up the road. How about a drink?' Kathy knew of no other remedy.

'Yes, I think so. I need something to steady me.'

Over drinks, Maggie managed to draw her unhinged emotions back within. She felt embarrassed to have been so overt in front of Kathy but losing Marcus was like losing a part of her self. How do you explain what forty years of taking someone for granted amounted to? She couldn't recall ever once fighting with him, but for that matter she couldn't recall the last time she had found him endearing either. They'd grown distant in recent years, Maggie and Marcus were more like brother and sister, a family bond adhering one to the other. If Kathy were to ask her there and then how she felt, Maggie would have simply said, 'hollow'. It wasn't in reference to Marcus' death, but a description of what Maggie amounted to as a person.

It didn't surprise Maggie that neither Patrick nor Isabel answered their mobiles when she called them yet again. Contrary to popular belief, she wasn't entirely ignorant of technology and knew without doubt that both children would be screening her calls, or perhaps Isabel's phone was off. Maggie never could quite work out the time difference. She chose not to leave another message for either, thinking she would try Patrick's home number later in the day when he might be home from work.

They sat in silence, mostly. Kathy was drinking too quickly and it was not until the fourth or fifth Scotch that either of them found the energy to speak.

'You can come stay with us if you'd like.'

'I might.'

'Should we call relatives?'

'Not right now.'

'Or Marcus' work?'

'Would you mind?'

'Of course not. I'll go outside.' Kathy couldn't explain Marcus' death while Maggie sat there listening.

Maggie sat there taking in the sounds around her, the sounds she would have expected from an old man's pub such as this. Oh, there was so much to do. What were the mechanics of death? The car, the hospital, the will, the funeral, the calls, the wake . . . the list was mind-boggling. Maggie ordered two more Scotches though she was struggling to hold the previous ones down.

Kathy returned with tears in her eyes. They were contagious; though neither woman sobbed, both their faces were wet. Maggie knew what dealing with death could do to a person and she knew that with each new death, past ones reared their ugly heads.

She woke to a spinning room. It took her a few moments to comprehend where she was. Leroy was at her feet, snoring. Ugh, she felt very ill. What would Marcus say? She turned to look at the dull glow of her bedside clock. It was past eleven o'clock. How could she end up like this? She racked her brain. Glimpses of Kathy helping her into bed. Leroy snuggling up to her. Maggie crying. Crying? Hospital.

Marcus' lifeless face. Marcus is dead.

She quickly ran from the bed to the toilet and began vomiting. Scotch, she could tell. She couldn't stop the vomiting, or the tears that stung her eyes. When was the last time she'd vomited from alcohol poisoning? How could she have got so drunk in the face of Marcus' death? Well, that was just it. She didn't have to be strong for anybody.

Patrick

The sound of her voice was grating. She was slurring, muttering something. Why would she call him when she was drunk? Patrick had been tempted not to answer the phone at all, thinking it might be *him*. It had been a shit of a day, topped by a worse evening and now he had been woken by a drunk mother who wasn't making any sense. But the fact that she was drunk made him instantly aware that something was wrong. His heart thumped – please don't let it be Leroy.

'Patrick, I have something to tell you.' He braced himself for the worst, something to top his already hideous day.

'So, are you gonna come home with me tonight?'

The question hung in the air between them like a lie. A strange vacuum of silence followed it and Patrick felt compelled to turn his gaze to the city skyline. Sydney looked stunning, the February dusk placing a veil of crimson across its metallic face, the windows reflecting Patrick's last glimmer of hope.

'I think you already know the answer to that,' Damien stared at him, revealing nothing.

Patrick did indeed know the answer. It stung like a slap to the face; somehow he had known the evening would end this way, its beginning had planted that in his subconscious.

It was unlike Patrick to be late; he was usually early for every appointment, cursing colleagues and friends for every minute he waited past the agreed meeting time. Work had been frantic in the morning and he had indulged far too much at lunch, turning off his mobile so his boss wouldn't be able to track him down. Feeling the perspiration slide down the side of his chest, he had stumbled out of the restaurant after five, so, of course, taxis were impossible to find. They weren't meeting until seven-thirty; if he walked home he would still have time for a nap and a chance to shake off some of the booze.

He hadn't counted on sleeping long but had lost all track of time and ended up meeting a very impatient Damien for cocktails closer to eight o'clock. Damien was cold and distant, unforgiving of Patrick's excuses and even less impressed by his drunk state. The conversation between them was stunted, the mood unpredictable. Patrick thought of the last conversation they had shared – no anomalies there. He concentrated hard and tried not to slur.

'Well, you're in a filthy mood.' Patrick antagonised him even further.

'I'm okay.' Damien sighed without conviction.

'Hey, I said I'm sorry I was late.'

'Really, it's okay.'

'Would you prefer to pass on dinner?'

'Kind of. But we're out now, so we may as well go.' He was giving nothing away.

'The restaurant's pretty exxy,' Patrick said. 'This was meant to be a special night. Why don't I take you when you're in a better mood?'

'For a special night, you sure took care of yourself at lunch. No, I think we should go to dinner.' Damien stood up to leave, his drink unfinished, announcing the end of that discussion.

The conversation over the three-course meal lacked energy and then, over dessert wine, Damien slapped him with his retort. You already know the answer to that.

Of course Patrick did. He should have guessed that this would end like all the others.

'This is it, isn't it?' Patrick whispered.

'Yeah, I think so,' Damien said flatly. 'Don't you?'

Patrick just smiled. What else could he do? Two weeks ago he thought Damien might be *the* one. How pathetic he felt now, to have invested so much hope in a man he barely knew. How ridiculous he was, to believe in everything they had discussed, he should have known it was futile.

On the first date, they went to a highrise hotel for cocktails and talked and drank so much they forgot to eat. Everything Damien said made perfect sense to Patrick at the time, even talk of a future together. Now it was all revealed for the hollow promise of something he so desperately craved.

Patrick paid the bill, drank in the view one last time, finished the remainder of his wine and stood to leave. They didn't talk.

To add to the sting, a cab was waiting outside the restaurant so there was no chance for further conversation, no last minutes to try to convince him to stay.

''Bye Damien,' he said to no one as the cab drove him out of Patrick's life. 'You fucking arsehole,' he muttered, before walking away with his hands in his pockets.

How could it have happened like that, with absolutely no explanation? Patrick searched for an answer and, as was usually the case when it came to his bad luck with men, the finger of blame was pointing squarely at him. He had no muscle definition. His teeth were not straight. He wasn't particularly good in bed. Whatever the reason, it was definitely his fault, right? Why else would an intelligent, successful, reasonably attractive guy with a good sense of humour be single at the age of thirty-two? The fact that Damien provided no explanation was surely another sign he was just trying to protect Patrick's feelings. Singledom certainly had its pros, but the past six weeks with Damien meant its flaws were high-lighted to Patrick. Now that he had a taste for relationships, he wanted more and the prospect of being alone again depressed him.

He wasn't prepared to deal with his empty apartment, so Patrick walked to a small bar hidden down a sidestreet in Kings Cross. Only locals really knew about the bar – and some of the backpackers from the hostel across the road. It was situated at the top of an old, worn staircase to the rear of a restaurant which was always empty. The owners tried to offload pot to anyone who looked like they might want it. The bar was small and friendly and the relaxed but dark atmosphere suited Patrick's mood.

It was fairly crowded, but Patrick managed to score the corner settee after buying a Crown Lager and choosing a few tunes on the jukebox. Number 1111 was his favourite so he punched in the familiar numbers. He didn't try to talk to anyone and was quite content to observe – catching snippets of conversation, mostly from British backpackers. After two bottles of wine over dinner, Patrick decided to get smashed and one beer turned into three. Drunk and in a less sombre mood, Patrick started to notice the barman. No longer a young Jerry Seinfeld, he now seemed an exotic Antonio Banderas type. He fantasised about asking him home to get some sort of private revenge on Damien. Damien, the dirty bastard. How could he do this when everything felt so right? How could Patrick have been so gullible? Jerry/Antonio would be great in bed, he knew, and Patrick began to respond to the fantasy.

He didn't care that the room was starting to spin or that he was becoming unsteady on his feet. The thought of going home to that empty apartment terrified him, willing him to take some drastic action he might ultimately regret. He stumbled towards the jukebox where a small group crouched, reading the song titles. As he approached, he tripped on the corner of a low-lying table and fell unceremoniously into the people, squashing them against the hard angles of the jukebox.

'Oi! Back off, mate,' a British voice said.

'Come on,' Patrick slurred. 'It was an accident, settle down.'

'I think you're a bit pissed, mate.'

Patrick stood staring blankly at the man for a while, not sure that he was following the thread of the conversation, or that there even was one. 'Are you British?' He attempted to start over.

'Mate, I think you should go home,' said one of the girls.

'Oh do ya, sweetheart?' Patrick mimicked her accent. 'What makes you think you can tell me what to do?'

'You're a real arsehole, aren't you?' She turned her nose up at him and whispered something into the ear of the girl next to her, making them both giggle.

'Let's play nice now,' was Patrick's feeble attempt at getting them back onside but it was no use, they weren't having a bar of him.

This rejection, even by strangers, affected Patrick more than he cared to admit. To put it simply, Patrick liked to be liked. He had a wide circle of friends, many circles in fact, but he failed to appreciate that these were mere acquaintances. He didn't know what true friendship was and while every weekend and most weeknights were filled with social events, each one saw him chat to one person for a few minutes, refuel with more alcohol and move on to someone else. On the whole, he was well liked, but that was probably because no one knew the real Patrick, no friend had ever been invited back to his apartment or knew a thing about his upbringing. If anyone ever challenged him on being aloof, he would retreat as fast as possible, or turn to more booze to build up enough confidence to turn defence into offence. Most people gave up trying after one attempt and learnt to enjoy Patrick Apperton for who he was: a good time, fair weather pal.

Noticing Patrick's lurking, swaying presence, the backpacker turned on him. 'You're not one of us, mate.'

'Hmm,' he mumbled. 'I'll be right back.'

Too drunk to feel embarrassed, he staggered to the toilet and made his way into one of the cubicles. On top of the cistern he detected a fine spray of powder, enough to form a thin white line when he collected it together using his maxed-out Amex. He snorted it up greedily, gagging at its acidity. That was a stupid thing to do, he thought.

Patrick was drunk, high and horny. A lethal combination, especially after being dumped. He decided to leave before he made the right moves on a wrong guy, whether it was Jerry/Antonio or the cute, straight tourist. A smack to the head was all he needed right now.

Patrick fumbled outside the apartment block digging into his pocket for keys, and heard the distinct sound of a departing cab. Could it be Damien? He turned around, but it was one of his neighbours. They smiled vaguely at each other and she stayed outside to finish a cigarette.

In the darkness of his apartment, Patrick glanced toward his answering machine. No messages. He turned on the hallway light and stumbled towards his mobile lying on his couch. If he had been able to call Damien to warn him he would be late, would they be together now? Four messages; three were from his mother. He couldn't deal with her now and besides, she'd be fast asleep at this hour. He would listen to them when he was sober. The other was from his office . . . he would deal with his boss in the morning if need be. Should he call Damien? No, it was best not to drink and dial; it would serve no purpose except to confirm that he was drunk and pathetic. Patrick was surprised to see that it was only eleven-thirty. He drank three large glasses of water, swallowed three aspirin, took off all his clothes and climbed into bed. His pillows did little to compensate for Damien but Patrick held them tightly, pressing their coolness against his groin. Despite the powder in his system, within minutes Patrick was asleep.

It took three rings to wake him. By then, the phone had gone to his answering machine and he was startled by the sound of his own, recorded voice. He staggered out of bed naked, and ran to the phone. Damien!

'Hello?' Silence. 'Hello?'

'Patrick, I have something to tell you.'

He was disappointed to hear any voice other than Damien's, but recognising the drunken slurs as his mother's deflated him even further. He wasn't in the right frame of mind to speak to her now. He considered hanging up on her but caught a slight tone of sadness in her voice and knew if she was drinking there'd be a very big reason for it.

'Are you there?' she asked timidly.

'Yes, Maggie, you woke me up. What's going on?'

'Marcus is dead.'

Patrick's heart dropped. He thought of Leroy having been hit by a car, of his playful nature suddenly ended. But then it dawned on him. Marcus. His mother never called his father that, it was always 'your father'. Hearing her say a name, he'd naturally thought she had said Leroy.

'How?'

'I...he...heart. It was sudden. I'm a bit vague, I'm sorry, Patrick.'

'Fuck, fuck...fuck! Sorry Mum...' He wanted to tell her that everything was going to be okay but he knew that was not true. He had a vision of his mother in two years, a frail old woman unable to care for herself, him visiting her in a nursing home. He pushed these thoughts aside. 'I'll come up, Mum,' and I really hope I don't get pulled over by the cops.

'Oh no, don't be silly,' she insisted.

'Well, I'm not gonna sleep now anyway, am I? I'll drive up now.'

'Be careful, Patrick, drive slowly.'

'Yeah okay, don't worry about me. Give me a couple of hours, okay?'

'Don't forget to bring that book.' It was a foolish thing to say and she knew it. A book he had told her about months before, that he kept forgetting to bring with him when he visited. Yet, it was only a foolish thing to ask given the circumstances and she still marvelled at how easy it was to temporarily forget Marcus' death.

'Ah, okay. I won't be very long.'

Patrick hung up. Though he knew it was wrong to think of it, he wanted to call Damien in the hope that sympathy might bring them back together. It made him sick to think of using his own father's death to his advantage and he cursed his mind for the course it chose. Had he really become this shallow?

He put on some music to distract himself while he hurried around his apartment collecting things to throw in an overnight bag. In the bathroom he paused to stare at his reflection in the cabinet mirror. He was looking older than thirty-two, he thought – fine lines beneath his eyes and on his forehead, a few grey hairs protruding through the dark brown. He had his mother's eyes, uncannily so. Steel, he referred to them as, though she insisted they were simply blue. Around the mouth, the contours of his nose. Yes, he could definitely see signs of his father too. It sent a chill down his spine to think that he would be carrying this dead man's legacy. Would it torment Maggie to see traces of Marcus in her son's face? He checked his teeth for food. How did other people respond to the death of a parent? Patrick hadn't discussed it with anyone before.

Patrick checked through his bag and made sure he had everything he would need. He had forgotten his toothbrush and a plastic toy for Leroy. He checked his pockets for his keys, wallet and mobile, quickly popped a Berocca and followed it with two glasses of water. He opened the door of his apartment and paused to glance at himself in the full-length mirror. God, he *was* putting on weight.

In the car he fumbled around for the right CD to match his mood. He settled on Cyndi Lauper's *At Last*. As he drove, his mind raced over a thousand things – failed relationships, marriage, his parents, and his father's death. Tears stung his eyes, making it hard to focus in the artificial light of the Harbour Tunnel. My father is dead.

Having a father like Marcus had always confused him. They had only ever communicated over superficial things and yet Marcus had provided the family with every material thing they'd ever desired; obsession with work was all in the name of giving to the three of them.

46

Patrick

What Patrick resented most about his father's death was that so many questions would be left unanswered. He knew little of Marcus' childhood, had no hint as to why his father usually remained quiet and was reticent about sharing affection. To Patrick, this was what all lives amounted to – the death of one person's memories, and one person's knowledge. And after Patrick, who would want to know anything about Marcus anyhow? More sobering was the realisation that no one would want to know Patrick's memories. His entire existence was leading towards a few moments' worth of ashes being scattered to the wind.

For his eighteenth birthday, Patrick's parents paid for him to visit Isabel in Paris. She was there studying at the Sorbonne, and though she'd almost begrudged his presence at first, by the end of the two weeks they shared a secret and became firmer friends. In recent years that bond had dissolved and now they rarely spoke but that winter in Paris had been an amazing one for both of them.

Patrick lost his virginity to a young Frenchman, a friend of Isabel's. He was studying music, Isabel studied French cinema. Isabel threw a dinner party in her tiny studio on the top floor of an apartment building in Alésia. Jean-Marc arrived before anyone else and was surprised to meet Patrick; Isabel had invited three friends and told none of them about Patrick's visit. Jean-Marc was pleased to have someone to practise his English with. (Isabel usually refused to speak English, preferring instead to attempt to perfect her French.) While Isabel fussed about in the communal kitchen at the end of the hall, Jean-Marc and

Patrick began drinking wine as they sat on Isabel's bed and got better acquainted.

Patrick thought Jean-Marc was attractive, his full red lips carefully pronouncing every English word and he had a seductive smile. Patrick had only ever fantasised about men, his fear of being an outcast at school forcing all his desires to remain within his mind. He was well liked by his peers and to admit his desires to anyone would have been social suicide. But in Paris, so far removed from everyone who knew him in Australia, he felt at liberty to speak of those desires and here, in Jean-Marc, there may have been the possibility to explore his sexuality for the first time.

As the others arrived, the room grew crowded and Patrick and Jean-Marc were forced closer together. The wine flowed more freely and, as Isabel and her other friends fell into French, Jean-Marc and Patrick continued in English, Jean-Marc often leaning in close to whisper hotly in Patrick's ear. Jean-Marc's shoulder length hair was pulled back into a greasy ponytail and he smelled of a vanilla and cinnamon cologne. Being close to him made Patrick excited and clammy.

Vincente, another of Isabel's friends, was an overweight mature-age student with a strong crush on Jean-Marc. As a result, he found Patrick's flirtations annoying and treated him rudely. It was Vincente's mission to destroy the young boy's confidence.

'So Patrick, what do you do in Australia?'

'I've just finished school.'

'Ah, so you're beginning to – how you say?' he said rather pompously, 'find your shoes?'

The fact that he had got the phrase wrong wasn't lost on Patrick, nor was his hostility.

'I reckon I can find them easily enough,' Patrick said with a smirk and raised his glass. 'To Paris!'

'To Patrick's visit!' Jean-Marc said.

'So, you are gay then? Did you know, Isabel?'

Isabel, who'd been trying to translate the conversation to Marie, the only non-English speaker, was taken aback. 'Sorry?'

'I'm . . . not sure what I am,' Patrick hesitated.

'And what does that mean?'

'I'm undecided, Vincente. I haven't been with a man or a woman.' Patrick's face coloured at the thought of having such a conversation with three strangers, and in front of his sister, but there was something in the air he found intoxicating and it encouraged him to be honest.

Jean-Marc said something in French to Isabel and then, turning to Patrick said in English, 'That's okay, I used to be undecided too. Now I know exactly what I want!'

'Patrick, can you come help me in the kitchen, please?'

Patrick followed Isabel to the end of the hall, fearing a confrontation. She closed the door behind them.

'What the fuck are you doing?'

'What?' He was genuinely surprised and defensive.

'Why are you saying that shit?'

'It's not shit, Isabel, I don't know what I want, I just want to explore all possibilities,' he said, though he knew exactly who and what he desired.

'Well, just be careful. Vincente's been in love with Jean-Marc for three years so he's pretty protective of him. And Jean-Marc's just told me he likes you. Make sure you know what you're getting yourself into.'

When they returned to Isabel's studio, Jean-Marc had pulled Isabel's guitar from beneath her bed, and was strumming it quietly. His hair was now hanging loose, covering one side of his face. Vincente was glued to him . . . as was Patrick. At eighteen, he could overlook the cliché of the moment because he was in France, the foreignness of it meant he knew no better and wasn't sceptical.

Later that evening they all went to a nightclub near the Bastille and it wasn't long until Jean-Marc kissed Patrick. It was Patrick's first real kiss and he was high on its effect, in awe of its power. It soon emerged that Vincente and Jean-Marc shared an apartment so there was no way Vincente would allow Patrick to go home with them. At four, they said their goodbyes and as Patrick lay wide-awake on a mattress on Isabel's floor watching the first grey light of the day creep its way into the room, he was unable to shake the shivers of excitement and the hollow pit of anticipation from his stomach.

Jean-Marc called him later that morning and they spent the following ten days meeting in secret, avoiding Vincente and Isabel whenever they were together. For Patrick, it was too good to be true and he cancelled all sightseeing plans to spend every available minute with his lover. It was a fairy tale come to life, impossibly romantic to a naive virgin but it seemed such a brief affair when the time came for Patrick to go home.

On the ferry to England, where Patrick had promised Isabel they would share his last few days in Europe, he was so morose, so sick with love, that Isabel eventually got him to talk about

Jean-Marc, to let down his guard for a few hours. Though the extent of their affair surprised her, it also brought her closer to her brother and the last night in London they stayed out until sunrise, getting intolerably drunk and talking incessantly about the affair, and their vastly different lives. They also made a solemn pact to keep this secret from their parents.

Though Jean-Marc and Patrick promised to write to one another, it wasn't long until Jean-Marc's letters to Patrick stopped and Patrick's heart broke at losing such a love. He spent months wallowing in his room, hating his first year of university, hardly eating and, for a reason he couldn't quite put his finger on, treating his parents poorly. Throughout it all, he and Isabel wrote long honest letters to each other, pouring out their hearts, their deepest thoughts, fears and desires. But when Isabel visited home later that year, she betrayed his trust by hinting to their parents about Patrick's sexuality and after she left, they waited for him to confirm their fears.

He sat them down one evening and said simply, 'It's true. I fell in love with a man in Paris and I'm still in love with him.' The statement made his parents fall silent and the tension in the room was suffocating. It was his mother who finally spoke.

'But that was just some silly holiday romance with a foolish European. Things are different over there.'

'That's not true at all. You don't know what happened – it's what I want.'

'Nonsense! You're eighteen for goodness' sake, how would you know what you really want?'

'I know I want to be with men.'

'Oh,' she dismissed him arrogantly. 'That's ludicrous, Patrick. You're in Australia now, stop thinking that choosing –'

'It's not a choice,' he interrupted her.

'Your choice will make your life a difficult, disparate one,' she spoke over his words. 'I suggest you think very carefully before you go parading your desires to all and sundry because once you do, you can never take it back. People don't forgive these kinds of indiscretions, Patrick. Nor do they ever forget them!' There were tears in her eyes.

'Indiscretion? Jesus! It's who I am.'

'Well, I don't care to know about it, quite frankly. What you do in the bedroom is never of any interest to me and I only ask that you don't become a militant and start wearing it like a badge. It would destroy your father and me.' With that, she abruptly left the room and went to her bedroom.

There was a painful lump in Patrick's throat. His face burned. With only Marcus left in the room, he barely dared to look at his father. After what felt like hours, he gathered enough courage to meet his father's gaze. Marcus was staring at him, streams of tears flowing freely, and when their eyes connected, he produced a gut-wrenching smile of sympathy but he said nothing.

His mother insisted a wall of secrecy be built between them. The next day, she pretended that nothing had been said and she laid the foundations for an unspoken rule: Patrick was never to discuss his sexuality at home again. He had been obeying that rule for close to fourteen years now. She never asked and he never told.

Two days later, his father brought Leroy home for Patrick. When the last family dog had died, Maggie had consistently resisted Patrick's pleas to get another. Leroy was his father's peace offering and the olive branch helped to heal a tension in the house. In a subconscious way, Leroy stood as a reminder of Patrick's confession and when he left home twelve months later, his mother's refusal to allow Leroy to go with him stood, more or less, as her unspoken acceptance of Patrick's 'lifestyle choice'.

He was halfway there by the time he realised he would be in for a God-awful night. At close to midnight, he knew nothing on the Central Coast would be open so he stopped at a liquor store to get some Grand Marnier. It reminded him of Jean-Marc, and of how they had sipped it together in the bath the last night they ever saw each other.

'I don't want to go back to Australia,' Patrick sighed. 'I don't think I'll ever be the same again.'

Jean-Marc splashed water playfully into his face. 'Do not talk like this. You are very beautiful, someone – many boys – will fall for you and you will love them more than you ever loved me.'

'That's not true,' Patrick said. 'Why do we have to live so far apart?'

'This is nature trying us,' he said. 'Giving us two weeks of intense love to make us realise how beautiful it can be. You will always be very special to me. If, some day, I make it to Australia, you will have to tell all your other boyfriends about me!'

Jean-Marc never made it to Australia. Two years after Patrick's Paris trip, Jean-Marc contracted HIV. On his twenty-fifth birthday, Isabel found the courage to tell her brother of Jean-Marc's death but it came long after Patrick had given up any hope of there being a future for them. Jean-Marc was right: there had been other men – just none quite as significant as him.

Patrick started to accept that he was more like his father than he had admitted to anyone. Patrick couldn't remember a single occasion when he had seen his father show affection. His parents' relationship was very much one of best friends, sharing a life, a business and a family, but never sharing open displays of love. When Maggie found a lump in her breast, Marcus had been surprisingly strong. For two agonising weeks, as Maggie waited to find out the test results, Marcus got her everything she needed, showering her with attention and gifts but never once kissing her. When Patrick watched this, he brushed it aside and thought of it simply as being his father's way. Now that it was too late, though, Patrick wished there was someone around to explain why Marcus was the way he was.

Why did Patrick push his partners away? It may have been through fear of rejection or, more likely, he may have pushed them away before it got to the stage where he was required to show them real affection. How did others see him? Was there some trait of his, some subconscious mannerism, that gave his partners the impression he was incapable of feeling love? There hadn't been one lover, after all, to whom he'd ever said 'I love you'. So Marcus' legacy, an inability to express emotion or love, would live on. This was not to mention Isabel who, Patrick thought, was probably still a virgin and who, he'd often noted, visibly recoiled when anybody touched her. The last time they had seen each other, a few years ago in London, she stiffened so much in his embrace that he thought she might break.

Then, of course, there was Maggie. She rarely embraced her own family, but with Kathy there was a bond like no other. The first time Patrick met Kathy, he was shocked to see his mother so lively and affectionate towards another woman. It was almost as if Maggie needed to be away from her family to express affection, probably because only other people, and their children, gave her affection in return.

As Patrick drove down the slope towards Mooney Mooney bridge, he thought it strange that he still didn't know how his father had died. He supposed it would have been a heart attack, perhaps he died while doing some heavy lifting at work. At least his employees would have seen to him immediately. It was sudden, his mother had said. Perhaps it was a car accident . . . no, 'sudden' implied natural causes. What if he'd been killed? Again, no, his mother would surely have said *murdered* rather than dead.

Patrick had no idea whether these thoughts were natural. They may signify the onset of grief, he thought. He knew there were distinct stages to grief. Denial was first. He thought she'd said Leroy. Confusion was second. His mind had turned to thoughts of winning Damien back. What was supposed to come next? Was it a sense of loss? Also, somewhere in there was anger.

Maggie had only cried once in front of Patrick, apart from his coming out, but they were more tears of anger and disappointment than sadness. One night, when Patrick was nine, Marcus was working interstate and Isabel was staying at a friend's house. Patrick cooked his mother dinner – a spaghetti bolognese he had ruined by using coriander instead of parsley – but Maggie ate it all and seemed genuinely pleased with his efforts. He even cleaned up afterwards, telling his mother to rest up for the evening. Later, they sat in front of the television watching a documentary about a family of gorillas. In it, one of the young male gorillas died in a man-made trap and its mother was so grief-stricken that she stayed by her son for two days, losing touch with the rest of the group, refusing to eat or sleep. She continually stroked her dead child. By the time the poachers returned to their trap, she was so weak with grief that she couldn't even run away. They beheaded her.

When the documentary finished, Patrick turned to his mother. She was crying so heavily that her chest was damp, two loud sobs pierced the air and she hurried from the room. Patrick was stunned; he'd never seen his mother sad before, let alone distraught. He had no idea what to do, how to make things better. So he made her a cup of tea and watched it go cold. Ten minutes later Maggie emerged with swollen eyes.

'Silly documentaries! I can't stand to see animals get hurt.'

Nothing was ever said about it again and Patrick doubted that his mother's extreme emotions were solely a response to cruelty to animals.

How would she react to Marcus' death?

Patrick turned into the familiar driveway and immediately noticed the absence of his father's car. He turned off the ignition and sat motionless for a while, taking deep, slow breaths, thankful to have arrived in one piece despite his drunken state. Now that he was home to face his father's death, he feared there would be a part of himself he would never be able to understand.

Maggie sat cross-legged on the rug in the centre of the living room. A box of photographs lay spread out before her. Leroy was lying with his back against her tailbone, serving as her cushion. He was snoring. When Patrick walked into the room, Leroy sprang to life but his instinct to charge at this intruder was immediately confused with the desire to leap all over him while whimpering with excitement.

'Hey, fella,' Patrick said quietly, trying to calm him. Maggie looked horrendous. Smeared make-up masked her skin and made her look ridiculous. Nearly all her hair had fallen from a hastily arranged bun so that all that remained atop her head was a knot of tangles and elastic. Her nose was red raw, probably from too much wiping, and her eyes were yellowed and bloodshot. Her entire face was bloated.

'Hi,' Patrick said, 'you look awful.' All the while, Leroy ran around in circles chasing his tail and turning the gravity of the situation into a farce.

'Leroy!' Maggie screamed in a high-pitched voice.

'Come on buddy, I'll put you outside. He's just being a dog, Maggie, he doesn't know.' Much to the dog's disappointment, Patrick led him to the back door. Leroy sat down, refusing to budge, but Patrick pulled the plastic alligator from his bag and threw it into the darkness of the backyard. In an instant, Leroy was gone and Patrick closed the door behind him. He turned back to his mother, who hid her face in her hands. This wasn't going to be easy.

Patrick took the Grand Marnier from his bag and poured himself a glass. Silently, he made his way over to her.

'Maggie?' Patrick whispered. 'I'm so sorry, I dunno what to say.'

'I know, Patrick,' she said, looking at him for the first time since he'd arrived. 'The silly thing is I don't know what to say either.' She let out a long sigh. 'I shouldn't have got so drunk today. I can't remember much, and one part of me still thinks this hasn't happened, that he'll be walking through that door in a minute, disappointed in me for drinking too much with Kathy.'

'I was thinking the same thing in the car, that this isn't right. I took Dad's existence for granted and now he's gone.' He took a sip of the orange liqueur.

'I suppose we all did. But he was like that. Never wanted any thanks, never expected recognition for all that he did.'

'How did it happen?' he asked her hesitantly, not wanting to sound morbid and unsure whether she was feeling strong enough to explain.

Maggie cried as she told him about the accident and described Marcus' face at the hospital. 'I tried to call you so many times,' she pleaded desperately, 'but you never answer my calls.'

'I'm sorry. I got drunk at lunch and I wasn't checking my phone and then I forgot to take it out with me tonight. I wasn't thinking straight. I really am sorry you had to do it alone.'

'I had Kathy,' she said. 'Thank the gods for Kathy.'

Of course Kathy had been there watching his father die. Of course Kathy had been there for Maggie, who else would have been?

'His face, Patrick, it was ghastly. I'm worried it will be how I remember him.'

In her trembling hand she held a photograph from their wedding.

'He looked good there, you both did. That's how you'll remember him. Young and handsome. It's so weird to think that you can't be together anymore.'

'Ah, together...' Maggie sighed heavily. 'I suppose he did love me, Patrick, but what does that mean anyway? You know, I never, ever thought I'd be referring to my husband in the past tense. It's so cold, such an impersonal way of talking about him. Silly, isn't it? It was always fifty–fifty that he would go first, but it was going to be me.'

'So, how are you feeling? Hungover? I mean, if you wanna talk about...oh shit, I dunno...'

'No, you're right. I'm not ready to talk yet. I have turned off my mobile. The answering machine is at bursting point because my lunch ladies keep calling, but I just can't talk now. I am hungover but I'll survive.'

'Why don't you go have a shower? You won't be getting much sleep tonight. I'll make you some toast with Promite, and let Leroy know I still love him.'

'Poor Leroy,' she said and smiled selfconsciously, regretting her previous outburst. With a small groan she got up off the floor and headed for the bathroom. Maggie turned around. 'Patrick?'

'Hmm?'

'Thanks for coming. You made good time.'

'Yeah, it was a good run.'

'You didn't speed did you?'

'No, Maggie, I never do. You really should stop asking me every time I come here.' He got up and made his way to the back door.

As Maggie showered, Patrick played with Leroy and gave him the affection he craved. How easy it was to show love to an animal. Patrick always found his dog's attention intoxicating and often on a Sunday, as he lay awake mid-morning, recovering from the night before, it was not a lover's presence he craved, only Leroy's.

Patrick made some toast and picked up his Grand Marnier, soothed by the familiar sound of ice rattling against glass. He walked over to the pile of photographs. Why had his mother never bothered to put them into albums? They weren't written on either, making it virtually impossible to place them chronologically, though Maggie never had any problem relaying perfect details of the events surrounding these frozen pockets of time. Though he never really liked his own appearance, Patrick couldn't help poring over photographs of himself, trying to assess his looks objectively, wondering how other people truly saw him.

His parents' wedding photos were on the top of the pile. His father looked so thin and young. Patrick had never known him as thin and his father looked quite dashing. Maggie looked fragile, a petite girl–woman beaming with an innocence which was now replaced by a detached wisdom, an acceptance of things without questioning, a quashing of her feelings and emotions. Or so Patrick thought. He recognised younger versions of the old relatives he rarely saw and supposed that he'd be forced to exchange niceties with most of them at his father's funeral. They all looked stern and awkward.

Patrick paused at one of the photographs featuring a stunningly beautiful boy on the verge of manhood. It was the kind of man Patrick usually fell for – defined masculine angles at the brow and jaw, full pouting lips and small deep-set eyes that could easily seduce. On his left cheek was a distinctively dark mole. He had no idea who it was, this tall, tuxedoed late teen with model looks and a pronounced Adam's apple. He stood alone, looking visibly out of place. I must remember to ask Maggie who he is, Patrick thought.

A photo of his grandmother came next in the pile. There were tears clearly visible in her eyes, and a mole showed on her upper lip. She wore horn-rimmed glasses and looked like every Australian woman he'd seen on Movietone newsreels of her generation. His only memory of her was lying in a hospital bed.

The next portrait was a solo shot of his father. The background was black and he stood, his head bowed, his hands on his hips. The look on his face seemed ... Patrick struggled to find the right word. One of defeat? Perhaps it'd been taken at the end of the evening? It was probably exhaustion. In the next one, though, he was smiling. With the beautiful boy–man, sharing some secret joke as no one else around them smiled.

'Ah,' Maggie said as she entered the room. 'I see you've succumbed as well. You know, I just can't help but feel that photos are the most . . . brilliant things. The hours I've spent, Patrick, just staring at those photos and reliving a thousand moments.'

It was a bizarre notion to Patrick, the fact that Maggie, his mother, had a lifetime's memories she revelled in, sorting through them and refiling after a brief turn around the dancefloor of her mind, choosing the ones she would entertain more regularly than others. Patrick was not used to seeing Maggie with her hair down, it made her look so much younger than when she pinned it up, despite its greyness.

'I guess we've got that in common,' he smiled over his glass. 'If there was ever a fire at my apartment, my photos would be the first thing I'd grab.'

'Thank goodness for them,' was all Maggie said.

Patrick searched her face for the innocence so obvious on her wedding day. She was still quite beautiful, though she was carrying extra weight. Her face was broad and pale, something she tried unsuccessfully to combat by painting her lips with a bright red lipstick too harsh for her complexion. The bridge of her nose was flattened slightly, adding a regal quality to the way she held herself and the way she looked down her nose to address you directly. Beneath her sharp eyes was a puffiness that gave her age away but aside from her neck there was hardly a wrinkle to see, though this never stopped her from covering her neck with a scarf or a high shirt.

'I made you some toast,' he said, pointing her to the plate in the kitchen. 'It's cold now, the way you like it.'

'I'm fine,' she said, sitting down awkwardly across from him. 'This is the one, Patrick, the one I wanted to show you.'

Maggie handed him another black-and-white photograph, it was slightly washed out. It was Marcus in the bath, with a toddler-aged Patrick sitting next to him. They both had shampoo in their hair which they had shaped into Mohawks. Marcus was looking down at his son, the hairs on his chest slick with bathwater. They were both smiling cheekily.

'I never meant for us to grow so far apart, you know.'

At first Patrick thought she was referring to Marcus and it took her stroking his hand for him to realise that she actually meant *him*.

'Maggie,' he said, as he often called her before thinking. 'Mum, we choose to keep to ourselves. That's just the way it is.'

She sat looking at him, her pyjamas damp against her still warm skin. 'I've been thinking,' she shuffled around some photos, 'maybe it's about time we dropped that barrier between us. Before ... before it's too late.'

'Yes, you're probably right, you know.' Patrick finished his glass with one loud gulp.

'Isabel too,' she smiled. 'Look at you two!' In her hands was a photo of the two of them at a parade in primary school. Isabel was dressed as Donald Duck and Patrick as Mickey Mouse. They were ad hoc costumes Maggie had made. The surreal image showed two bright, smiling children – looking nothing like Disney characters, but dressed from head to toe in Maggie's brave attempt at creativity.

'Jesus!' Patrick laughed. 'I'd forgotten about that. One year you dressed me up as Old Father Time. One of the teachers asked how old I was and I answered stupidly, "ten". 'Member that?'

'Yes, I remember.' Maggie half-smiled. 'The same year I dressed your sister up as a witch and her school wasn't very impressed.'

'Have you told Isabel? Does she know about Dad yet?'

'Oh, my goodness, no.' Maggie looked around for the phone guiltily. 'Patrick, do you think you'd be able to call your sister? I just don't think I've got the strength to tell her now.'

Isabel

Isabel hung up, shocked to have heard those words. That certainly wasn't the news she had been expecting. What the hell was she going to do now? She wasn't sure whether she was going to cry, vomit or faint. Of all the things in the world to happen, why this, why now?

Paris was her home now. Isabel hardly ever spoke English, needing to only when her mother called. Her father's insistence that she learn French at high school was probably the best advice he'd ever given her, and continuing it at university in Sydney had laid the foundations for a new life overseas. She had arrived in Paris in 1989, bright-eyed and virtually penniless; her only contact had been a Sorbonne professor she had met in Sydney. He set her up with a bed-sit in Alésia and she had stayed there for nearly five years until her possessions began to occupy more space than she had.

She had finished her masters degree in French cinema by then and begun her cadetship at *Le Point* magazine. Even now, she led a relatively isolated existence in Paris, choosing to spend the majority of her time researching and writing. Isabel took any opportunity to immerse herself in the darkness of a cinema, not only to escape the world's social niceties, but also to prepare reviews and articles for the magazine where she currently worked, *Cine-film*. Unlike the horror stories she had heard, Isabel found getting a work visa in France quite easy given that she had sponsorship from a local magazine. Her French was impeccable and, without doubt, it helped to secure her way through all the red tape.

Most of her time outside work was consumed with writing her thesis, a comparison of the treatment given to sexuality in European and American cinema. Whatever social time she had was spent with Nicolette, a sixty-three-year-old woman Isabel befriended at *Le Point*.

Nicolette was one of those people who talked so much about herself that she allowed others in her company to remain relatively quiet if they chose, but she always managed to include them in her conversation. Nicolette had led the most fascinating life, listening to her was like watching a film come to life.

'Darling,' she would say to Isabel, 'my life is not extraordinary in the grand scheme of things. It is just out of *your* ordinary and that is likely why you find it so fascinating. I'm just a rich old whore with lots of kids and a keen eye for turning the mundane into compelling dinner-speak.'

The fact that she was the opposite of Isabel didn't seem to deter either woman from forming an incredible bond with the other. Nicolette rarely asked any personal questions of Isabel and yet she relished any intimate details that slipped from the younger woman's lips. Not that there was much intimacy to divulge. Much like her mother, Isabel kept her emotions safely locked deep inside, far from prying eyes and judgements.

In the early years, being alone to explore a foreign city felt bearable because there was always something new to see or try, a palate for the senses. Isabel wasn't interested in trying to permeate the highly structured French society, nor was she the type of woman to venture out alone at night in search of something other. Loneliness was a state of mind she refused to entertain and whenever it reared its ugly head she simply found a new book or hobby to explore, jumped on the Metro with no destination in mind, or sank into a seat at the rear of any darkened cinema.

Isabel felt that befriending people only led to being disappointed by them in the end. At least she knew she could rely on her own mind to keep her challenged. This is why, when she interviewed actors, she couldn't fathom why the drug of fame was so addictive. Who would want to be surrounded by people wanting to get to know a version of you that simply didn't exist? Who would want their every public move scrutinised to the Nth degree, their uneaten tacos placed for auction on the internet?

At university in Sydney Isabel had kept to herself on campus. Aside from her lack of trust in others, her looks made her a natural outsider. Her maternal grandmother's namesake,

Isabel also bore a striking resemblance to the dead woman. Her shoulders were too broad for her thin frame, her long spidery limbs moved awkwardly and her hair was an unruly mess, a mousey tangle of abandon. If studied for long enough, her face might be considered antique, a classical angle and colour, as though she'd stepped straight from the pages of a Jane Austen novel and had somehow managed to forge her way into the modern world without anyone noticing.

Isabel felt she understood people, women especially; there was no mystery in coming to grips with what made a person tick. It didn't take much to keep a distance; all Isabel felt she had to do was keep her thoughts to herself. In-fighting and unpopularity usually only happened when people said what they really thought of others or, hedonistically, themselves.

Family was an entirely different beast to society. It frightened and perplexed her and she chose to avoid the poison of its venom as often as possible. Physical distance helped secure her position remarkably well.

Avoiding intimacy was easy until Alain. Their affair had been continuing now for eight months and no one knew, not even Nicolette. Alain had transferred from the Brussels office a year ago, bringing his wife and three children with him. He treated the staff poorly, except for Isabel, whose accent enthralled him. While he was stubborn towards the other women, to Isabel he was gentle and full of encouragement. Though she found his flirtations entirely inappropriate, there was something about this man she couldn't quite identify. One day she went to him to suggest he keep his innuendos to himself.

'I am glad you are here, Isabel.' On his face was the usual smirk.

'Oh yes? And why is that?'

'It saves me the walk to your desk. I want to discuss your future here at *Le Point*.'

Isabel couldn't believe it. Was he going to fire her?

'You know the Associate Editor position has been open for some time,' he began teasingly. 'And how we've had trouble filling it?'

'Yes,' she answered, waiting to hear news of combined roles and redundancies, *her* redundancy.

'I wondered why you haven't applied for it.'

Isabel was flabbergasted. There had never once been talk of promoting her. 'I, well, I just assumed . . . I suppose with my doctorate I didn't think I'd have the time, or make the ideal candidate.'

'The board and I would like you to apply for the position. Off the record, I strongly urge you to. Naturally, it would come with a pay rise,' he continued, 'and I would support you in writing your doctorate. So, will you apply?'

What else could she say?

The following Friday after she had been given the role, he insisted on taking her out for a celebratory drink and she knew she couldn't refuse. At drinks, he apologised profusely for his behaviour but explained his strong feelings towards her. Things at home weren't good for him, his children didn't respect him and his wife wasn't very attentive.

At dinner, he unbuttoned his shirt slightly and Isabel found herself intrigued by the taut hairiness beneath, her first glimpse of his sexual appeal. She rarely drank, and had forgotten its aphrodisiac qualities.

Isabel assumed the affair could continue forever. She never asked him to leave his family because she truly didn't want him to. Being his mistress meant that Isabel still had time to herself – when she wanted to be alone, she could be.

Now this phone call from her doctor. Surely it would change things – she was a French citizen, but perhaps she should return home to Australia for good? In light of everything, she knew she'd want to spend some time with Maggie. It would give them a chance to allow old wounds to heal, to share certain secrets and, perhaps, some fears. She rarely thought of Maggie as a maternal figure but felt that in order to accept this news and feel equipped to deal with its aftermath she would have to see her again. If Maggie couldn't fill Isabel with knowledge, the least she could do was show her how *not* to behave. Already, Isabel could feel the ulcers beginning to form in her mouth. Maybe going back to Australia right now was the last thing she should do – she could continue life in her real home, Paris, come what may. They didn't even feel like her family anymore.

As usual when she felt like this, she decided to go for a walk, though it was cold outside. She put on her favourite red coat, grabbed her journal and a pen, a few francs and her keys. At her door stood a cactus, one she had had since coming to Paris. Something about it caught her eye – one of its limbs was hanging limp. She bent down to inspect it and her heart sank to see that it was rotting from the inside. Had she over- or under-watered it? And why today of all days? Was it a warning she was rotting from the inside herself?

Isabel opened the door to her hallway and was immediately met with a rush of cold air and the smell of freshly baked bread. She found it surprising how quickly her body adjusted to the cold and, once in the street, she saw the day's brilliant blue sky and a light layer of sleet had covered cars parked on the street. Isabel never wore gloves, she hated the sensation of not being able to feel things on her fingertips. She headed straight for the Jardin du Luxembourg, the place she always went when she needed to simply sit and think.

As soon as she walked though the gates of Luxembourg, it was as if she was passing into another world, one whose beauty allowed her to see her own life more clearly, now unaffected by the constant bustle of the city. The sky was a wonderful misty blue, the sun casting long shadows from her pen as she wrote in her journal. This place felt like her paradise, its serenity calmed her. In her usual spot, Isabel felt so utterly content she often wished she could spend the remainder of her life simply sitting here.

The constant fall of water from the fountain and the occasional cry of gulls as they took flight from their semi-frozen pond echoed the sounds of Paris. How could she go to Australia now? Why had she thought instantly of her mother upon hearing this news? Maggie was little more than a caricature for Isabel, a voice on the end of the phone, harshly Australian. No, she knew she'd have to deal with this in Paris, whether that be alone or with Alain's support. Isabel knew Paris, and all it delivered to her, was her destiny.

She'd never really thought much about having children. Whenever she saw Nicolette's grandchildren they generally left her alone, most of them too intimidated by their grandmother's made-up face and garishly coloured clothes to interrupt their conversation. Maybe she wouldn't be a mother after all? There was still time to change a certain course of events, take a different tack. It was unfair of her to expect Alain to change his role in their affair, becoming a father again wasn't his end of the bargain.

'He has the same eyes as you,' an elderly lady said and smiled at Isabel.

'Pardon?'

'My grandson, you look mesmerised by his eyes. I said this is because they look much like your own.'

Isabel became conscious of the fact that she was staring at a group of children playing with pebbles and sticks. How long had she been locked in his gaze without even realising it? Had his eyes, his infancy, been the catalyst for her thoughts?

'Your grandson is very beautiful,' Isabel smiled in reply. 'You must be very proud of him.'

The old woman took hold of the boy's hand and slowly led him away. It was time for everyone to leave, the park would be closing soon.

'Who was that lady, grandma?' Isabel heard the little boy ask as they walked further away. 'Do we know her?'

'No, I do not think so.'

'She looked –' Isabel didn't catch the last words but she guessed, by his slow backward glance, that he'd said *aux yeux tristes*. Sad-eyed.

Isabel

Was she sad, was that the impression she gave to strangers? Isabel rarely suffered from depression, life was just something you were dealt, and got on with. There were always people in the world far worse off – a life imperfect was hardly worth taking a handful of pills for. By the same token, when was the last time she had laughed out loud? She couldn't remember, and though Alain often made her smile, they weren't in the habit of rolling about on the floor in hysterics.

On the way home, she stopped for a cheap bottle of wine. Bulgarian red usually did the trick. Though she knew she shouldn't, she felt like getting intolerably drunk tonight. Studying should have been the only thing on her mind, this was a study day off work after all, but given today's phone call, that would have to wait. Alain was non-committal about tonight, unsure which woman he wanted to spend his Friday evening with. That was his luxury – lie to his wife about a premiere screening to spend the night with Isabel, or tell no lies and leave Isabel alone while he played happy father. She had sometimes thought of ending their affair but had trouble denying she was addicted to him, addicted to his virility, his masculinity, his sex. In bed for the hour or so after sex before he had to leave, he'd tell her of his past sexual experiences and she knew from these stories he was inviting her to experiment with him, and on him, tempting her to push both of their boundaries.

In many ways, Alain was one of the best things that ever happened to Isabel. He never questioned her motivations and while at times she felt like screaming at him to ask her about her thoughts, ask her anything at all, she knew her guarded nature was one of the things he liked best about her. He could

73

talk about things usually taboo in his life, ask her to perform favours he could never ask of his wife. It was as if her relative shyness shielded both of them from the outside world and anything that occurred between the two of them was erased from history each time he left her to return home to his wife and children.

Back in her apartment, she opened the red wine and made herself a snack of crusty bread and pickled herrings. Processed fish was one of her greatest weaknesses – smoked, canned, dried, salted – her cupboards were always full of the stuff. More or less waiting for Alain to call, she sprawled across her shagpile rug and searched through her bookshelves for the journal she had kept at the time of Patrick's first visit.

She placed a soundtrack in her CD player, sat cross-legged on the floor and flicked through her journal. Her relationship with Patrick had been great for those few days, it had been such a revelation to her. Patrick's eyes were opened to the world by the beauty of Jean-Marc. Isabel thought back to his funeral, how desolate she had felt sitting in the tiny church near where he grew up in Fontainebleau. She had not known anyone else at the service. Isabel had only been close to Jean-Marc her first year in Paris but they had kept in touch as he continued his studies in New York. It was there that he fell in love with an actor, a love that also bore the infection which eventually killed him. He finished nearly every letter by asking after Patrick, questions she never knew the answer to. Was he happy, was he in love?

Isabel looked through her journal for a particular passage she wrote about Patrick's last night. As she read, the tears

74

welling in her eyes made it difficult to focus. She thought of Jean-Marc, a friend she'd lost to distance and disease, and she thought of Patrick, a brother she was losing to distance and long-held family grudges.

Isabel lost all track of time. Before she knew it, she was three-quarters of the way through the red wine, onto her third CD and had devoured more than nine months of her journal life. When her doorbell buzzed, she was jolted out of her reverie. Isabel wasn't really in the mood for a visitor or prying neighbour.

'*Oui?*' She spoke impatiently through the ancient speaker next to her door.

'*Oui? C'est moi!*' *Moi* being Alain. He never, ever came around unannounced. Something must be wrong and the last thing she felt capable of right now was coaching her lover through the trials and tribulations of adultery. Isabel buzzed him into the building.

As usual, Alain opened her apartment door without knocking. In his hands he held a bottle of champagne and three long-stemmed roses.

'I think my wife is having an affair!' He was beaming.

Isabel was a little unsteady on her feet, her words slurred. 'And that is something to celebrate?'

'Don't you see, Isabel?'

'Obviously, I don't –'

'It is her acceptance of my infidelity, her understanding that nothing will change between you and me.'

'How do you *really* feel about some strange man in bed with your wife? Isn't that supposed to be a man's greatest fear, being compared sexually to someone else?' Isabel liked to challenge him in a way that gave her a small shot at holding the power in the relationship.

'It's not a fear of mine,' he dismissed it with a shrug.

'You don't care that he might be fucking her right now?'

'Ugh, why must you be so vivid, so disgusting?'

He was right, of course. What Alain's wife got up to in bed was no business, and no concern, of Isabel's. She relented.

'Sorry, my day has been terrible.'

'But now I am here to make it better!'

'Yes. You are, I suppose.'

'Suppose? *Suppose?* Come here!' He held out his open arms and they embraced, sharing long, wet kisses. As habit would dictate, within minutes he was removing his clothes. She looked over his body, wondering if she'd ever grow tired of seeing it naked. Though slight, he had barely an ounce of fat save for a little paunch, the very early beginnings of a belly. He was hairy all over, except for his balding head.

The strange arousing power he held over her made her feel helpless, as though every time they were together would be their last. Perhaps she was in love with this man after all, with the promise that he'd continue to fulfil her until her death.

As they made love, she thought about her body, of his thickness entering her and of how he felt perfectly suited to her own shape. His face in the moment of climax was vulnerable yet powerful, every hair on his body seemed to stand on its end.

'It makes me so hot to think of her with someone else,' he groaned. 'I love thinking of it.'

'Pardon?' Isabel asked calmly, not sure if she'd heard correctly.

'My wife, her lover. I know who he is, I've met him many times and I find it erotic to share her, it makes me feel strong.' It was his way to say whatever was on his mind.

'I want you to leave.'

'No, it's okay. Tonight I told her I was not coming home.'

'No, Alain, you misunderstood. I *want* you to leave.'

'But –'

'Get the hell out!' she screamed, feeling his stickiness in the hair between her legs, suddenly feeling repulsed. He'd practically just told her that her presence during his climax was incidental.

Confused, hurt, and still hard, Alain began to gather his clothes. Isabel couldn't bear to look at him. Listen to me, she felt like screaming, listen to what I have to say, what I found out today! Does that change how you think of me? Will I be more than just a place for you to be relieved? But she couldn't yell at him, not now, she lacked the energy. Her unpredictable emotions made her angrier – at once loathing his indifference yet always infatuated with their sex. It was an impossible situation, one she felt too dizzy to face. It was best that he leave.

Within moments he had slammed the door behind him. Isabel held her hands to her face and began to cry but, of course, there was the smell of him – sweet, musty, earthy. The tears fell more freely and she went to the bathroom to run herself a hot bath. She'd finish off that red, too. Her telephone rang, just audible above the thunder of the running water against enamel. Isabel was tempted not to answer it, one of his little tricks was to call her from the phone booth across the road after they fought, hoping she had cooled off enough before he moved too far from her apartment. She would usually apologise for yelling and allow him to come back. He liked to think that if she didn't stay angry for long he would get another chance. His predictability and persistence enraged Isabel. She turned off the taps and hurtled towards the phone.

'What?' she screamed into the receiver. She only ever spoke English to him when she was angry.

'Isabel?' a timid, resigned voice. English. No, Australian. Patrick.

'Patrick?' she asked in disbelief.

'Yeah. Are you okay? You sound kinda –'

'Not really. I, I . . . it's not a good time right now Patrick, I'm sorry. It's great to hear your voice, I was just thinking about you today actually, wondering how you were . . . are . . . but I just can't, I'm not up for a social chat right now. I truly am sorry, maybe –'

'Isabel! Slow down for a second. This isn't a social call, I'm calling with bad news.' He sounded somehow older, wiser than she remembered. Gone was the impatient naive boy. It sounded like he was making a business call. They were both silent. 'Mum left you a message on your mobile this morning. Isabel, it's Dad. He died.'

For the second time that day she was actually stunned. She feared she might go into shock. But why? Isabel had never really been close to Marcus, but somehow she had assumed he would always exist, that their Australian lives would continue without her whether she showed interest in them or not.

'How?' No, that was too morbid. She immediately added, 'Maggie. How's Maggie?'

'Not great, but okay, I guess. She got really pissed this afternoon.'

'Patrick!' she heard her mother feebly protest in the background.

'He died of a heart attack,' Patrick changed the subject. 'Mum had to turn off his life support and he couldn't survive without it. He crashed his car and had massive internal injuries, he suffered brain damage. We haven't done much about it yet, you're the first one we've called.'

'Oh, Patrick, this is so messed up. I'm sorry you're there dealing with this alone,' she said, not believing her own words. She wouldn't trade places with him for the world. 'What can I do?'

He lowered his voice and shuffled the receiver around, obviously turning away from Maggie. 'I think you should come home.'

'Yes, of course,' she blurted out without thinking. Yes? Just like that? Christ, of course it was yes, it was her father's funeral!

'You wanna speak to –?'

'Patrick, no! I couldn't. I'm so . . . cold. No, not . . . I just have no idea what to say to her. I'd better . . . Look, tell her I will call her later, I should organise a flight, time off work, you know?'

'It's four in the morning here.'

'Oh shit, yeah. Can you tell her I'll call her the second I know what I'm doing? Once this has all sunk in and I can think straight. I'd probably just upset her if I spoke to her now, I –'

'Yeah,' he said, feeling foolish for expecting that his sister might actually do this as a favour to him. 'Maggie's waving her hands about. Either she's telling you it's fine, or she's telling me to stop with the long-distance call.'

'Patrick!' their mother said again.

Despite the circumstances, or perhaps because of them, Isabel and Patrick couldn't help sharing a brief chuckle.

'Are you going to be alright?' he asked her, thinking she had little to worry about.

'Yes, I'll be alright,' she said without thinking, 'It's just so hard to believe . . .'

'See ya soon then,' he said, before hanging up without waiting for her response.

Isabel's gut instinct was to go and take that bath, make it a long one, then call her brother back after an hour or so and insist that every flight out of Paris was full. They could work through this just fine without her. No one need ever know that she'd lied. How could she face the familiarity of them now? How could she pretend to them that everything was fine and rosy in Paris when really she felt like melting into a heap? But then again, how could she ever live with the guilt of not going to her own father's funeral?

She picked up the phone again and dialled Nicolette's mobile.

'Hello, darling!'

'Hello. Where are you?' Isabel asked her flatly.

'It is Friday, at the hairdresser's, of course.' Nicolette went every Friday evening.

'And after that?' She clung to a thread of hope that Nicolette might actually be free for a change.

'You're not alright. I can tell.'

'No, something's happened. Well, a few things actually...
Nicolette, can I see you tonight?'

'Well of course, darling.' To the hairdresser she said
abruptly, 'You must finish up, I am needed,' and then to Isabel,
'I'll be there within the hour.'

Nicolette had become a sort of mother figure for Isabel,
replacing what should have been Maggie's role, someone she
could turn to whenever it was required, but someone who also
knew to give her space.

Isabel rang through to the operator and asked for the
numbers of Qantas, British Airways and Air France. It was only
six o'clock, surely one of them would still be open. As it turned
out, only Air France had something other than a recorded
message on the other end of the line. Shamelessly, Isabel utilised
her circumstances to get the cheapest, next available seat
(silently hoping for a compassionate upgrade). If she paid by
credit card over the phone, she could fly out at two the next
day. So fast, to be on the other side of the planet within about
forty-eight hours, when yesterday a visit to Australia hadn't
even raised itself in her consciousness.

Isabel started to feel nervous knowing she was getting on a
plane. She wasn't a great fan of flying, couldn't comprehend
how something that large and heavy could, usually, keep itself
up in the air. But she was also a believer in Fate, and she knew
that when her time was up it would all end, whether that was
a few kilometres in the air, or sitting alone in her apartment.
Then it dawned on her...if the flight was at two, she would
have to get to the airport by about twelve. Which meant that
she'd have to leave for the Metro at ten, just to be on the safe

side. This all meant that she would have to set her alarm for eight, which also meant that she had better start packing.

She pulled down an old suitcase from her closet. It was full of letters, photographs, tickets and maps from her first years in Paris. Nostalgia swept over her but it would have to wait. She upended the past onto the floor, noting the case in her hands was the very one she originally packed in Sydney all those years before. Rather fitting that it should see her through the trauma of her return. Where to start? Nope, she couldn't do it, not just yet. Time for that bath after all.

Isabel lay in the bath for half an hour, relishing the soapy warmth. She tried to remember the last time she talked to her father, but couldn't. The most she heard from him was a brief question shouted in the background as her mother talked to her on the telephone. He'd asked her if she'd seen snow falling this Christmas. No, she had not. 'How is the business?' she asked Maggie to relay in response. Cookin'! His standard response. The last time she'd seen him was three years ago. They had dinner together while he was in Paris on business for a few days. She thought about that trip now, its revelations based on chance and how it led to father and daughter finally beginning to understand each other.

What a relief it was when Marcus revealed the person he truly was, not simply the role he played in her life. Unlike Maggie who'd never shown anything remotely human. Though she had discovered it quite by accident, the revelation brought her closer to her father as she finally began to understand what made him tick, who made him laugh and who made him feel alive. She tried to imagine how things would have been had she not run into him on the street, the gods conspiring to force a truth. If only her mother could learn to embrace truth as her father had done. Marcus wasn't perfect, she knew that, but his willingness to allow her into his life meant more to Isabel than he realised. Even before she had glimpsed him at one with himself he had been so approachable, as though once removed from Maggie's controlling influence he could finally be the man he always longed to be.

'So, this is what's happened to your life,' Marcus said into her hair as they hugged hello. 'You've fallen in love with a fairytale called Paris. Isabel, what a city!'

It was unlike Marcus to be so poetic, uncharacteristic to be so encouraging of her choices. It'd been Isabel's intention to have dinner with him once, but they got along surprisingly well, so she volunteered to be his sightseeing guide the following day. They went to the Arc de Triomphe and admired the view from its roof. Marcus gazed at the bas-reliefs on its walls for close to an hour, saying he had never known they existed. They walked up the stairs of the Eiffel Tower together, Marcus occasionally stopping to regain his breath. His middle-age spread had grown since she had seen him last but she took this as a sign of the business' success, and him enjoying its rewards.

That evening, after criss-crossing Paris several times by Metro, they dined in the Latin Quarter, getting quite drunk. The more they drank, the less censored they became.

'Are you truly happy, Isabel?'

'Actually, yes Dad, I am pretty happy here.' Compared to where I could be, at least, she thought.

'You look it.' He stroked her hand. 'I want you to know how incredibly proud I am of you. I'm envious, actually.'

'Oh, come on, Dad!'

'No, it's quite true. I'm envious of your freedom.'

'And my *egalité et fraternité*?' she said before laughing cheekily.

'Yes, those too,' he said with a smile. 'Speak some more French for me.'

'Dad, no . . .'

'Please. Just . . . I don't know.' He turned to the wall behind him and took a magazine from the rack. 'Read me just a few paragraphs, anything at all.'

She read him a review of an opera and not a very good one, at that.

'Ah, yes,' he said with his eyes closed. 'I'll never stop being amazed by how beautiful it sounds.'

He walked her home before catching a taxi to his hotel. 'I hope you have a special friend in your life,' he said by way of goodbye. 'You deserve to be loved.'

Isabel watched the back of his head as the taxi pulled away, wondering what thoughts were filling it. How unexpected that the following day would provide a watershed.

For the second time that evening, the door buzzer interrupted her thoughts. Even as she was telling Nicolette about her day, Isabel was feeling a huge weight lift from her shoulders. It felt wonderful to finally confide in the woman she'd long considered her best friend. Isabel spoke without pausing for an hour, starting first with the news of her father's death, how it felt, and her plans for flying to Sydney the following day. She talked as Nicolette helped her pack, adding a sense of order to things and doing all the folding while Isabel went from drawer to cupboard, picking what clothing she thought appropriate for an Australian summer.

Once she started talking, it all kept flowing. Isabel told her about her affair with Alain, their fight. It all led to her telling Nicolette about the call from her doctor. She had felt nauseous for days; her period was heavy and had come late. Isabel hadn't even considered that it was possible to bleed while being pregnant. And besides, she was on the pill.

'Oh, darling, that's fabulous!' Nicolette hugged her. 'Being a mother makes a woman's life fulfilled, it all starts to make sense.'

'You know, in all my confusion and fear, the fight with Alain, my father's death ... I've barely had time to contemplate the fact that I'm pregnant. I never ever thought I would have children.'

'The pill, sweetheart, it is not foolproof. Nothing is certain in matters of contraception. I even heard of a woman who had her tubes done and still fell. She sued the doctor.' Nicolette was full of these kinds of stories, a tale to tell or a proverb to live your life by.

'Nicolette, I'm so scared ...' Isabel finally admitted.

'What of?'

'Life. Australia. My mother. Alain. Where would you like me to stop?'

'You have not told him, angel?'

'I haven't decided whether I want to.' Isabel knew how hopeless she was sounding but could do nothing to push her fears aside.

'But you must. He is the father; he is also your boss so you will have to tell him eventually. Actually, no. It is not a question of *must*. You can do as you please, I will help you.'

'What would I do without you?' Isabel asked her friend.

'Survive just like everyone else, I expect. Only you wouldn't have brunch as often.'

'No, I mean it, Nicolette. I wouldn't... I mean...' Tears started to flow down her cheeks.

Nicolette came to comfort her, stroking her back delicately.

'I'll tell him,' Isabel whispered. 'I don't know what he'll say, but I think I want this baby more than I've ever wanted anything.'

'Men are unpredictable beasts in the matter of commitment, that much is certain.' Nicolette spoke often of the troubles she'd had with men, her horror stories were a great source of amusement for them both but, in essence, they served to remind Isabel that not everything Nicolette lived through was enjoyable.

'I feel this is some sign.' Isabel moved away from her embrace, more composed now. 'Being told of a new life and a death in the same day. It's a chance for me to love, to share with this child what I never really shared with my father.'

'It's good, this,' Nicolette said in English. ''S marvellous!'

''S wonderful.' Isabel joined in on their familiar pick-me-up song.

''S what I like to see!' The two women laughed.

They both jumped at the buzz at Isabel's door. Nicolette walked towards it.

'Nicolette, what are you doing?' Isabel whispered harshly.

'Letting him in,' she said matter of factly. 'What else would I be doing?'

'But –' Isabel looked down at what she was wearing and the state of the apartment. She would have to tell him everything.

'I know men, darling. It will be Alain. Probably with flowers, definitely a little boozy.'

'I can't –' she tried her best.

'Hush!' Nicolette said. 'Make amends with the man. Tell him of Australia and your father. Make love to him and tell him about his child, or not. But see him before you go.'

Isabel knew she was right and nodded for Nicolette to let him in.

'Now, spare keys for me and I will look after everything while you are gone.' She pressed the button for Alain to enter. 'Remember your own words, Isabel. In Australia you must make up for lost time, show your mother and your brother the love you have, the love you want to show your own child. This could all be very good for you, no?'

Isabel kissed her and handed her a set of keys to the apartment. 'Well, you know I love *you*.'

'But of course, darling. I'm fabulous!' Seconds later she passed the handsome balding man on the stairwell, she eyed him up and down, and she approved. It would be a beautiful baby.

Isabel knew she would have no trouble telling him everything as Alain peered from behind a bunch of yellow roses.

Jack

He ignored the whispers and giggles of the teenagers as he paid for the magazine. What in hell did he care what they thought? It was a small town, he had nothing to hide. Not that it was possible to hide anything in Daylesford. Everyone knew everything. Well, almost. Some secrets were important enough to protect.

'How are you today, Jack?'

'Not bad,' he said to the woman behind the counter. She was new in town and he had never bothered to learn her name. Ever since Bev stopped running the newsagency he shopped there less frequently. Bev was good about things, even getting in some special magazines for him on occasion. They became firm friends and would often share a beer, chuckling at the images. Just because he bought magazines of naked men from her every once in a while, this new woman assumed she could call him by name, everyone knew it after all.

Bev once asked him why he stayed in such a small town where everyone knew his business, and commented on it. In a city no one would know the difference, and no one would give a 'rat's cadoodle', as she put it.

'Because I've lived here most of my life, Bev,' he answered her simply. 'I belong here just as much as the gossips, maybe more. To be honest, I don't like cities much.'

He really ought to get out to the home to visit Bev again. Not that it would really mean much, it'd been eight months since her stroke and she had all but lost her memory. He missed his old mate.

Jack said goodbye to the new woman who had subtly placed his magazine in a brown paper bag and taped it closed. For Christ's sake! It wasn't that the locals' idiosyncrasies offended him, he just found them annoying. How refreshing it would feel to face up to a brand new insult!

He was making his mother a special meal tonight, her eighty-sixth birthday. Jack was constantly in awe of her, she was still sharp as a tack with a wicked sense of humour and an outlandish habit of consistently speaking her mind. He couldn't help but adore her, also appreciating that together they made quite the pair of town freaks. He was the lonely, old, perverted poof, and she the old motor-mouth with the acid tongue. Would he have it any other way? Somehow he doubted it. Well, perhaps he'd have done some things differently if he'd had the chance to live his life over, but as for his status in Daylesford – it suited him just fine to be the focus of such suspicion and innuendo. One thing he always prided himself on, since turning forty, at least, was that he refused to run or hide. In the words of his favourite singer, 'I am what I am'. Screw 'em all. Perhaps there was even a part of him that thrived on the attention, a celebrity of sorts in a small town which had nothing better to gawk at. Cities were so impersonal. It would be easier to meld into the background in Sydney, just as Bev said, but who wanted anonymity? Not Jack.

It was a habit of his to stand in the fresh produce section of the supermarket and wait for inspiration. He would use whatever was in season to form the basis of his menu. Jack loved to cook. Since retiring, it was one of the few pleasures he could indulge in – reading infuriated him because he couldn't concentrate on the words, each sentence led him to his thoughts and memories and though his eyes scanned every single character on every page, not one iota of it held any meaning for him. The process of reading merely triggered self-reflection. Television made him want to be sick – Jack hadn't ever liked it, not even as a young man. And the notion of flicking a switch on a wireless in the hope of finding something that he might like was too much of a stab in the dark. But cooking, despite the countless hours he had stood in some metallic workspace aboard a stinking ship or in some tiny restaurant, attempting to create something remotely palatable with limited ingredients and utensils, despite having learnt everything he knew in a space which forced him into a permanent hunch, and despite the fact that he had lost two fingers while chopping carrots, of all things, in a storm at sea ... despite all of this, Jack found cooking the most therapeutic, challenging, rewarding and satisfying pastime there was. While cooking and preparing in silence, his mind was a void. It was his only art, his escape and salvation.

When he saw the plumpness of the Roma tomatoes he knew what he'd make. Jack always loved puttanesca and the way its taste stayed on his tongue for days; he believed it meant 'old whore', appropriately enough in his eyes. It had so many strong flavours, its unapologetic stench was complemented with a perfect balance of texture and taste. His mouth was beginning to water.

For dessert he wanted something subtle, a watermelon and vodka granita would be perfect. To finish, he would serve bitter Belgian chocolate and strong black coffee with a nip of Benedictine. His mother would be thrilled. Jack had given her her first sip of the stuff and now she had a glass of it every night. She said it was her dessert.

It didn't take him very long in the supermarket – he had most of the ingredients at home and the rest he could buy at the delicatessen. Its owner, Maureen, had an eight-year-old grandson who loved to marvel at Jack's missing fingers, the youngster was always dumbfounded, but never scared.

'Saturday again already, Jack?' she greeted him as he entered through the plastic streamers which served to keep the flies at bay.

'Guess so, Maureen, I can't believe it's come around again so quickly but I suppose there's no doubting it.'

'So, what's on the menu tonight? You always do something nice of a Saturday.'

Nearly everyone had to tilt their heads at a sharp angle to look Jack in the eye because he stood several inches over most.

Maureen was no exception. A rotund little woman who had married a Greek man in an attempt to dilute some of her raw Australian-ness. It hadn't worked. Though they'd moved to town twenty years ago to open Daylesford's first real delicatessen, Maureen knew nothing of European produce and it had been Anton who had done all of the buying... until he ran off with one of his young shophands. For the past six years, Maureen operated the deli alone and though the locals noticed a sharp fall in the quality and range of the goods on offer, most still shopped there out of a sense of loyalty to the town's original delicatessen if not out of a sense of pity for its sadly single owner.

Maureen stared up at him blankly, her eyes mere slits. She had never been able to open them properly, some defect forcing her to peek from beneath the lids as though she were afraid of what she might see. The thickly applied bright aqua eyeshadow did little to hide her affliction.

'I thought puttanesca. I haven't made that for ages.'

No sign of recognition.

'It's a pasta sauce,' Jack elaborated for her benefit. 'I'll need kalamata, purple olives, a jar of capers, some of these small fish pieces here in front of me and a quarter-kilo of that cheese there,' he said, pointing to the parmesan block. Such was the custom of shopping out of pity. Perhaps it was time to find a new deli after all. There was one near the supermarket, staffed by greasy-haired high school students, but surely they'd be trained to know what products they sold, whereas Maureen's customers and suppliers chose to forgive her ignorance.

'Where's the little tiger today?' It was Jack's nickname for the grandson.

'Oh, he's visiting his dad in Bendigo this weekend. Terrible thing, divorce. It ruins the children.'

Also ruins a fucking deli, Jack felt like adding, but he bit his tongue and smiled inwardly, knowing it was something his mother would find funny. 'I'll need some Belgian chocolate too, if you've got any,' he added instead.

Jack hated her routine, his charade of tolerance. Then again, his routine was just as predictable – venturing into town every Saturday to buy ingredients for his special weekly meal. Did people find his predictability annoying? He had never really thought to contemplate what life would be like post-retirement.

Jack joined the crew of a cargo ship at the age of nineteen after working as a kitchenhand at various cafes and restaurants around Daylesford and Melbourne. At that time, he had been trying to get his mind off certain events. Back then, Daylesford was a painful reminder of a lost love, an almost embarrassing time of misguided desires. He'd felt it impossible to share his anguish with anyone and this encouraged him to stay at sea for months on end. By the time he was twenty-one, he was the only chef on a ship making regular trips between Mombasa and Perth, working for a company that imported coffee from the beanfields of Africa, and textiles and crafts from its exploited population.

Jack was the cook for the crew of twelve – they were an odd array of souls, either lost or in pain, men who could go for weeks at a time without uttering a single word. It was the therapy that a young man grappling with rejection could never afford. Confronted by silence and with no one to share his secrets or his pain, his own thoughts eventually provided him with an agreeable companionship and it was during those years cooking in the dark, cramped galley that he called a truce with himself. He'd grown into a man surrounded by men who, at close to twice his age, had failed to discover themselves.

When the gin did flow among them, the mood turned lively and jovial until juniper depression set in. They'd tease Jack about his beauty and long hair; telling him his looks were wasted on washed-out bums on a ship that reeked of coffee, when he should be at home among the fillies of Australia and their newly emerging sexual liberation. Jack merely blushed, pieces of his heart still stuck in Daylesford despite the fact that it had been two years since he'd last laid eyes on the object of his affection, or even, obsession. Although solitude helped him come to terms with what he wanted, and allowed him to learn from mistakes, that very solitude also prevented him from meeting someone new, anyone to free him from the self-imposed prison of lost first love. Now he was shy and aloof, much younger in mind than his twenty-one years.

On one of the gin-drinking evenings, the mood turned sour between the men and what started as a mocking of Jack's beauty turned more toward envy. There was one particular crewmember Jack never trusted, one he rarely acknowledged. He was the laziest of the men, often alluding to the fact that the ship merely provided him with a means of escape from what he called 'the blue law'. What law he had broken he never did say exactly, but most of the other men guessed he was just big-noting himself, and it was probably little more than unpaid fines or basic fraud. Whatever the rest of the crew thought of Harry, the gin-soaked stench of the man was scarred into Jack's memory.

Most of the other men were already snoring but because Jack was younger and had the duty of tidying up, he was usually the last to fall. Whereas the men drank where they slept, Jack's bed was in an alcove off the kitchen so that his early morning preparations would not wake them. As more snores began to fill the room, Jack started to gather the empty and half-emptied gin bottles from the floor. While kneeling close to one, a thick, strong hand bolted out of the darkness to grab his hand. The grip was so strong Jack thought the glass would burst beneath his fingers.

'Alright, alright,' he said, thinking the man was just letting him know the bottle was not yet done with. Jack was also responsible for keeping the alcohol under lock and key. 'I'll leave you this one.' The hand released its grip, leaving Jack's fingers pulsating.

'You really ought to be careful, boy,' Harry said in the darkness. 'Something as pretty as you among these lonely confused men . . . must be tough sleeping at night, never knowing who might come a-callin'.' The hand briefly brushed his face, sending goosebumps over Jack's flesh. He didn't respond, but merely grabbed the bottle and left the room.

Three nights later, Jack was woken by a weight lying across the length of his back. As if in a dream, he allowed the events to unfurl without moving, offering no protest, no sound at all. Within minutes it was over and the lack of emotion did nothing to lessen how momentous an occasion it had been for Jack. There in the cramped darkness of his room, if Jack closed his eyes tightly enough and closed his mind to the sounds he heard, he could almost pretend this was someone else. In the surrendering of his liberty Jack was able to find the strength to embrace a new direction for his life. His first love had never reached this level of intimacy and now that Jack had crossed this line he felt more sure of himself.

The following day, as he made breakfast, feeling undeniably changed, he started to make plans for an escape. Although it had been painful and he burned with shame, he couldn't ignore the fact that he'd been aroused by this form of physical contact with another man. The violation gave him a confidence he thought he'd lost. Some part of him almost wished that it could happen again, but not with Harry; next time it would be on Jack's own terms.

When the boat docked in Mombasa later that day, Jack gathered all his possessions and pretended to head into town to fetch supplies.

He spent six months in Mombasa, finding work as a cook in one of the few tourist camps dotting the coast. Only the wealthy travelled to Africa in those days, paying locals a pittance to take them on safari and to cook and clean for them. A westerner who could cook western favourites soon garnered a reputation and, before long, the camp where he worked was one of the tourists' favourite places to eat.

Like the cargo ship, working in Mombasa was a lonely time for Jack. The local cooks respected and liked him, and were pleased to learn some of his techniques, but they generally didn't talk to him, the language and a presumption they made about his social status forcing a barrier between them. As he began to relax into his surrounds, Jack started to relate more to the tourists who poured through the camp. Many of them offered him drinks, and several females offered him something a little more personal.

One night, in the sticky humidity of his cabin, as the occasional shriek of a monkey signified yet another piece of fruit or jar of jam had been stolen, there was a timid knock at his door. Because it was the only way to sleep in Mombasa, he made his way to the door naked and opened it a fraction. There stood the young husband of a rich French tourist. She looked like an older version of Elizabeth Taylor and the husband, Jack now saw, was very good-looking indeed. While Jack was preparing the meals that evening, he had looked into the dining room often to see this man staring at him seductively. Then, when his shift was finished, Jack was sure he had sensed the man following him back to his room and though he had left his door open for some time, either the man's courage had waned or else Jack had imagined the whole thing.

'Excuse me, sir,' he said in a thick accent reminiscent of Jack's long-dead grandfather, and then burst into tears.

With little regard for his modesty, Jack ushered him into the room and placed a consoling arm around his shoulder. As the man continued to weep, Jack found himself a pair of shorts and poured each of them a glass of vodka to which he added a shot of honey and a stick of sugarcane.

'Tonight as I watch you in the kitchen...' the man said quietly, 'I think to myself – I am same age as this cook but I can tell he happy and me so very sad.'

African heat did strange things to people and Jack wasn't surprised by this unexpected midnight visit, or the outpouring of emotion. In fact, Jack frequently comforted a homesick tourist, or one who feared returning home to a civilised society where capitalism reigned. Usually the tourists were women – young and old – crying at having their advances rejected by someone who appeared to be worth taking the risk for. But this was the first male tourist to unravel before Jack and, while sensing they may have similar histories, he knew that should it come to it there was no way he would reject *this* crying tourist.

'Why are you sad?' Jack asked. 'You have a beautiful wife, you're rich . . .'

'She marry *me* for beauty. She tell me this all the time. I marry her for money but I tell her it is also for beauty. It all lies. We are very sad, we both.'

Jack handed him the vodka, knowing the man must've been craving company for months as the wife shot for ivory and mingled with similarly pretentious Europeans. 'What's your name?'

'Elijah.'

'I'm Jack.' Jack shook his hand.

'Oh, Jack,' Elijah jumped up quickly as though the personalisation of the conversation brought him to his senses, 'I no should have disturb you. I am fool.'

'It's fine,' Jack reassured him. 'Sometimes it feels better just to talk about how you're feeling. I wasn't sleeping anyway . . .' It was a shameful come-on but Jack had been celibate for months and he desperately needed relief.

Jack and the Italian talked until sunrise, occasionally kissing and fondling, their skin sticking together with perspiration. Elijah talked mostly about Paris, a city brimming with life, culture and beauty. As Jack lay there in the sanctity of another man's body heat, he felt an excitement that suggested he was wasting his time in Mombasa, the world had better things in store for him.

The following morning, Madame Froideur was none the wiser about her husband and as Jack watched them leave the camp hand in hand, his heart sank for the poor Italian and his ridiculous situation. The sight of the woman harshly instructing locals how to stack her ivory on a truck was the last straw for Jack. He knew he couldn't stay serving the likes of Madame Froideur a moment longer, so, for the third time that year, he gathered together his possessions and sneaked away from the life he'd created. Three hours later, he was on a train bound for Nairobi, looking to start over yet again. Tucked safely inside the pocket of his shirt was a matchbox across which Elijah had hastily scrawled his Paris address. At the time, Jack had absolutely no intention of going to Paris. The last thing he wanted was to try to convince a married man that choosing happiness was more rewarding than conforming to society.

In the six months he'd been in Africa, Jack hadn't ventured further than Mombasa. The train journey was a revelation to him, an introduction to the vast beauty of the continent and just a small taste of what it had to offer. A long way from home, he was in a place where every sight, smell, taste – every single sensation was foreign and completely awe-inspiring. A flock of ostrich running from the noise of the steam train, two distant Masai warriors dressed in red walking in the middle of nowhere, an army of vultures pecking frantically over some newly dead animal. Closer to Nairobi, he saw a group of giraffes silhouetted against the distant horizon, majestically making their way across the plain in search of water.

In the heat and disorganisation of the capital, Jack spent three long days searching for work. Organised kitchens were few and far between, and the small number of international hotels hired inexpensive locals for their kitchens. He visited the produce markets often, looking for restaurant owners, harassing them for work amid the overwhelming smell of meat warming under the blazing sun, African spices prickling the hairs in his nose, and succulent, exotic fruits sweetening the air. On the third day, a Dutchman took him in for an interview but the grill he owned specialised in the preparation of African game and Jack's experience was considered too western.

Dejected and worried about his dwindling savings, he boarded a plane for Cairo in the hope of eventually finding work in the port of Alexandria. It would have been cheaper to travel overland, but he figured that spending most of his savings on the flight would allow him to start working for real money sooner. On arrival in Cairo, he made a deal with himself – the only indulgence he would allow was a detour to the Great Pyramids at Giza.

The following day, with the mayhem and squalor of Cairo behind him, he stood at the foot of the Pyramid of Cheops, dwarfed by its enormous mass, physically unable to move an inch. Standing silently with his mouth agape, he ignored the pestering locals around him and simply contemplated existence.

He was proud of himself for making it so far, for seeing parts of the world most Australians would never get the chance to see. There was no time for him to see much more of Cairo, he desperately needed money and he knew he'd never find work there. He hitched a ride north and it took him less than three hours in the chaos of Alexandria to locate a crew of British men in need of a cook. They sailed from port to port in search of cargo – any cargo to be taken to any destination in the world. At each destination their search would begin again, no cargo refused, no port too far. The *Halcyon* had never had a cook before. Each man took his turn to cook but it was creating tension among the vessel's crew and the captain jumped at the chance to employ 'a pretty young convict' for a minimum wage plus a bonus paid as the ship pulled out of each port. They were setting sail the following day, carrying African art, Egyptian artefacts and tonnes of ivory bound for London.

The men spent their final night ashore getting drunk together in a bar near the ship, drinking a local brew and smoking hash. Jack was a welcome addition to their crew of eight and they sat listening intently as he told them about Australia. He described its vastness, of feeling overwhelmed by its mass. He talked of a country bursting with opportunity, hope and excitement where mateship was held in the highest esteem and people still slept with their doors unlocked. It was a fantasy for Jack, who had always felt disappointed by Australia's small mind, but there was no way he would deride his own country in front of a bunch of Poms. Frederick, the captain, was most interested and Jack promised him he would show him his homeland one day.

Jack spent the next four and a half years aboard The *Halcyon*. These years provided him with countless sexual experiences but none that he dared speak of. His beauty gave him a privileged status in the gay quarters of the ports – when he could locate their hidden doors. None of the crew knew of his persuasion, so bringing any conquest aboard was impossible. Often, his encounters took place in darkened alleys or public toilets and, on rarer occasions, in a local man's home. They were generally an hour or less of frantic movement with little or no conversation due to the difference in language and yet it seemed almost universal that a certain look shared between two men, even two strangers of opposite cultures, would inevitably lead to one thing. Jack supposed he liked it this way, these dalliances were free of restraint, clear of complication or commitment. They allowed him to hone his sexual skills without getting hurt, allowed him long yearned-for relief from those lonely weeks spent at sea.

In the fifty months of couriering, though, not one job led the *Halcyon* to any port in France. Jack began to develop an edginess, a desire to move on from his home of the past few years. It was time to say goodbye to his adopted family and begin anew, perhaps find some stability on land for a change. When the captain announced at Piraeus they were heading for Calais to collect a shipment of wine bound for New York, Jack knew it was time to move on from a life at sea. He went to his quarters and rummaged through his few possessions. When he found what he was looking for, Jack got an overwhelming desire to start facing up to the man he'd become.

At Calais, he took his modest wad of British pound notes, carefully folded his few clothes into an old canvas bag, added a few kitchen utensils he thought he could make use of and assured the captain he wouldn't miss the five o'clock deadline the following evening. Being the cook, he didn't have to work during those days at port; it was up to the other men to perform the labour of loading and unloading. They always ate on land when they could, leaving Jack free to roam until it was time to set sail again, his only task to buy the provisions for the ship.

Now he had to find a local market and arrange to have supplies delivered by four the following day. It would have been unfair to leave the men without food and to keep the ship's kitty for himself. After changing all his pounds, he found a merchant who could speak English and arranged for the delivery. When the groceries arrived without Jack the following day, the captain would understand. Frederick never held the *Halcyon* back – that was one of his few rules. If a man hadn't returned by sailing time it was assumed he'd abandoned ship. If it was the case that the sailor had rather got lost, or drunk, then it was up to the crewman to make his own way to the next port of call. If he didn't greet the *Halcyon* there, Frederick would immediately go about recruiting a replacement.

In the early evening Jack boarded a train for Paris, unsettled by the different rhythm of the journey after four-and-a-half years at sea. He began to suffer from motion sickness, and spent the majority of the journey with his head in a reeking, rusted toilet bowl. He purged until there was nothing left in his stomach. Weak and hungry, he practically crawled through

Gare du Nord and when he finally emerged onto the Parisian streets at eight o'clock, he burst into tears. He couldn't explain it, nor control his emotions, but he'd never felt so alone or so helplessly foreign in all his life. He sat on the front step of a closed *fromagerie* with his head in his hands, wondering whether he should turn back and make a mad dash for the familiarity of the *Halcyon*. Then, unexpectedly, he began to laugh. How many times had he moved on and never felt helpless, seeing each new start as a challenge to engage with and be rewarded by? He'd become settled on the *Halcyon* and he hadn't even realised it. Of all the ports and cities he'd been to, why should Paris be any more intimidating? Elijah had spoken of its endless wonders and Jack wanted to experience as many of them as possible. He rose to his feet, shook off his fragile state, and searched until he found a place to lay his head – an apartment building with a sign for 'cheap roms' tacked inside a shop window in its basement.

First thing the following morning, he sat down to a breakfast of *croque monsieur* and a bowl of coffee. He simply couldn't believe that bread with ham and cheese could taste so good. With a renewed strength of mind and body, he dashed about town taking in the famous sites of Paris, but his heart wasn't really into being a tourist and he felt disgusted at the filth to be avoided every second step. Shit, rubbish, rotting food, street bums, he had almost forgotten that cities (especially inland ones) could be allowed to fester away in their own insidious juices. And yet, there were certain aspects of that very filth he would actively seek, so he couldn't complain that he found some of it disagreeable.

He found the sex district later that evening and spent a few hours watching shows and cruising for some action. He eventually got the look in an adult shop and within minutes was being led to a stinking alleyway for yet another meaningless encounter. But this wasn't just another port of call, this suddenly felt inexcusable and Jack felt a sudden urge to cry again. Was this honestly what his life had amounted to? He knew he was better than this; he should be in bed with someone he loved, not in a cold alley full of rubbish. He filled with rage and for the first and only time in his life he punched out another man. Stunned by this sudden change in attitude from someone who had initially seemed so eager, the man collapsed to the ground and began whimpering for mercy. At once sickened and excited by his actions, Jack hastily zipped up his pants and ran from the scene. He knew this night was a turning point and that he would never again indulge in sex which was so blind to attraction, so utterly meaningless.

His self-disgust that evening prompted him to take affirmative action. The following day, Jack negotiated a good long-term deal with his landlord. Though the room was small and airless, it was very clean and at just five francs a day he could easily afford to live there for a few weeks without a job. Jack paid a month in advance and hit the street again, pounding the pavement to peddle his skills as an international chef. He started with the English-owned hotels he'd highlighted on a cheap map of the city. He knew his lack of French would serve as a distinct disadvantage and as a result he would be screwed over with an abysmal wage – but he truly didn't care about money; as long as he had enough to live on for this new start.

A small boutique hotel named The Belvedere eventually offered him shift work preparing the following day's meals and delivering late-night room service. It paid better than he had hoped and enabled him to take French lessons in the afternoon. He worked hard at learning the language and drove the hotel staff insane by insisting they help him learn as much as he could. Jack settled into his life in Paris just as easily as he had settled into life at sea.

As he became more comfortable in his new skin, Jack wrote a letter to Elijah. He decided on French knowing that Elijah's English was slow and, with the help of his teacher, he wrote a brief but inviting note. Jack wasn't even sure if Elijah would remember him, it'd been so many years, but he was bored of having no social life and was looking for companionship as well as someone to show him some of the hidden excitement of Paris.

It took Elijah several weeks to respond to the letter and Jack was pleased he was able to decipher it without his teacher's help. They exchanged telephone numbers and eventually agreed to meet at a small cafe near Villa Seurat.

At first they weren't quite sure of what to say to each other. After a few minutes of awkwardness, they began to tell each other about the past few years. Had their night in Mombasa been significant enough to rekindle any feelings? Jack described the places he'd seen, Elijah talked about the riches Madame Froideur gave him, his justification for staying with her. It was true, he conceded, in some ways he did love her, he loved the attention and affection she showed him, but their sexual relationship was virtually non-existent. They shared intimate conversations and Elijah had become accustomed to his new lifestyle just as Madame Froideur was increasingly proud of the trophy husband she flamboyantly paraded around her social scene. But Elijah couldn't deny his lifestyle was still a lie, just as it was when he last spoke to Jack that evening in Mombasa. Elijah told Jack his father had recently bequeathed him enough money to purchase a tiny bedsit near Montparnasse. He was spending more of his time there to escape from the Madame who, though well into her forties, was beginning to demand a child from Elijah. It would spell the end of the marriage, he insisted, if only he could tear himself away from her money and companionship. Without her, he felt alone and helpless.

For Jack, the meeting brought mixed emotions. He was pleased to be speaking English with someone he knew, however superficially, and just to see a familiar face was comforting. But he began to appreciate the futility of Elijah's situation with the Madame and rather than feel attracted to him, Jack could only pity him. The last thing Jack wanted to do was to lead Elijah on, to build a false hope that he could serve as his saviour. Coffees turned to beers, however, and by late that Sunday afternoon the flirtations began and Jack could do nothing to control his beer-induced sexual urge.

The sex was heated and frantic, both men eager for relief and to finish what had been started in Mombasa. Jack knew it was a foolish thing to do, knowing that he didn't really care for Elijah as more than a friend. Despite this, or because of it, as Elijah hurried back to Madame Froideur before she grew too suspicious, Jack gave in to his insistence that he move into the bedsit and use it as his own. If he could just maintain their status as friends, with occasional sex, he saw no conflict of interest and besides, he could do with a place with its own bathroom.

They settled into a routine of making love when either of their libidos demanded and as often as Madame Froideur's paranoia would allow. He and Elijah spoke mostly in French and after four months or so, Jack was fluent enough to rarely use English.

Jack eventually grew to admire all facets of the city he was now beginning to consider his own, and his culinary skills grew under the watchful eye of the hotel's sous chef. He began writing letters home to his mother, finally willing to reclaim his tenuous connection to Daylesford.

Though he tried to keep some emotional distance from Elijah, for the first time in his life Jack knew he was the recipient of a genuine, adult love. He never questioned Elijah or tried to assert his own feelings about their situation because he knew that Elijah would never make the decision to abandon Madame Froideur. Besides, the bedsit was so incredibly small, he doubted they – or any couple for that matter – could live there peacefully for any length of time before its cramped space would suffocate them. The arrangement lasted well into its second year but although Madame Froideur was a little on the sluggish side, she wasn't completely stupid and she eventually grew less tolerant and more suspicious of Elijah's distant nature. She employed someone to have him followed and it took her spy less than four hours to discover the truth behind Elijah's frequent disappearances. From the instant she was told of the other man it took her twenty-four hours to have every single reminder of Elijah removed from her house and hence from her life. He returned to the apartment late one evening to find all his things piled along the sidewalk and the door locks changed. No amount of screaming would bring the Madame to the window and eventually the police came to move him along. Rather than feeling relieved that his deceit could now be buried, however, Elijah sank into a deep depression. Although he was addicted to Jack for his love and sex, he was equally addicted to Madame Froideur for her wealth and without one, the other began to crumble. At the root of it, Elijah wasn't able to admit his homosexuality and being known in certain quartiers as *Nounours Froideur* afforded him, in his own eyes, a more agreeable reputation.

It was soon obvious to Jack the love Elijah had for him existed only if Elijah was happy, and Elijah's happiness was contingent upon his wealth. For nights they argued, throwing things at each other, Jack demanding that Elijah be reasonable. But Jack also knew that the money he earned as a chef wasn't anywhere near enough to keep Elijah in the lifestyle to which he had grown accustomed. It was a life, after all, in which the young Italian had never worked a single day. Almost instantly, Elijah became a completely different man. By turns pathetic and whining, he began to speak of finding a way to punish Madame Froideur. Jack tolerated this erratic behaviour for six weeks, trying to believe their friendship was strong enough to cure Elijah of his sudden personality shift. When Jack delivered his ultimatum, Elijah took it silently, merely nodding as Jack explained that Elijah must return to the Madame and his opulent life because Jack couldn't care for him as well. Besides, he had no desire to be with Elijah fulltime. Elijah picked up his keys and left the bedsit without uttering a single word. When Jack left for work six hours later, he still hadn't returned.

Jack got home from his shift in the early hours of the morning to find his keys no longer fitted the lock of the bedsit. His rucksack sat on the stairs, filled with all he owned. He thought of kicking the door in or pleading reason with Elijah but instead he just gathered up his things and turned to walk away. He had never been in love with Elijah and that wasn't going to change. Jack was too proud to be his other lover, too independent to enter into that hopeless triangle again. He wasn't ready to move on from Paris, however, and he began to dread the thought of upheaval once again.

Too confused to think beyond the moment, he walked for hours that evening, not caring that he had nowhere to go. As the rising sun turned the sky from black to grey, he decided to keep moving, taking the first southbound train from Gare de Lyon. By late evening he was roaming Marseilles, searching for yet another place to begin again, and a restaurant with a 'help wanted' sign.

As a child, his mother repeatedly told him he was like a cat. He'd have many lives, of that she was sure, and no matter what life threw at him, no matter how hard he fell, he would always land on his feet. Up until Marseilles, her prophecy had proved true enough and, several weeks later when he moved into a room above the restaurant where he worked, her prophecy continued.

Jack worked his way through many different restaurants, each one teaching him new skills, adding more dishes to his already considerable repertoire. Lovers passed through his life and he refused to allow himself to feel too much affection for any of them, no matter the temptation. He was generally a solitary man and he preferred it that way, the locals accepted him for the outsider that he was. By his sixth year in Marseilles, he opened his own brasserie and was, for all intents and purposes, accepted as a local businessman *avec pas femme*. As his thirty-fifth birthday loomed, he experienced a sinking feeling – for though he had crammed so much into his existence, he still felt there were things he needed to do, places he still needed to see. As he watched his mother's script grow shaky, and read of her battle with pneumonia, he felt a real desire to see her again, to know her as a person, not just as his mother. While he considered his options, he stayed in Marseilles, continuing the lease on his successful brasserie and making enough of a living to add considerably to his savings.

When Sir Freddy glided through the doors of the brasserie in search of a British beer it was as though the gods provided him with the direction he'd been seeking.

Freddy took one look at Jack and burst out laughing. 'Well, I'll be blowed!' he slapped Jack on the back. 'It's been about ten years and you're still the prettiest darn convict I've ever seen.' They stayed up late into the night getting drunk on Italian beer because Jack never served British.

'Bloody cooks,' Freddy said with a sigh. 'Unreliable bunch. Never had one who stayed as long as you did Jack – not one! You know, when we sailed out of Calais, I thought against all logic that we'd see you again in New York, knowing of course that you'd never be back. After four years and about thirty fucking cooks, I gave up. Went back to a roster for every man. Had a few women too, over the years. On the crew, I mean!'

'I thought that was one of your rules, Frederick, no female crew.'

'Well, times are tough, I have to say that Jack. No one finds the idea of boat couriering as romantic as they once did. Big business is moving in, not to mention fucking planes. Faster. Everyone wants things there faster. It's not as easy as it was. More often than not we're leaving ports empty, moving on with blind hope.'

'So, what brings you to Marseilles?'

'Blind fucking hope!'

It was strange that their conversation seemed more personal now than it ever had in all those months they'd worked together. It was comforting for Jack to be speaking English again, and to be reminded of the freedom of being surrounded only by the sea.

'Going to see a man tomorrow, about taking a shitload of liquor down to some fuckhole called Perth.' He was smiling broadly.

'You can't be serious!' Jack shoved his shoulder.

'Sure am. Still haven't been to that colony myself. I've heard they breed pretty homosexuals down there though.'

'You bastard, you knew?'

'Mate, of course. It's a captain's job to know everything about his crew. And besides, no woman wants a man as pretty as you.'

'Fuck off.' They drank silently for a few minutes. 'Frederick, if you can call me a pretty homo, I can call you Sir Freddy to your face.'

'Oh, everyone does now. First man that did it ended up going overboard, mysteriously, mind you, but I've mellowed with age.'

'Like a good red, Sir Freddy? Would you ever take a cook again? I mean, it's a bloody long way to Australia, you know.'

'Oh, I might.'

'Well, if you get this job, I might know of someone who'd be interested.'

'Let him know there's been a new rule added,' he said, sounding very official.

'Oh, yes?' Jack asked sheepishly.

'No peeking on the other men in the shower.'

Jack smiled. 'This guy might not be so interested after all.'

She was early. Though she'd been early for everything all her life, Jack never got into the habit of telling her a much later time.

'Happy birthday, you old bag!' He embraced his mother at the door.

'Thanks, you little shit. Now show me some respect, it's my birthday!' She sniffed the air. 'Smells like old whore to me!'

'Mother, your talents never cease to amaze, nor your charms. Now come in, sit down, I've got your favourite wine.'

'Oh, thanks love.' She looked around his modest three-roomed cottage. 'You always keep it so clean, Jack. Do you have too much time on your hands?'

'Maybe, but I get it from you, you realise? You were always moaning about clutter around our house. I think that's why you didn't stay with Fat Frank for long...you told me once you felt he was like a big piece of clutter!'

'Did I?' she chuckled. 'I don't remember that. I dreamed about your brother the other night, in it he kept reminding me of some abuse I once yelled at your father.'

'What?'

'Oh, I can't remember,' she said with a shrug.

'I miss Stefan.' Jack forced a smile.

'Me too, love. Me too. I find I'm always wondering what he'd be like today but in my dreams he's always a teenager.'

'Yeah.' Jack dismissed her before sentimentality took hold. 'And I wonder whether he'd be speaking to me again. Anyway, I got you a present –'

'Ja-ack!' she protested.

'I know, I know. What do you give the woman who has everything?'

'Besides a new liver?' She raised her glass of wine.

He saluted his own in response. 'Well, you wouldn't want mine, trust me.'

Liz opened her present excitedly. It was a large coffee table book on African elephants. Her bookshelves were full of books about elephants, she was obsessed with them.

'Hope you haven't got that one? I searched eBay for weeks looking for one you don't already have.'

'No, I don't have it! It's wonderful, thank you.' She got up to kiss him gently on the cheek. 'I was sort of hoping you'd buy me that gift voucher for the tattoo parlour, make my mind up for me.'

'Well, I did think about that,' he said jokingly, 'but I doubt they'd be able to find any wrinkle-free skin.' Deep down he was mortified that a woman her age would even consider getting a tattoo, but that was just like her.

She was one of his best friends, had been for years. Jack had got seriously ill a few years before and was hospitalised for weeks, ending up in intensive care. When he had recovered, Liz had insisted he begin telling her more about his life. The saddest, most painful thing about losing him, she had said, was the thought that he could have died a stranger to her. After all these years, she was prepared to hear all of the details – if it was a part of him, she wanted to know. He granted her wish, and though it felt strange confiding in her at first, usually requiring a lot of wine to loosen his tongue, eventually it became second nature. In return, Liz told Jack more about her own life. Why she'd married Emile (to annoy her own father), and why she'd gone with Fat Frank (to get Emile out of her life).

Now she and Jack met regularly for dinner, and to gossip about the locals and who was screwing whom, both actually and metaphorically.

The meal went flawlessly. Jack genuinely enjoyed spoiling his mother. Without her, he would be quite lonely in this town. Not Liz, though, she had her lawn bowls and housie and about a million friends asking her to various social functions. People her own age adored her, the rest of the town thought she was bizarre.

She got up to leave at about ten. 'What are you doing tomorrow?' she asked by way of goodbye. 'I thought we could go to that sale in Bendigo or something.'

'I can't, Mother, I already told you. I'm going up to Newcastle again tomorrow.'

'Oh yes, of course you are. My mind is like a sieve these days. I ran into George Apperton this morning.'

'Really?' Jack asked, his heart skipping a beat at what would follow.

'We got talking about the family, he says Patrick called him and left a very strange message. He's worried something is wrong.'

'It's unlike Patrick to call anyone in the family. I'll give Marcus a call and get things cleared up, I might pop around to see George before I go, let him know things are fine.'

'Well, enjoy your time up there.' She kissed him goodbye and added, 'Sort it out as soon as you can. George said he heard something about an accident but Patrick's mobile phone was cutting out so he couldn't get the whole message and he said there's no answer at Marcus' house.'

He watched her walk to the end of the drive and shuffle off down the street. For some reason he knew to expect the worst and his heart told him that Patrick could only be calling for one reason.

Wake

Though she hadn't the faintest idea what made a wake successful, Maggie insisted that Marcus' be held at the house, and that she do all of the catering for it. Because she kept insisting, Patrick left her alone on Sunday and for the first time in her life, she felt totally isolated. He had been absolutely perfect, though, arranging the funeral and calling the necessary relatives and acquaintances. How Patrick had known a thing about organising someone's burial was anyone's guess but Maggie knew she was grateful to her son. In the two days they had spent together she couldn't deny that she was beginning to regret some of her past behaviour towards him. Perhaps Maggie had been selfish in her rejection of his choices. No, she chided herself, she wasn't allowed to use the term 'choice' when it came to Patrick, he'd argued that often enough. There was no denying the fact that what she craved most in life now was a chance to get to know her children before her own time was up.

Maggie had slept most of Saturday. Well, she had refused to get out of bed at least, though the few moments she'd drifted off could hardly be considered sleep. Patrick disappeared for most of the day taking Leroy in his car, a treat the dog adored but rarely received. Regardless of the circumstances at home – a family meal, a heated argument, a dead father – it was normal for Patrick to take his dog and disappear for hours. Mostly, Maggie suspected the two of them sat at Macmaster's Beach gazing out over the ocean, the master pondering a thousand different thoughts, the dog humble and content. When Patrick was younger, he and Maggie were quite close, often spending school holidays together, shopping for knicknacks or seeing the latest film. But in his early teens Patrick pushed both of his parents away, preferring to spend hours isolated in his room, poring over pop magazines and analysing the weekly Top Forty. Who could blame him though? Maggie thought. Patrick didn't trust anyone with his secrets. Maggie knew he had good cause too, for even his *revelation* as a young man was met with her disdain. It seemed there was nothing at all to keep the family together once Patrick grew old enough to rely solely on himself.

How on earth could Maggie still pretend that his sexuality was a shocking revelation? She had long suspected it, and often followed his eyes as they gazed a little too longingly over other men – at the beach, in magazines, on television. So what, then, had caused her to react so dismissively to it? Her own fear, or perhaps a concern for his wellbeing? No, certainly not the latter. Patrick was more than capable of looking after himself. The disbelief, the tears and rejection were indeed selfish responses.

When Patrick finally returned it was close to dusk, and Maggie was still lolling about in bed just as he had left her, struggling with her thoughts and searching desperately for a reason, any reason, to get out of bed.

'I brought you some food,' he whispered when he saw she was awake.

'Thanks, but I don't think I can eat.'

'You have to eat, don't be silly. You can't just waste away.'

'I was thinking a lot while you were away. Where did you go?'

'Here and there,' Patrick said with a shrug. 'What were you thinking?'

'Oh, this and that.' Maggie shrugged too, unconscious of her mimicry. 'Patrick, where did you go?'

'Funeral home, Mother. I've chosen the casket and booked the chapel, there's a chaplain free on Friday. I thought you'd want me to get things organised.'

'I hadn't even thought –'

'My point exactly!' he interrupted her.

'– you were grown up enough for this,' she continued. 'I suppose I hadn't even realised that you were an adult, a man.'

'I think it's time you got out of bed.' Patrick certainly wasn't about to allow self-pity.

'Will you ever forgive me, Patrick?'

Before he could answer, the telephone rang. The instant she heard its shrill tone, Maggie's heart sank with the fear that she'd never find the courage to ask her son's forgiveness again.

It was Isabel. She told Patrick she'd be arriving in Sydney a little after eight on Monday morning.

'So how is she?' Isabel asked tentatively.

'A bit slow; she stayed in bed all day today and she's not eating anything.'

'God, it's as though a part of her has died too.'

'We have to make sure she doesn't think like that.'

Overhearing Patrick's side of the conversation, Maggie felt pitiful. She pulled herself up off the bed and went to have a cool shower. Under the water she began to feel vaguely human again, though her tears were indistinguishable from the shower water.

In the kitchen, Patrick felt useless. This insight into having to care for a decrepit parent scared the hell out of him because he didn't have any idea what to do. He didn't want to indulge her, but that was because he was too scared of tapping into the emotional turmoil she must be hiding. He thought the liability of looking after Maggie would never be his but with Isabel in Paris and Marcus gone, there was now only one candidate.

He was relieved to see his mother looking more animated after her shower. Leroy bounded over to lick between her toes and instead of being impatient and abrupt, she showed affection to him for the first time since Patrick had arrived.

'Feeling better?'

'I suppose so.'

'Can I get you anything?'

'You know, actually, I think I'd like a beer. I think Marcus put some Crown Lagers in the fridge.'

'You're not hungover?'

'Not anymore. And I think I can decide for myself.' Maggie raised a suspicious eyebrow.

'Yeah, yeah. All right, I'll have one too.'

They sat on the back verandah sipping their cold beers and eating cheese and crackers. Leroy sat at their feet, waiting to be thrown scraps of cheese. Facing the same direction, they looked out over the greyness of the water. It was a typical summer's evening, full of the sound of crickets, a distant sprinkler and Leroy's occasional sighs in protest of the heat or not getting enough cheese. Five minutes passed in silence as though they were watching a film and had agreed not to speak.

Maggie broke the silence. 'When I first met your father, I thought he was the most dashing, well-mannered gentleman. We met at night, some outdoor party, and the only light came from a big bonfire. It was on a property outside Bendigo; my cousin dragged me to the party because she had a crush on some stockman. Your father was manning the bar, you know, a few buckets filled with ice and countless bottles of beer.'

Patrick was listening intently to his mother. It wasn't often that she spoke about the past and he read between her words to find some deeper meaning as he casually stroked Leroy's fur with his bare feet.

'So there he was,' Maggie continued, 'this charming man. I asked for a juice and he made some remark about sweetness. Really corny stuff, I suppose. My cousin went after her stockman and left me alone. I was sitting there, getting more bored by the minute, and my eyes kept wandering over to your father. He was so polite, he treated everyone with the utmost respect, and they responded to his kindness with genuine affection.'

Maggie looked over at Patrick and sighed. 'Oh, would you listen to me? You must be bored out of your brain!'

'I'm not bored, keep going. I want to hear this, I want to know.'

'Well, he walked me to my car at the end of the night and said goodbye and I presumed I'd never see him again. I was a bit timid, and would never have suggested anything. I fell asleep waiting for my cousin and early in the morning I was woken by a tap at the window on the driver's side. It was your father; he'd brought me a sausage sandwich for breakfast. I was just so touched by that, by the fact that he'd kept a distant watch on me all night, knew which car I was sleeping in and had waited until the decency of morning to make further contact.'

'I don't think you'd get that these days,' Patrick teased. 'Your car would've been surrounded by a mob of horny, pimply-faced hicks.'

'Patrick! Anyway, not if your father had been there,' Maggie said and smiled, her profile making her look more like the girl of whom she now spoke. 'In the light of day, I was surprised to see exactly what he looked like. You see, he wasn't my type at all – or so I thought. He had freckles which I never liked, but there was something, Patrick, a generosity of spirit and a longing to be nurtured. You will know when you meet the right one . . .'

'I reckon I've just about given up on that,' Patrick sighed. 'I'm getting old and fat –'

'Stop talking such nonsense. Anyway, appearance won't mean a thing to someone who genuinely loves your spirit.'

Her retort forced them back into silence so they sat, drinking their beers faster than before.

During their fourth beer, Maggie and Patrick decided to look through Isabel's vinyl collection. Isabel loved disco, and though Maggie couldn't understand what the craze was about, she had heard Isabel play her records ad nauseam. By default, she became quite fond of disco. To her, disco was something that couldn't be taken seriously and though it may have been in their subconscious, both Maggie and Patrick were eager to keep their spirits high. The beers tinted the evening nicely, allowing each of them to ignore the tensions they shared, and the fact that they were from entirely different generations. The only conversation that took place was the occasional 'Oh, remember this one?' Or 'Isabel loved this!' They took their time going through the collection of forty-fives.

Midnight came and went, as did the last two lagers in the bar fridge. They were a little unsteady on their feet by the time they agreed to go to bed. As soon as the stereo was turned off, Leroy bolted for the room where Patrick slept.

'Cheeky thing,' Maggie said. 'Thanks for staying up with me, Patrick.' A spontaneous hug took them both by surprise; it was an awkward embrace. Maggie refused to let go and before long she started to sob. 'I'm so sorry,' she whispered.

'Don't be sorry, it's okay to be sad, Mum.' Patrick rubbed her back, the intimacy completely foreign to him.

'No. No, not that,' she pulled away from him and looked up into his face. 'I mean... I've wanted to tell you I'm sorry for pushing you away, for not supporting you like a mother should.'

'I can look after myself, don't worry.'

'Patrick,' she said firmly, 'I mean it! I'm deeply sorry. I want to be . . . I want things between us to change before . . .'

'Before what? Why would things change all of a sudden?'

'Before it's too late. It mightn't seem it from all this drinking I've been indulging in, but I still need to grieve; I'll need some time alone. After that, I want us to start over, resolve things. Is that asking the impossible?'

'I'm really not sure, Maggie. If that's what you want, we can give it a try but I'm not sure how I feel, to be honest. We've been strangers for so long . . .'

Patrick had been waiting for this moment for a long time, but things were so strained between them, he didn't think he'd suddenly be able to share his feelings openly. He asked himself whether this was something he wanted, to befriend his mother after more than ten years of distancing himself from the impact she had on him. He was tired of the effort involved in continually pushing her away. Could solving the issues between them help him find happiness, assist him in his own self-realisation?

'I think you should go back to Sydney tomorrow.' Maggie wiped tears from her eyes.

'Nah, I think I'll stay here a while longer if that's alright?'

'What if I asked you to do it for me? I need the time . . . just to think straight. Besides, I have so much to do with organising the wake and preparing the house. And I have Kathy. I feel so awful for not talking to her today, she must be worried sick.'

'I don't think you should be on your own,' Patrick protested.

'Well, to be frank, I have to get used to being on my own just as you have to get used to not having a father. Patrick?'

'What?'

'It would mean a lot to me if you were to meet Isabel at the airport, let her stay with you for a few nights instead of in some awful hotel.'

He was silently disappointed to be cutting short their bonding time but could understand why she wanted it this way. He knew Isabel was another nut he needed to crack. 'Okay, but only if you're sure?'

'Yes, yes,' she slurred. 'I am sure.'

'Shit! I just remembered. I'm supposed to be going to Brisbane tomorrow.'

'Oh?' Maggie began gathering the empty beer bottles.

'For work,' Patrick continued. 'I'm gonna have to find someone else to send.' Patrick worked in a recruitment agency which specialised in placing new graduates. At the beginning of each year, he was sent to scour universities across the country, setting up information booths and meeting with graduates.

'Surely your boss will help you out?' Maggie shouted from the kitchen as Patrick began to put away the records.

'Not a chance,' he said. 'I may as well ask for the whole week off. That way I'll get some time with Isabel, and we'll come up on Wednesday night to help you with everything for Friday. Is that alright?'

Hearing their noise, Leroy prowled cautiously down the hallway to see if it was safe to stay in the lounge room, or close enough to bedtime to fear being pushed outside. The unspoken rule of the house was that if he made it to a bed before the lights were turned off, he could stay inside all night but if he was in the lounge room or on the patio, he'd generally be put outside. He continued watching as Patrick finished putting the vinyl discs in their correct sleeves and the instant he stood, the dog bolted again for the spare room.

'He's such a cunning thing.' Maggie shook her head in disbelief. 'You know, he only ever really responds to discipline from you or Marcus. I suppose he'll run riot now.'

'I just can't believe he's dead,' Patrick said blankly. 'I know everyone says that, but I keep expecting him to walk in the room. Do you think this is gonna hit me hard at some point?'

'I honestly can't say. You strike me, Patrick, as the type of young man who can hold his emotions well.' There was a moment of awkwardness between them as Maggie waited for him to respond. When he didn't, she said, 'I'm off to bed.'

''Night, Maggie.' For the briefest moment he felt an ember of affection for her, glowing deep within.

Cordial was the word he used to describe his relationship with his mother. They rarely scratched any further beneath the surface and, rather than cause confrontation, Patrick tried to treat her with respect. He was never mean to her like Isabel could be and he didn't ridicule the shallow nature of her social observations. When she tried to be funny, on those incredibly rare occasions, he found a polite laugh to humour her. Greetings and farewells weren't accompanied with a kiss, in fact, there was never any touching. Patrick avoided looking into her eyes because he didn't want to see the connection that existed no matter how far they drifted apart. He knew they were more similar than either of them cared to acknowledge and as a result he thought he understood her – her motivations and fears, her desires and innermost thoughts. But Patrick couldn't have been any further from the truth.

He went around and turned off all the lights and locked the door, gulped three large glasses of water and went to the toilet. A shiver ran down his spine as he remembered listening to the night-time sounds made by his father, the final ones being urine splashing into water and a half-flush. It disturbed him that he was now echoing his dead father's routine and that evening, despite the humidity, he spent the majority of his sleep tightly hugging Leroy.

Patrick talked on the phone for hours on Sunday morning. First, he called his boss to explain the situation and ask for leave. Patrick didn't like his boss and asking her for compassion made him feel weak. Though she was understanding about his desire to be with his family for the week, she nevertheless hesitated for some minutes over his request that she find a replacement for the Brisbane trip. Her compassion was rather limited, as it turned out, and she insisted that Patrick find a replacement himself, and arrange the necessary changes with the airline. Just before passing on her sympathies, she reminded him that company policy stated a maximum of three days compassionate leave were allowable but as she thought Patrick had been performing well of late, she'd consider extending it to the five days he'd requested if he found a suitable replacement for Brisbane.

The third colleague Patrick managed to track down, to beg (by that stage), was Simon Harlen. It should have come as no surprise to Patrick that his colleagues would be so unaccommodating. In the past he had found the majority of them spectacularly unsympathetic to the plight of any of the other employees. Those rostered on for weekend work had Buckley's chance of ever finding someone to cover for them. In the end, compassion came from the least likely of sources.

Simon was a young innocent when he began at the company and it took Patrick no time at all to start flirting. It was the game Patrick usually played – show enough attention in order to get some in return but once he had his target hooked, he'd ease himself away, retreating before anyone could penetrate his carefully constructed exterior. If sex happened at any point during the cat and mouse struggle, that was a bonus but he rarely thought about the impact on those he courted. In Simon's case, although it was against his rules, he had relented and agreed to a date.

He made Simon do all the talking. Simon took Patrick to a bar which made him feel old and ill-at-ease. Patrick insisted they sit in a darkened corner irrespective of the fact that Simon might take this as a move toward the romantic.

As he sat making banal chat, Patrick knew the only thing he wanted was sex – devoid of emotion, a purely physical exchange. He knew it was unfair of him to take advantage of Simon as he sat there innocently talking about his family and his dogs. He talked about his harsh Croatian stepfather, his absent mother who ran a teashop in the city and his uncaring older brother who was addicted to methadone. The hours passed and Patrick kept drinking, trying to ease his insecurities. Simon ordered bread and tzatziki and the stench of the yoghurt and beer on his breath made Patrick want to heave. He politely excused himself from the table and went to the toilet. Then he left – he simply snuck out of the bar and left Simon sitting, waiting, two fresh drinks before him. There seemed no logical excuse Patrick could use; it just felt the easiest, most sane thing to do.

They rarely spoke after that unless work required it. For weeks Patrick avoided the look of hurt in Simon's eyes, a look which implored an explanation. But none would be forthcoming. Then, as Simon came into his own, blossoming into a bright, energetic, popular man on the gay scene, Patrick developed a hatred towards him. Envious and rejected, the tables had turned and Patrick searched for anyone to blame but himself. He was playing a dangerous game, seeking approval in order to gain the strength to reject.

Calling Simon two days after hearing of his father's death and being dumped by Damien was, for Patrick, an exercise in swallowing hurt pride. Simon was surprisingly understanding: of course he would go to Brisbane for Patrick. This was one of many unexpected moments surrounding the events of Marcus' death which highlighted the generosity of others to Patrick, and, indirectly, encouraged him to make contact with his family's past.

Patrick had shed few tears for Marcus, there'd been no gut-wrenching outpouring of emotion, but there had been a tacit recognition within him that things were fundamentally changed – nothing could be the same again. Mixed with that inescapable sensation of deep loss, like an amputee moving to scratch a limb that no longer exists, Patrick also knew a fatherless future would bring new realisations. Perhaps of self, perhaps of humanity. Though things between him and Maggie had been strained for many years, perhaps his father's death could be the key to unlocking the reasons behind their mutual antagonism. He now felt sorry for her, in her new status as a widow, and he knew the sadness he felt at losing his father was also anchored in his own unhappiness with who he had become as a man. In light of being fatherless, and the recognition that he knew so little about his own history, he decided he would try to remain patient as Maggie peeled away her layers. He was sure this would help him be a better person and it might go some way to solving his state of loneliness. He was so grateful for Simon's generosity, he also knew he would make friends with him, apologise for his abysmal behaviour and attempt to regain his trust.

After forty minutes on hold to an obviously under-resourced airline, he called Simon back to confirm the arrangements. He was careful to show Simon genuine gratitude and he detected a warmth in the voice on the other end of the line suggesting that perhaps they could form a friendship after all.

Patrick ensured Maggie had everything she needed until his return with Isabel on Wednesday, took Leroy for one last walk and left what had recently become his *mother's* house. It was a vacant drive for him, one of those apparently done on auto-pilot with barely a conscious thought. Had he known that at the exact instant he entered his empty apartment, both he and Maggie crumbled into sobbing heaps – kilometres apart, yet feeling the same – perhaps they would have been able to find words adequate to console the other; two hollow shells of life, reflecting, but barely comprehending, the past forty-eight hours.

Maggie finally surrendered to her sense of guilt and made the effort to return Kathy's call. In a matter of minutes, Kathy was at the door and both women embraced. Maggie realised the next few weeks would demand she exhibit the same emotion many times, as each new person fought to find the right words to say. Kathy was as sensitive as always and allowed Maggie to steer the conversation and mood. There was no reminiscing this evening, just a need to get certain tasks done. Kathy called the lunch ladies and even a few of the other unreturned messages that had filled the answering machine yet again. She helped compile a menu and shopping list for the wake and made them both a chicken and broad bean salad for dinner. They stayed up late into the night, playing Scrabble and drinking herbal tea and Maggie was silently grateful when Kathy offered to stay the night.

The flight proved more exhausting for Isabel than she could have guessed. Never a big fan of flying, with the heightened threat of terrorism, deep vein thrombosis and increasingly frequent reports of mechanical failure, she was now even more afraid. Who would have ever thought that Concorde would simply do a back flip and explode? What sadist could have predicted two planes being flown deliberately into two of the world's tallest buildings?

Her sleep on Friday evening had been littered with nightmares of crashing planes – it happened to her every time she needed to fly. She had, over the years, developed petty superstitions like having to have her arms crossed during take off, never looking out of the window until the captain turned off the seatbelt sign, always requesting an aisle seat and, after reading a certain novel, she had conformed to the faith theory. What kept a plane in the air was the faith of its passengers – if a majority of them lost faith in its safety, it would crash. If she ever found herself thinking negative thoughts, Isabel quickly forced them aside as she needed to stay firmly on the side of the silent faithful. These terrors generally only lasted for the first thirty minutes, however, and then her heartbeat would gradually return to normal, her face would stop burning with fear and she would long for a strong Bloody Mary.

Isabel squirmed in her seat. To her dismay, she was sandwiched between a screaming child and the toilet. She alternated frequently between being irate, compassion for the poor child, annoyance at the mother, pity for the mother and a nauseating headspin at the constant stench coming from the toilets. Having a child growing inside her did little to help the situation. How on earth could she even contemplate mothering a child whose father was married to the mother of his three children? More than anything, she feared that her child would see how transparent she was as a person, casting aspersions on every decision she made and growing, ultimately, into an adult without an ounce of respect for its mother. Naturally, she thought of Maggie and of how she had placed so much distance between them, how she still couldn't forgive her mother certain things. Having this baby would only be repeating the cycle, of this she was becoming certain. Nicolette's words echoed through the back of her mind – perhaps this baby could change Isabel for the better. Was it too selfish to hold onto that hope?

By the time Patrick met her at the airport she felt vile. Angry, irritable, dirty, ugly and completely exhausted. She wished she had been able to look nice for him, seeing that he had made an effort to look good for her, and would probably judge her appearance within seconds. He had always been like that, a vicious tongue to ridicule any poor fashion sense, any obvious defect or flaw. She knew the dark rings under her eyes would look like bruises.

'Good flight?' he joked with her.

It came from nowhere, a sudden sinking feeling that he was a complete stranger, and she was an alien in a land with nowhere to hide, no one to turn to. Isabel burst into tears, standing before a stunned Patrick, wanting to punch something and wishing, somehow, that she had been able to stay hidden in Paris. If only she had the determination to sever all ties with Australia, would her life be easier then?

He put his arms around her shoulder and carried her bags. 'It'll be alright,' he said as he rubbed her arm. 'Honestly, it's not as bad as you'd think. Maggie is coping okay and at least he went suddenly.'

'I'm so sorry,' she managed to sputter into his ear, resisting the habit of speaking French. 'I'm so tired and emotional, it's not just Dad. I had a crappy flight and I feel so alone and things in Paris...' Isabel censored herself. 'Oh, would you listen to me? Typical. Patrick, how are you?'

'Okay. Better than you, I guess. At least I'm not crazy!'

Isabel stopped walking and stared at him, about to erupt. How dare he! Then she saw that twinkle in his eye, the mischievousness she remembered from childhood and they both collapsed in a helpless heap of giggles. Like children, they stood laughing, unsure of any alternative and desperately trying to ignore the feeling that the air between them was stale.

After a few minutes of walking past row upon row of parked cars, they got to Patrick's car and regained some of their composure.

'I feel so guilty,' Isabel whispered. 'Laughing so much when Dad's not even buried yet.'

'I know, it's weird isn't it? I just keep telling myself that it's alright, that Dad would want it this way. I mean, he wasn't the most emotional or sentimental of men, was he? He'd want everything to continue as it was.'

'But it can't.'

'I don't know about that. Time will tell, I suppose, but I reckon that's what he'd want.'

As they drove towards the city skyline, a wave of nostalgia swept over Isabel. 'My God, it's so strange to be back in Sydney. To be speaking English is so weird! And look at you, you're a man! I've been away so long, Patrick, I feel so... removed from all of this.'

'You wail till jetlag kicks in and you'll feel like you're on drugs. I've been really emotional too. I forget he's dead one minute, and burst into tears the next. I've got no idea what I'm doing half the time and I think I'm reacting the way I should, but not the way I really want to.'

'Same,' she said with a nod. 'It just feels like it's a job to be done, you know? Like the priority is to help Maggie, do the funeral and the wake, do the relly thing . . . and then I suppose I'll deal with my feelings after that.'

'I think Mum's pretty much the same at the moment.'

'How is she? Really, I mean.'

'Like I said, it comes in waves. I don't think it's properly hit her yet. Saturday she was like a zombie, then at night she got a bit pissed and played some of your old records. Yesterday she was very quiet and a bit teary. It's like she isn't herself – she's become all tender and craves affection. Can you imagine? Maggie Apperton being affectionate? My heart goes out to her though. I know she hasn't been a perfect mother but it's going to be so hard on her being alone. Marcus was more than her husband, he kept her strong. Now she's going to need her friends, and us, more than ever.'

Isabel groaned. 'I'm exhausted already. This is going to be one hell of a week.'

'Are you only staying one week? I think she needs more of a commitment than that.'

'Depends on Maggie,' she lied. 'It's an open ticket. Alain, my boss, is fine with however long it takes.'

'Jeez, wish I could say the same about mine. She was an utter cow.'

'My boss owes me a few favours so I guess this is one of them. How's your work going?'

'Oh, you know. It's a job. They pay okay. I wouldn't say I'm thrilled to get out of bed every morning, but it's bearable. They're talking about laying people off but I should be fine.

It's so surreal to have you home, Isabel. I suppose we need
to . . .'

'What?'

'This is so strange,' he said, stopping at some lights.

Isabel sat watching him, noticing that he was fatter in the
face. They were getting older and Patrick was beginning to look
more like Marcus. She thought it would be a cruel joke of the
gods to make her start looking like Maggie.

Patrick continued, 'I've known you my whole life and yet –'

'– we're basically strangers,' she finished for him.

'Yeah, sort of. We've got the same history but we don't even
really know each other. I was going to say I think we need to
put things behind us. We've been a bit slack about keeping in
touch and there's no excuse for that. Maggie tried to call a kind
of truce with me; she's decided to get over herself a bit. I think
it's time we all got over it. Whatever *it* is.'

'You're right, Patrick, I know you are, but I don't think it's
as easy as that. It's going to be hard for me to be friends with
Maggie and be part of a family I've never really felt was mine.'

'But because Dad's gone, I feel I have to act now before I
become a stranger to myself.'

'I never talk about our family to anyone in Paris. I just don't
want to have to explain anything.'

'Well, we've got that in common. I don't feel the need to
discuss my family with anyone but sometimes I feel so lonely,
not that Mum or Dad could have filled that void but, I
dunno . . . our family seems to have made me wary of people
and I don't want to feel that way anymore.'

Isabel wasn't quite ready to travel down that path, certainly not with Patrick just minutes after stepping off her plane. They travelled the rest of the distance in silence, Isabel stunned at the amount of new residential development, the new tunnels and motorways – just how new the entire city felt. She had assumed Patrick would drive her to the hotel she had booked, and when they pulled into the carpark of an apartment block, she couldn't hide her look of surprise.

'You didn't think I was going to make you stay in a hotel, did you?'

What she really wished for now was a big, sterile hotel room with a pristine bath and starchy sheets. There was still awkwardness between them and her desire was to be alone, to soak indulgently in a hot bath and sleep for twelve hours. She could remain anonymous in a hotel, reduced to nothing more than a room number, but with Patrick, she would have to be herself, or at least a version of it. They were indeed creatures of the same family; surely Patrick could appreciate her need to be alone. Isabel thought of ways to protest, of excuses to leave for the hotel, but once inside his apartment she saw that he had made his own bed up for her, complete with folded towels and mini soaps still in their plastic wrappings. For tonight, she wouldn't create tension but she would insist on going to the hotel tomorrow.

They spent the day watching bad television and hardly speaking. Patrick made some futile excuse and disappeared for a few hours while Isabel sat motionless in front of the television, unable to find the motivation to do anything else, even sleep. Determined not to lay down her head until a resonable hour, she sat like a statue until nine, mourning the loss of her own space and independence, longing for Alain as she had rarely done before and wishing to be in no other place on earth but her cosy little apartment in Paris.

They both slept restlessly. For Patrick, it felt strange to have a family member in his apartment and he feared any noise he made would keep her from sleep. Although she hadn't slept for forty-eight hours, Isabel was beyond fatigue, her body still stuck on European time, her mind throbbing with an endless stream of thoughts. There were so many things she could tell Patrick, so many things she still tried to forget.

In the morning, Patrick lay in bed past eleven reading. When he thought he finally heard Isabel making some noise, he virtually bounded out of bed. He was surprised to find no trace of Isabel, the noises he had heard were just his wooden venetians being blown by a gentle breeze. He started feeling frustrated, she could have at least told him where she was going, and what time she would be back. Of course, Isabel was guilty of Patrick's same crime, being overly considerate by sneaking out of the apartment silently to let her brother sleep undisturbed.

No matter where she went, Isabel managed to navigate her way around. It was something that both frustrated and impressed Alain. He hated the fact that she was always right when it came to giving directions. Even in foreign cities, Isabel never got lost. In some respects, Sydney had become a new city to her, it was forever changing, continually growing outward. It was unlike the Paris she knew, a city that had been able to resist highrise almost completely; in Isabel's mind the city's boundaries were defined succinctly by its *arrondissements*. But to her, Sydney, with its almost limitless access to land, continued to stretch its almighty limbs. Patrick lived in one of the most densely populated suburbs of Australia, so there were always people to be seen, there were always man-made sounds, but they were not the city sounds she was used to. She knew being close to Kings Cross was just the way Patrick liked it, mirroring his own social life, surrounded by people but always alone. He'd hated going to the country as a child, would get scared if he couldn't hear the sounds of a family next door, or a distant freeway. An isolated house disturbed him. It awed Isabel to think of the immensity of Australia, and of how it made France feel like a postage stamp on its postcard.

Isabel walked without purpose. It was something she liked to do when her thoughts confused her, saving her from having to address pressing matters as each new sight led her mind to less demanding thoughts. By the time she found herself at a small park on the foreshore, she knew her walk had come to its turning point so she sat on the ferry wharf contemplating what the next few days would hold. Though she had told Patrick that her airline ticket was open, the truth of the matter was that she was tentatively booked to return to Paris in a fortnight's time. She knew her mother would want her to stay longer, but Isabel just couldn't face more than a week or so with Maggie. Isabel touched her stomach – would her own baby follow in that tradition? Nicolette was right about using this as a time to show her family love, but it was easier said than done and Isabel knew communicating honestly with her family would end up causing her pain.

'Next ferry's not in for a while, love,' a fisherman informed her.

The accent startled Isabel, jolting her back to thinking and talking in English. 'Oh, that's okay.' She got up to leave. 'I was just having a think.' Then she followed what she remembered was the Australian tradition and asked, 'Any nibbles?'

'A few . . . Had to chuck 'em back though. Too small.'

'Well, good luck.'

'Yeah, thanks love. Think I might need it today.'

Me too, Isabel thought. She took a last lingering look across the beautiful harbour to Taronga Zoo. One day, hopefully, her child would get to see that stunning view.

It didn't take much for her to convince Patrick to go to Maggie's house right away. Aside from their concerns about their mother, they also knew that helping Maggie organise the wake would keep them occupied, and keep to a minimum awkward silence between siblings.

Though Isabel knew she should have used their time together in the car to get to know more about his life, she feared Patrick would see this as an invitation to ask about her own. She had thought the drive would be one of wonder, travelling vaguely familiar roads, but it took no less than ten minutes for the motion to put her to sleep and for Isabel to start dribbling.

The only thing they managed to talk about before she fell asleep was whether or not Isabel still played her guitar. She hadn't thought about that in years and wondered aloud why Patrick asked about it.

'Dunno.' He shrugged, eyes on the road ahead. 'I suppose every time I think of you I think about Paris, and Jean-Marc. And I guess I got to thinking about when I knew I was in love with him.'

'When he sang that cheesy ballad?'

Patrick didn't answer her for a while, his mind replaying the events of that evening. Then it struck him. 'You loved him too, didn't you?'

She thought about that for a moment before shutting her eyes. 'Yes, I did.' It seemed odd that the thing to have brought Patrick and Jean-Marc together was an object she had bought on a whim, determined to teach herself to play. She had barely touched the damn thing, let alone been able to produce music. It had eventually served a purpose though, and long after Patrick's trip, Isabel spent many nights utterly rapt in Jean-Marc's songs. They would inevitably end up in giggles at his unintentional misuse of English. How many other brothers and sisters had fallen in love with the same man? Isabel fell in love with Jean-Marc precisely because he would remain unobtainable and lurking somewhere in her subconscious was the realisation that her envy towards Patrick led her to force his outing.

The house was empty when they arrived, apart from Leroy, who leapt around wildly, forgetting that he'd seen Patrick two days ago. As usual, Patrick let himself in with the spare key 'hidden' inside an obviously plastic rock.

Isabel watched in awe as Patrick showered Leroy with affection, the dog whimpering like an overwhelmed child. She had only met Leroy for a few days during her last visit and now realised what an integral part of the family he had become in her absence, perhaps even replacing her. For all the dog's clumsiness and theatrics, Isabel was glad to know Maggie had him for company. Leroy treated her with caution, recognising her as someone he should know, but not quite being able to place her. Isabel wasn't good with animals; she didn't really see the sense in talking to something that couldn't understand her, though it was fast becoming apparent Patrick believed otherwise.

'Who's a good boy then? Yes, it's you, isn't it Leroy Brown? The maddest dog in the whole damn town,' he sang in his pooch voice.

As Isabel took a look around the house, Patrick went to get their bags from the car, Leroy his constant shadow. She tried to immerse herself in her mother's existence, and imagine what it would be like for Maggie to live without Marcus. It didn't take long to appreciate that Maggie must be petrified of the great unknown: life without a companion. It was ironic that Maggie's children were afraid of the exact opposite. Watching Maggie face this was going to be excruciating. Isabel hoped that her mother wouldn't be able to simply sweep this under the carpet as she did so many of the challenges that life presented her – her daughter's abandonment of the family, Patrick's sexuality . . . and those other secrets she was trying so hard to forget, now more than ever.

Isabel decided not to go with Patrick and Leroy on their drive to the beach. Fatigue was gradually winning the fight and, with no sign of Maggie, she went into one of the spare rooms to take a nap, planning to wake at seven for dinner.

꩜

She woke to find herself back in her apartment in Paris, disoriented and grumpy. Of course she had dreamed the whole thing, from the horrific flight to watching Patrick and his dog. When she heard movement coming from her kitchen, she walked slowly towards it, unsure of who it could be. A man was cleaning out her oven, wearing nothing but a woman's apron. His naked bum was floating a few inches above the tiled floor, shaking to each stroke of his hand. She then recognised the soft down on the small of his back – it was Alain, but this was a distorted vision of him, taller and with long hair. He turned to face her; he was wearing lipstick and eyeshadow.

'Isabel, darling, you must get dressed.' Isabel hadn't even realised she was naked.

'Wh... Why?' she hesitated. 'Why are you...? What's going on?' Why the hell was he dressed like a woman?

'Your father's here, remember? He's putting in the new skylight so you can see the zoo.'

'But I thought –' Isabel shook her head, now utterly confused.

'Thought what?' Her father walked into the kitchen, miraculously speaking French.

'We thought you were dead.' Isabel burst into tears, so relieved that she would have another chance to connect with him.

'Oh sweetheart, you poor, poor thing.' He took her in his arms and rubbed her gently on the back. 'You are confused, aren't you? It's your baby, Isabel, that's what we've lost, we can't find it anywhere. No luck in the oven, Alain?'

'No luck. I must return to my husband,' he cried in falsetto before rushing out of the room.

'I just want you to be happy,' Marcus said to Isabel. 'You have to go surfing tomorrow and the next ferry leaves in one hour. But whatever you do, just make sure your mother doesn't find out.'

Maggie got home at nine, marching through the door with Kathy and several shopping bags.

'What are you doing here?' she asked Patrick in an accusatory tone.

'We, ah, it was Isabel's idea. We wanted to...' It was easy to pass the buck to the renegade daughter.

'Well skip to it, sonny Jim.' Kathy took her cue, defusing anything likely to become a situation. 'There's more shopping in my car. Boot's open.'

There was much shuffling and cataloguing of groceries in the kitchen as Patrick tried to watch an episode of Benny Hill on cable. The whole family used to sit and watch it on Sunday afternoons but as he watched it now, he got bored. He had never realised how blatantly misogynistic it was, little more than an excuse to show tits and arse... without a laugh. How could Maggie have sat and watched it without jumping up in outrage? How could entire nations let it go to air? Because things were different then. Patrick was beginning to get agitated, not only by the appalling television, but also by his mother's constant reading of labels, connecting goods to recipes, and then instructing Kathy where to put them. 'Right. Sour cream. Potato cakes with salmon. Second shelf of fridge, left. Right. Coon cheese...'

He roused the lightly sleeping Leroy, felt in his pocket for some secret ingredients of his own and took the dog to sit with him on the jetty. As the moon sparkled on the flat surface of the water, he reached into his pocket for the pre-rolled joint and lighter and lit up at an angle to ensure his mother wouldn't be able to see the red glow from the house. Patrick didn't smoke very often, just at times like these when emotions and banalities were making him feel tense and when he came to this house he found being stoned at night was the only way to relax.

'I forget how beautiful it is out here.' Kathy had sneaked to the end of the jetty without him noticing and he visibly jumped.

'Oh! Jesus! Shit Kathy, you scared me.'

'Sorry, buddy,' she said with an evil chuckle. 'You didn't even have time to put that away.'

'I needed it,' he said a little too defensively. 'Sorry, are you okay with it?'

'You're a grown man, Patrick, you don't need to apologise to me, or get my approval. I was just telling the ladies on Friday maybe I should give it a go again.'

Patrick turned to her and motioned for her to take the joint.

'I shouldn't...' she hesitated. 'Brett's started it up and I want to strangle the little mongrel for it. If he turns out anything like his father I'll kill him.'

'He'll be alright,' Patrick dismissed her with a shrug, though images of the teenage potheads he had gone to school with flashed before his eyes. Arrogant, stupid dickheads the lot of them.

'Well, maybe just a toke then.' Kathy giggled and took the joint. 'For Christ's sake, don't tell your mother though.'

'Don't tell me what?' Maggie called from the edge of the jetty. 'That my son and best friend are out here doing marijuana?' She marched up to the two of them, managing to instil a fear in them both, sprung like teenagers. 'I'm not entirely stupid, you two, and at this stage, given everything, I'm too old and tired to really care what drugs you are doing out here. Just don't let the neighbours smell them.'

'They're joints, Mother, and we're not *doing* drugs, we're sharing a social smoke.'

'You want some?' Kathy said jokingly.

'No, thank you!' Maggie chided her. 'A woman of your age ... out at nearly ten –'

'Shit! Is it really? I gotta go, Maggie. I promised the babysitter I'd be home by nine. She'll probably ask for overtime now. Is everything put away?'

'It's fine, Kathy, honestly. You go. The kids are here now ... we'll be fine.'

Kathy got up awkwardly and kissed them both goodbye. Maggie chuckled to herself again. After Kathy's departure, Maggie slowly lowered herself to sit next to Patrick. She huffed through her nose, shaking her head in disbelief.

'You don't have to hide absolutely everything from me, Patrick. Especially ... not now. I may not approve of everything you do, mostly because I worry, but you are who you are.'

'It's gonna take me a long time to get used to the new you,' he said cautiously. 'I hope you get that. After thirty years it's like getting to know you all over, so bear with me.' He breathed out smoke and shut his eyes. 'I am here for you, Maggie, and

I want things between us to be better. I'm tired of feeling like I have to blame you for things you have nothing to do with.'

'Like what, can I ask?'

He sighed. 'I don't know. There are so many things I don't understand about myself, I suppose it's just easier to blame your parents than accept any of the blame yourself.'

'Is that why you smoke drugs, to make it easier?'

'Sort of. It's a bit more complicated than that, though.'

'What are they like?'

'Joints make you float. It's like being dizzy without getting sick, and every muscle in your body relaxes. It makes it impossible for me to feel tense or angry.' His voice sounded distant.

'Your father always wanted to try it, even recently.'

'Seriously?'

'My word. He said it would help him sleep, though a good herbal tea usually works for me. I was always scared he'd get addicted or something.'

'Unlikely. It's pretty cool that Dad was interested, though.' Patrick thought about this for a minute and relished the snippet, another thing he didn't know about his father.

'I suspect he has done it. Probably did it behind my back, just like you. Maybe he just wanted to get it out in the open. Have you ... have you done other things?'

He groaned.

'Tell me honestly, Patrick, I won't say a thing. I won't worry.'

'*Some* other things, yeah.'

'Like what?'

'Mu-um.'

'Pat-rick,' she imitated.

'Okay . . . most things. At one time, lots of things. But not anymore, it doesn't really interest me now.' He avoided saying the word drugs.

'Why did you try it in the first place?'

'I don't know, really. It's not like I was searching for some fantasy escape hatch or anything. I guess the people I associated with were trying it so we had support if anything went wrong. And I wanted to know what the experience was like. It came with the territory of becoming more comfortable with myself, and learning to let go.'

'I see . . .'

'And that's all drugs do, Mum. They help people drop the barriers that society makes everyone live behind.'

Maggie was silent, trying to digest this information, trying to imagine which drugs Patrick had actually tried, and which hopeless, filthy situations he'd got himself into. It melted her heart to hear him speak of drugs so nonchalantly. She wasn't stupid, she knew that most kids tried them at one time or another but the way Patrick spoke with such resignation in his voice made her desperately want to know why her children were such lonely souls and why they felt so at liberty to dismiss her.

Patrick responded to her silence. 'See, I knew I couldn't tell you things like this!'

'It's not that you can't,' she said, shaking her head. 'It's just that I get glimpses of a whole side of you I know nothing about, and I don't mean that in a judgemental way, not at all. You telling me these things makes me feel so out of touch. But I'm also proud of myself that I won't go to bed and worry tonight, proud that I'm pushing away some of my own fears to try to understand some of yours. This is good for us, Patrick, just talking openly like this.'

'Yes, but it has to be a two-way street.'

'Meaning?'

'Meaning: if you and I are going to be open with each other now, there are things I'm gonna want answers to, you know?'

'I'll do my best if you promise to try too.'

'Yes, Maggie, I promise. I reckon this has gone on long enough.'

When Isabel woke early the following morning, the sounds of Australian suburbia filled her with childhood nostalgia. The distant songs of magpies and cicadas, and the coughs and splutters a lawnmower makes before roaring into action – these weren't the sounds of Paris. Waking in Paris, Isabel was met with the sounds of garbage trucks and scooters. In Paris, it was the sound of rusty pipes heating up for the day, ancient buildings slowly creaking to life and the soft murmur of the Metro metres underground. By contrast, waking here was waking to nature. Even the lawnmower was a sound of nature to her. When was the last time she'd heard one? Who ever needed to trim grass in Paris or, for that matter, who even *had* grass? At last she was feeling refreshed after her draining journey. She slowly got up, ready to face the days that lay ahead, ready to face Maggie.

The first one awake, Isabel quietly made herself some toast and walked down to the jetty to bask in the warm morning sun. She missed Australia's weather, but enough to return? Alain had reacted soberly to her news; her pregnancy was neither welcomed nor rejected, specifically. He kissed her, told her he loved her and would support her in whatever choice she made. Of course, he couldn't be expected to have as much input, or excitement, in this child's life. Isabel guessed that, really, he wanted her to have an abortion. It suddenly saddened her to admit that Alain would never leave his wife and Isabel would never become his only love. Though she insisted solitude was important to her, she had begun to wish Alain would choose to be with her permanently. Either way, what she really wanted was to make that decision for him. With a baby there would be no such thing as solitude, so why not ask Alain to make a commitment? The baby would consume her existence twenty-four hours a day. If she could handle that much of an intrusion into her routine, then living with Alain would be easy. Films, wine, uninterrupted love-making – these would all become things of her past. But what of the joys? The bond of breastfeeding, first steps, first words and perhaps the ability to express unconditional, boundless love? Alain could certainly be a part of things but only if he wanted to; only, she suspected, if everything was on his terms.

'I thought you'd stay sleeping forever!'

The sound of Maggie's voice made Isabel jump, and she dropped her last piece of toast into the water.

'I'm sorry, Isabel, I seem to be in the awful habit of scaring the wits out of people on this jetty.'

'That's okay.' Isabel smiled dryly, then got up to hug her mother awkwardly. Maggie smelled like a grandmother and the thought sent shivers down Isabel's spine. 'How are you?'

'Oh, you know. Okay, I suppose, all things considered.'

'I don't know what to say. I'm sorry.'

'Isabel, just having you here is enough. Patrick is the same; he should stop trying to think of something profound to say. I'll survive. I will miss your father terribly, but I will be okay.'

'Well, now that I'm here, whatever you want or need, just ask.'

'How was your flight?'

'Hellish! Just awful, as I expected.'

'It's good of you to keep getting up in the air though, keep confronting your fears. You look different, Isabel.' Maggie sized her up and down.

'Fatter, probably.' Isabel knew mothers possessed uncanny instincts.

'No, different. It's in your eyes, something . . . some knowledge you've recently gained.' Isabel blushed, praying her mother wouldn't guess immediately. 'If I didn't know any better, I might even say that you were in love!'

'Maggie! You and your motherly intuition . . .'

'It's alright, you don't have to tell me. You kids don't have to tell me anything at all. But you can, you know that? I want both of my children to know they can tell me anything. You should be more open with me.'

Isabel kissed her mother again, not knowing what else she could say or do and hoping desperately to change the topic of conversation. Some strange emotion was obviously affecting Maggie and Isabel knew she wasn't equipped to deal with it.

The relationship between the two women was infected with mistrust and secrecy and Isabel would require more than a token peace-offering to begin looking to Maggie as a confidante. Isabel was here to offer her support, be amicable and sympathetic, touch base – how difficult it was going to be to form a new bond with someone she blamed for her scars.

From Tuesday morning until Thursday night, the details of the wake consumed each of them in differing ways. Maggie and Isabel spent long hours in the kitchen absorbed in individual tasks that didn't require them to speak much. Maggie would merely inform her daughter what dish to prepare next and Isabel set about creating it, using the preparation as a kind of therapy. The mood in the house was stilted, if not sombre. There was no music, no laughter and very little conversation. They were expecting around fifty people at the wake on Friday and Maggie was determined to feed all the guests well.

Patrick spent the days running errands for his mother, picking up glasses and crockery, and organising the delivery of tables and chairs from the hire company. He also returned the steady flow of messages banking up on the answering machine. They'd decided not to adjust the volume on the telephone since Maggie had turned it down. A few times a day, Patrick pressed the play button and took down the numbers of distant relatives who wanted to know if there was anything they could do. It was also a time for Patrick to prepare a eulogy for his father, and he spent hours in Gosford library searching for an appropriate poem. He also spent hours at the beach with Leroy, taking long aimless walks as his dog chased after gulls and avoided the white foam of new waves.

Aside from Kathy's occasional visits, what remained of the Apperton family was left alone, as though there was some cushion of courtesy requiring them to be kept in quarantine before their public appearance at the wake. The situation suited each of them perfectly because it meant they weren't forced to reveal anything of themselves before the inevitable probing questions on Friday from curious relatives, many of whom they had never even met before. That was the thing about death, it encouraged obligation.

Patrick and Isabel spoke briefly each evening after Maggie went to bed. In some ways, Patrick wished the lighter, sillier Maggie of the weekend was still around. Neither sibling had any idea how to empathise with Maggie's peculiar form of grief.

'Who arranged the funeral?' Isabel asked Patrick the night before the event.

'I did.'

'What, alone?'

'Yeah. Dad didn't have a will. He'd told Mum a few weeks ago that he thought wills were morbid. They agreed to leave everything to each other.'

'So how'd you know what he wanted?'

'I didn't. I guessed.'

'Such as?'

'I decided he shouldn't be buried next to his mother's grave – there's some family plot in Daylesford. He's being buried locally.'

'Well, the family plot can go to hell. I assume you're making all the right decisions but I would've chosen cremation myself. I hope Mum doesn't become obsessed with tending to the grave.'

'That'd be pretty hard for you to deal with, all the way from Paris, eh?'

It was a cutting comment and Isabel felt the full force of its sting. No one in the family had ever challenged her decision to live so far away, or her motives for doing so. Though the bitterness in his voice was duly noted, Isabel decided not to bite back because she lacked the energy and felt no need to answer her younger brother, whether his questions were actual or merely implied.

'How did you know how to organise it? Who to call, I mean, what choices to make?'

'I organised a friend's funeral last year.'

'A friend? Who?'

'No one you know.' Patrick struggled to hide the agitation in his voice.

'Was it a lover?'

It was all Patrick needed to snap. 'Isabel! I don't want to talk about it! You come over here for the first time in however many years, you refuse to divulge anything at all about this foreign life you lead and yet you want to know everything about everyone else. Are you married? Are you happy? Do you have children? Are you a virgin?' His voice began to waver as the intensity of his argument grew. 'I wouldn't know. None of us would. Dad died having no idea who his own daughter is. I'll probably die the same, never knowing a single thing about any of you.'

'Yeah, well, the question remains . . .' Isabel said calmly, 'do you even *want* to know?'

Patrick sat silently, unable to answer the question because he couldn't deny he rarely considered her at all and it was only in the face of his father's death that he thought to ask.

'I thought as much,' Isabel shrugged in answer to his silence. 'You don't even make a token effort to find out about my life, and you know why? Because you're so caught up in your own little secrets. All you care about is being free to prance around being gay. You attack me because I can deal with keeping things to myself. For some reason you just can't wait to force your secrets down everyone else's throats. So what's better, Patrick? That Dad died not knowing my secrets, or that he died knowing yours?'

'You're just jealous, Isabel. You always have been. You make my life sound disgusting so that yours can sound so fucking noble. Get over yourself.'

'It's all about you, of course. Did you ever stop to think that maybe there's another reason why I'm like this? Just maybe it doesn't have a damn thing to do with you!'

'How could it have anything to do with me? You've made sure that we stay as far apart as possible. *Au contraire*,' he mimicked her French. 'You've cornered the market on self-pity.'

Isabel was about to explode when she saw her mother standing at the end of the hall. Maggie was shaking her head in disbelief. Patrick turned to follow Isabel's gaze and was instantly silenced.

'How could your father's soul be resting in peace knowing that the two of you don't seem to give a damn about him? Why on earth do you both find it so hard to respect the ones you're supposed to love?' Maggie turned around and went back into her bedroom, closing the door firmly behind her. Within moments Isabel did the same and Patrick went to the jetty with Leroy and a big fat joint.

Because none of Marcus' immediate family members were talking to each other, an air of a melodrama was added to his funeral service. Outsiders viewed this as overwrought emotion.

Maggie walked straight to the front of the chapel hand in hand with Kathy and sat directly in front of the small, raised lectern. Within seconds the lunch ladies had her surrounded with solemn faces of support. It felt strange to Maggie that these women had become the family she'd always craved, one free of tension and bonded by mutual admiration.

Isabel and Patrick stood at the entrance to the chapel silently shaking strangers' hands. They'd been instructed to do so by the chaplain, who failed to notice they had no idea who many of these people were. Very few people in the room seemed to know anyone else, to the extent that most mourners were alone and awkward, unsure where they should sit, or who should be acknowledged.

The chaplain was pleasant enough, not creepy in the way Patrick found most priests to be. As Isabel and Patrick took their seats in the empty left-hand row at the front, it felt wrong to see their trembling mother being comforted by a group of middle-aged women neither of them knew. Kathy was once again Maggie's rock-solid base, her unquestioning, unwavering support. As the chaplain spoke in generalisations about Marcus' life, of his wife and children, his successful business and loyal customers, Patrick shuddered. They were here to bury a virtual stranger. There on the stage was a wooden box holding the man who'd given him life. Patrick tried not to picture how he'd look in there, but gave life to the memory of the last time he'd seen his father. 'Drive carefully,' were the last words Marcus said to him, 'call your mother when you're home safely.' Patrick had, as usual, disobeyed him.

Maggie sat staring through watery eyes, clutching Kathy's hand in clammy tightness. How typical of her children to abandon her now. How morbid this whole scene felt, tinged with a foreboding sense of deja-vu.

Isabel watched her brother walk awkwardly to the lectern, his gait visibly affected by the weight of so many eyes staring expectantly at him. She'd apologise to him when all of this was over. How absurd for her to be sitting in the front pew, alone. No one needed Isabel to be here, of that she was certain. And if Isabel was here for herself she was making a bad attempt at reconciliation.

Patrick stood before the congregation and swallowed audibly. He didn't feel like crying for the loss of his father, but the air of grief in the chapel was stultifying, taking his breath and forcing water to his eyes. In the last row, Patrick caught a glimpse of a young man he recognised, one of the only familiar faces present. Simon Harlen nodded to Patrick, forcing a burst of adrenaline which allowed him to regain his composure and find his voice.

'My mother, sister and I,' he began quietly, his voice tremulous, 'thank each of you for coming to farewell a man who lived his life simply. Providing for his family was paramount and his second love was the business he fought to make successful. It's a testament to his hard work that many of his staff and customers are here today and it's obvious Marcus Apperton was a well-respected man. Speaking personally, I can say –'

Patrick's train of thought was interrupted by the appearance of a man in his peripheral vision. The tall figure was silhouetted against the sun glaring through the glass doors to the right of the chapel. The man stood hunched for a moment, his head bowed.

'I can say,' Patrick repeated, watching the figure disappear as though it had only been an apparition, 'speaking personally, that death takes with it many answers. Death holds the answer to who I am, why I'm here, how we are all here together today ... Often life hides the virtues of love, trust, humility and comfort. Death keeps these things for itself and it has turned my father into a stranger to us all.

'I would like now to read a poem by Emily Dickinson, one my father and I discussed when I was studying it at school.

As imperceptibly as grief
The summer lapsed away,
Too imperceptible at last,
To seem like perfidy.

A quietness distilled,
As twilight long begun,
Or nature spending with herself
Sequestered afternoon.

The dusk drew earlier in,
The morning foreign shone,
A courteous, yet harrowing grace,
As guest, that would be gone.

And thus, without a wing,
Or service of a keel,
Our summer made her light escape
In to the beautiful.'

Patrick paused to fold the poem away into his jacket pocket. It took a lot of strength to look his mother in the eye, but for an instant they connected about the meaning of his eulogy and he sent her a look of compassion, filled with as much love as he could muster.

'We now ask those closest to Marcus to step forward and place a white rose upon his coffin and for everyone to please join his family in a reflection upon his life at 29 Waterford Place.'

As swiftly as it had begun, Marcus Apperton's simple service was over. The mourners filed up the narrow aisle and out into the world to continue living their lives.

'It was a lovely service.' One of the uncles was patting him on the back. Patrick struggled to remember the man's name, his mind on other things. 'Who wrote that beautiful poem?'

'Dickinson,' Patrick whispered, adopting the accepted tone of the occasion.

'Oh, I never realised he wrote poetry.'

'Moron.' Patrick said under his breath before walking away. Even then it occurred to him that this was one of the subtle privileges of grief, most forms of erratic behaviour would be forgiven.

Maggie was utilising this privilege herself. She was too exhausted to speak to anyone except Kathy, barely even acknowledging the chaplain. If she happened to find herself stuck in a conversation she found boring, she simply walked away, even if the person was mid-sentence.

Aside from the hosts' unpredictability, it felt like it was a successful wake; compliments on the food were abundant, as they were on the simple service Patrick had arranged. Though the house was full to brimming, mostly with people Maggie knew she'd never see or hear from again, it was coping well enough. Everyone looked content given the circumstances of their gathering, except poor Leroy. He'd never seen such a large group of people and was starting to get grumpy. Could he be trusted not to bite before the end of the day?

Maggie's only real solace was Kathy. Patrick and Isabel were waging their cold war and Maggie had become one of its incidental victims, neither of them having spoken to her since the previous evening. If not for Kathy, Maggie would have felt hopelessly alone. The other lunch ladies were all rallying around Brigette, who had been a total mess all day, trembling with grief and sobbing hysterically at odd moments. Since she had only met Marcus two or three times, it was unlikely she was grieving for him but rather for the loss of her own son which, after so many years, still affected her as much as the day he had died. Maggie envied her self-indulgence, how blissful it would be to absorb one's self in a grief so absolute, especially over the loss of a child.

As Maggie thought about her own children, her eyes connected with Isabel's. There was some unspoken recognition between them that made Maggie's chest tighten. Maggie saw it then: her daughter knew many of her secrets – how could she not? Isabel's return home wasn't only for Marcus, Maggie could see as plain as day that she'd be a grandmother soon, and that Isabel was here to get some answers for herself. That sparkle in Isabel's eye wasn't love after all; it was the sparkle of new life. This fact frightened Maggie more than the idea of being on her own.

Marcus

It didn't come as a surprise to her friends when his mother died of heart failure. She started smoking at fifteen and drinking at twenty-three. From fifty-one, the drinking and smoking were practically constant. The surprise, if any, was that she lived until the age of seventy. By then, her teeth had yellowed almost to the point of decay; she was heading towards obesity and was drinking two litres of wine every day. Despite the gradual destruction of her physical health and appearance, however, Mabel O'Connor remained a very popular woman, a stalwart of her community.

In her retirement, Mabel enjoyed working for a number of causes – war veterans, free education, honest politics, the Red Cross, Australian heritage, nature and, though she strongly disagreed with its doctrine, the Catholic church. She supported the church for its local charities, its willingness and capacity to care for those less fortunate – albeit at the price of indoctrination. Mabel liked that it was a well-structured organisation, even though that very structure allowed for corruption. If she was being honest, Mabel would admit she was just trying to guarantee herself a place with St Peter, figuring she'd need as much help as possible, given her many vices and that she rarely attended church or prayed.

Depending on who you asked, Mabel was described as 'a good old stick', 'a sweet bird', or 'strong as an ox', she never suffered fools gladly and was praised for her ability to drink any man under the table. She had an Australian robustness that appealed to the people in the small town where she lived. The years of vice had weathered her face so it was heavily wrinkled and coarse to the touch and her loud voice was deep and caustic, her words regularly interrupted with heavy, audible breaths. People would remember her most by her laughter – it was an infectious reminder of her love of life and her wish to enjoy living it to the fullest.

As a mother, Mabel was an anomaly. By turns warm and tender, then becoming a strict disciplinarian who refused her children the indulgence of showing their emotions in public. Her husband died abruptly – leaving their house one evening in a drunken rage never to return. It wasn't unlike Alfred to leave her for days at a time so Mabel raised no alarms until well into the second week. By then, she could barely even remember which argument drove him from the house in the first place. Usually they fought over intangible things – politics, women's rights, whose work was worth more to the family.

His, at the nearby brickworks bringing thirty pounds a week, or her unpaid work in the home.

The shed at the back of the property was his private room, a place where he was never to be interrupted and, in search of clues to his possible whereabouts, local police had suggested they look there first. Alfred had been missing for nine days by then and he had been dead just as long. He was found hanging from the only beam in the large shed, a recycled railway sleeper thicker than a man. One of Mabel's children discovered the body and it changed the boy for the rest of his life.

On the evening of the fight, on his way out of the house, Alfred crossed paths with his youngest child. Drunk and angry, he didn't think twice about venting his frustration to anyone he saw.

'Your mother is an evil woman,' he warned his son.

'No she's not.' The youngest dared to stand up to his father.

'I'm leaving this time for good and I ain't ever coming back. Don't you tell your mother, fella, but this is the last time you'll ever be seeing me. Good riddance to you all, I say, you sure know how to ruin a man's life.'

Marcus burst into tears and immediately ran to his mother to tell her his daddy was leaving them forever. Blaming himself, he cried inconsolably as his mother tried to reassure him that his father wasn't himself, he would return to them all within a day or two. Everything would return to normal as soon as the liquor wore off.

Mabel now knew she was wrong and, at thirty-eight, the prospect of raising six children alone terrified her. A quiet man until he started drinking, Alfred led his life with a soft gratitude. He had a naturally muscular build, his work made him strong and lean. Mabel, on the other hand, had retained her pregnancy weight from the first child, and each one thereafter, so by the time the last one was born she weighed fifteen stone. As young sweethearts they had been the perfect couple – lean and beautiful, each full of driving ambition and fierce intellect. Their courtship lasted one year, the engagement six months. Mabel fell pregnant three months into the marriage. She wanted to be a veterinarian, had always loved animals, but motherhood and the Depression changed that, and soon Alfred also had to give up his dream of becoming a chemist so his new family had shelter and enough to eat. After the first child, he reassured himself, things could change, there would be enough time to save money and hopefully one day he would be able to return to his studies. But just three months after the birth of Harold, Mabel announced she was pregnant again.

'But how could that possibly be?' Alfred asked.

'Alfred, please don't start that again. I'm pregnant! I have to deal with that; by contrast you've got it easy.'

'If you had any idea how hard the brick –'

'D'you want to raise the children, Alfred? Go ahead, I'd trade places with you in an instant.'

'What's that supposed to mean?'

'I had dreams too, you know. You think I want to be twenty-two with two kids? People have sex, pregnancies happen.'

'It's just . . . not how I planned, is all.'

'Planned? Oh, you poor man. Life isn't meant to be planned, it's meant to be *lived*.'

It continued like this, a more or less dysfunctional marriage getting weaker with the birth of each child – all six neither planned nor celebrated. Alfred never did make it out of the brickworks, but Mabel paid her price too. She'd lost her vigour, her slim body and her youth. What shocked her most about her husband's decision to take his own life was she had had no prior suspicion, not even the slightest inclination he was heading towards such a destructive end. Mabel had taken their marriage for granted, had wrongly assumed their relationship was so predictable that nothing could ever come as a surprise. She was now furious as a result, angered by Alfred's selfishness and disgusted at herself for wasting her life on such a worthless man. How repulsed it made her feel that a man could indulge himself so thoroughly in his own emotions. Her inability to predict that she would be abandoned made her a harder character and her children would suffer this change the most.

Her youngest child was the most inquisitive and she supposed he was her favourite for that very reason. The day Alfred's body was discovered, he followed the detectives around the house as though he was a member of their team. A chatty and sociable six year old, Marcus took an active role in the hunt for clues. Running ahead of the detectives, Marcus eventually led them to Alfred's shed – he was expressly forbidden to go there by his father. The rule had long been established that no child could enter the shed without knocking, and only then, upon express permission to enter. The presence of the detectives following behind Marcus gave him a sense of security and he burst bravely into the shed.

It was Marcus, therefore, who first laid eyes upon his father's lifeless face. Though he knew little of death first hand, it was one of the topics he often pressed his mother about. Where do people go when they die? Why do people die? When will I die? He was able to process that his father was gone, but not the science behind it, nor the emotion. His first instinct was to laugh – his father looked so silly hanging from the rafter. Only gradually did the smell get to him and it added gravity to the situation. Marcus knew he was to blame for his father's death; if only he had been strong enough to stand up to the old man when he told him he wouldn't be returning. Marcus should have made some effort to make him stay; offer him some reason for wanting to be with his family. But all he'd done was burst into tears, a weak little boy whose actions had ruined the family.

He vomited just as the first of the detectives entered the shed. He heard shouting and felt someone wipe his mouth with a camphor-scented, snot-drenched handkerchief, these new smells inducing another round of vomiting.

'Get that kid outta here,' the older detective yelled to his colleague.

The next minute, Marcus was once again outside and he could remember running through the bush to the fading sound of his hysterical mother screaming in the shed far behind him. Determined to run away for good, he stayed crouched behind a solitary grey rock well into the night, ashamed of himself for vomiting and feeling entirely to blame for making his mother so upset. He fell asleep, cold and hungry, the taste of vomit still on his tongue. It was a restless night full of nightmares –

of feeling tiny in the arms of his father, his father's face larger than life scaring him and making him cry. Somehow, he woke in his own bed the following morning, the sun warming his damp cheeks as it shone brightly through his opened window.

In the days after Alfred's death, the household continued as normal. There was no time to grieve, no down-payment on misery. The children were expected to continue with their chores; Mabel stopped laughing, stopped embracing her children. Although Marcus overheard many whispered conversations mentioning his name, some between his mother and strangers, some between his older siblings, no one ever sat him down to talk about what he had seen, and what he felt. He burned with shame over his vomiting, and his initial desire to laugh at his father's face. He cried over his failed attempt at running away. Though no one pointed the finger of blame at Marcus, he knew the order of silence in the house had come because all this was his fault. Alfred had left the family, betraying them all, and Marcus was his unwilling accomplice, a witness to the act that now silenced them all.

Mabel's actions over the next few weeks were erratic. Any mention of Alfred by the children was met with a reminder to never mention his name. They soon learnt he simply wasn't to be discussed. Photographs of him were removed, presumably to some secret place. His clothing and belongings were given, or thrown, away. Two days after the funeral, Marcus' oldest brother was instructed to burn down their father's shed. Alfred was removed from all but their memories and even they began to fade with time.

Marcus

Marcus was a different person from that day forward. He rarely spoke, stopped asking the probing questions that had previously driven the whole family to distraction. He was no longer outgoing, didn't make friends with other children as he'd always done before. He shied away from adults too, especially men, hiding behind Mabel's skirt. When men talked to him, he rarely spoke back and his cheeks burned in their presence. The only thing he seemed to enjoy doing was copying what his mother did around the house. He cleaned and cooked just like her, he listened to the radio, just like her. Marcus was rarely more than a few metres away from his mother. Though she knew that his behaviour wasn't normal and was evidence, perhaps, of a deeper issue, she hoped the new school year would help him return to his old self and force him out of his shell.

School was utter torture for Marcus, it left him feeling more miserable than ever. He was now too afraid to speak in front of the teacher and he rarely participated. When specifically called upon, he would mumble and stutter his way through and, on occasion, simply sit in his seat and wet his pants. This, coupled with his red hair and freckles, was more than enough to make him a target for the other children. Even six year olds can be cruel, somehow knowing to pick on the weakest in the litter, targeting any child who stands out from the crowd. Marcus carefully marked the passing days in his mind. A bad day was being hit or pinched, having his hair pulled, being spat upon or having his lunch stolen. The worst happened one day when he went to use the toilets. He didn't shut the stall door properly, allowing three older boys to enter close behind him. They pulled off his grey shorts and pissed all over him – in his face, on his penis, all over his shoes and soaking his shirt. All the while, they were laughing at him, laughing, Marcus thought, at his penis. He went back to class smelling like a urinal, confused and guilty over the sudden attack. As the other children smelled him, the taunts in the classroom began, accusing him of wetting his pants again. His teacher was so appalled by Marcus' appearance that he made the child leave the room and stand outside until he dried. There he stood for hours in the sun, holding back the tears he feared would suffocate him.

That, however, was only the worst day for now because Marcus fully understood his enemies would create new, awful tortures for him the older he got. So scarred by his experience in the toilets, Marcus never used a toilet again at school, and even as an adult he was unable to perform standing at a urinal, anticipating humiliation at any moment.

Marcus never discussed what happened at school with his mother or siblings. He spent most of his lunchtimes in the library, absorbing himself in books, or sneaking snippets of news from the radio as war raged in a far-away land. The boy was so full of doom, so confused by his thoughts, he assumed the war would spell the end to his pain, that death would come to save him just like it had done for his father. He misinterpreted stories he heard, of Hitler taking little boys from their homes and turning them into soldiers – young boys fighting against grown men, each with real guns. These thoughts excited him, exhilarated him almost as much as looking at the pictures he had found hidden beneath his brother's mattress. Men with hair in funny places, their things huge and stiff, women with something different between their legs. He longed to be an adult, to be a man who possessed real strength and the will to be unafraid of other men. But most of all, he just wanted to live one day, two days, a whole week . . . without being teased and feeling every person who looked his way was laughing at him.

Books were his solace, his escape route to another world where he became the hero. The librarian treated him nicely, showing him the newest books and letting him sneak in his sandwiches as long as he promised not to let the other children see. It surprised her that a boy so young could read so much but any attempt she made to talk to him failed, as he squirmed in his seat and kept his eyes cast to the floor. She even gave him permission to call her Betty, but that secret between them provided no incentive for him to speak to her. Betty spoke to his teacher, who said that Marcus Apperton was a complete and utter failure when it came to interacting with others and yet his test results showed a firm grasp on the three R's and his work in art class hinted there could be a lot of creativity lurking deep within. He went on to explain Marcus' incontinence, the way he often pretended to be dumb, and confessed that he really couldn't tolerate the child.

Betty Dwyer knew, however, that books were the key to opening the poor boy up and she hoped they'd eventually encourage him to blossom. A brief visit to Mabel proved to be unhelpful, the mother insisting that Marcus taught himself to read though Betty couldn't see one book in the house. When she asked Mabel if she ever read to her children at night, the woman chuckled.

'Sweetheart, I'm workin' for the best part of twelve hours down at the brickworks every single day. I get home and I make dinner for my six kids, I clean up dishes, clean up children, clean up after children...no, I don't quite have the time nor the energy to read to my kids at night, and nor do I have money to buy them books.'

'What about the library?'

'It's closed whenever I'm not at work. My kids'll be okay, Miss Dwyer, I'm teaching them to survive, it's the school's responsibility to teach them to learn.'

Such ignorance made Betty irate. She loathed it when parents refused to help their own children develop. If Mabel O'Connor wanted her children to work dead-end jobs for the rest of their lives like their mother, then somebody else had to do something about it. Betty began sending books home with Marcus, letting him keep them so he could build up his own library, allowing him to read his favourites over and over. She gave him two new books each week, on the proviso that when he finished them, they could sit for five minutes to discuss the best parts – only five minutes, no more. The first few times, Marcus was shy and polite, answering her questions but not initiating any of the conversation himself. After a few months, however, Betty was able to work out what kind of books he liked best and soon enough, Marcus' face began to display passion and excitement during those five-minute sessions. Before long, the sessions extended to ten, then fifteen minutes. It seemed at last Marcus had found himself a friend, someone he could trust. At the end of that otherwise mortifying year of school, Marcus exchanged gifts with the librarian – he painted her a bookmark featuring scenes from some of his favourite books, and she gave him five brand new books in return.

Betty knew she was showing this child an unreasonable amount of interest. But she believed in his capabilities and if Mabel didn't object, then surely no one else would. In her heart, though, she knew there were also some selfish reasons for giving Marcus the books when they weren't hers to give in the first place. She wanted him to stay at her house when he felt comfortable enough because she wanted to introduce him to her husband. She'd been trying to convince her husband for years that a child would bring joy to their lives but he insisted he didn't want children, he had made that clear to her before they got married. Though Betty married him knowing he had no desire for children, they'd been so young she hoped Dick would eventually change his mind. It was her intention that he would form a bond with the boy, hoping it might trigger her husband's change of mind.

The first evening began brilliantly, save for Dick getting stuck at work. Marcus requested, and received, his favourite meal of curried rabbit followed by rhubarb crumble and they talked constantly about books, especially Marcus' favourite, *Biggles*. She ran him a bubble-bath and read to him as he soaked and played with the water. They stayed up a while longer, listening to music on the radio and chatting a little bit about the war, and her hope it might soon be over. She explained that Dick would have gone to war except for the fact that he had a limp. By eight o'clock, Marcus' eyes were getting heavy but Betty kept talking about her family, and how she hoped she'd have children of her own one day. She was completely oblivious to the fact that Marcus had fallen asleep until the sound of her husband entering the house interrupted her one-sided conversation.

Marcus' enthusiasm for nights at the Dwyer house waned as soon as he met Betty's husband, a brutish man who rarely acknowledged him, making him feel insignificant, a nuisance. It was Mabel who insisted he continued going, that he show gratitude for the gifts Betty bought him. In truth, Mabel felt that her youngest needed to get over his fear of adults, of people in general, and because he had no friends his own age she was comfortable in allowing the librarian to have him for the night. He had grown too attached to Mabel and she knew the time apart could only serve to make him stronger. Marcus tried to fight, but Mabel wouldn't have a bar of it and there was no avoiding the dread of walking up to the Dwyers' front door, no avoiding that the taste of curried rabbit, Betty's face and the very act of reading were now all linked to a feeling he couldn't quite define. Being around the man and his wife was like accidentally wearing your pyjamas to school and Dick looked at him in a way that made him blush with shyness.

On his fifth visit to the house, Marcus was uncharacteristically quiet. He seemed to have returned to being his former self and there was nothing she could do to snap him out of it. How on earth was Dick going to form a bond with a mute? Only when Betty said Dick probably wouldn't be coming home did the boy's spirit seem to improve. She suspected Marcus was slightly jealous of Dick, and the way her attention was divided whenever the two of them were in the same room. When she asked if Marcus would like to share her bed as a special treat, he positively beamed. But Dick came home after all, and, as he slid into bed to find the boy in his place, a fight started almost immediately. The truth came out in the argument, her giving him books which belonged to the school, her desire for him to bond with the boy because she wanted to have a child of her own. As their voices rose in volume, Marcus cowered in a corner of the room, shutting his eyes as Betty burst into tears and Dick ended his rage by bloodying her nose.

The following morning, nobody spoke in the Dwyer household. Betty walked Marcus back to his house in silence, too full of sorrow to open her mouth or attempt to explain things to the boy. At the Appertons' hollowed tree-stump letterbox, they stopped.

'I understand your silence. I'll be okay. But you must promise not to tell your mother,' she mumbled to him, her blackened eyes wet with tears. 'I'm sorry you saw us fight. It doesn't hurt, Marcus, truly it doesn't. He was just upset at you being in the house, that's all.'

Marcus retreated into his familiar coat of guilt and shame. The following day Dick and a policeman arrived at the Apperton house to reclaim all of the stolen books, neither man looking at the boy, who blamed himself. Marcus never saw Betty again, she left the school suddenly and whenever he passed their house it was all closed up and unwelcoming, as though warning Marcus to stay away. Betty had added to Marcus' sense of shame and he felt he would never be a normal boy, as though he would remain an outcast his entire life.

At school, his mistrust of people was painfully obvious but he could do little to overcome his fears. He made no friends, looked at people from under a creased, suspicious brow and spoke so rarely that the sound of his voice made the other children giggle. His shame grew so intense that Mabel considered sending him to a psychiatric hospital to cure him of his shyness. Ultimately, however, she refused to indulge his silences and instead reacted by smothering him alternatively with aggression and affection. A few sharp slaps to the face would be followed by her smoothing down his hair as he lay sobbing in bed. A rare purchase of a surprise gift, just for him, would be followed by shouts of disgust at his lack of gratitude. Though she did still consider him her favourite, Mabel had lost the ability to communicate with the family. Since the day Alfred took his own life, she had found it difficult to show any form of affection. Her reputation around town was gaining momentum by now. Mabel was usually found at the pub after work, her loud bravado making her a natural drinking companion for the other men at the brickworks. Mabel more or less became an independent machine, rarely seen in public with her children, or anyone for that matter. It wasn't long until the other women in town looked down on her behaviour with scorn and, by and large, the Apperton children became the town's scapegoats.

Things began to change for Marcus when a new boy started at St Martin's. The boy looked weak and fragile, a new runt in the school litter. Marcus had endured four years of cruelty and had never entertained the notion that the bullies' attention could eventually be turned on someone else. Not until Jack Catalano moved to Daylesford.

The shortest in his class by many inches, and painfully thin, Jack had inherited more than his share of his Sicilian grandfather's genes. Though only quarter Sicilian, Jack's skin was deep Mediterranean olive and his thin greasy hair hung to his shoulders. He was so slight, so soft-featured, that most people wrongly mistook him for a girl. That fact alone made him a new target at St Martin's and, quite deliberately, Miss Briggs chose Marcus to show Jack around the school – the first time he'd ever been chosen. Their initial meeting was awkward and clumsy, the new boy shy and cautious, the old school target quiet and uncomfortable. They didn't talk much – Marcus through force of habit, Jack perturbed by the way the boy looked at him so suspiciously. As they walked past the small but crowded classroom buildings, Jack began to overhear what he had heard a thousand times before at his last school . . . the usual taunts and whispered guesses as to his gender. But there were also some new cries and it took him some time to appreciate not every word was being thrown his way. Once the class clowns were out of earshot, Jack decided to make a new friend.

'You don't listen to them, do you?'

'N-no.'

'Nor do I. Bunch of idiots, if you ask me. Thick as a piece of four-be-two, my dad says.'

'I thought you would sound Italian or something,' Marcus said, almost accusingly.

'And you thought I was a girl, too?'

'I never!'

'Well, most people do. I get it all the time – they talk to me real slow because they think I'm a wog who won't understand English, or they embarrass themselves by treating me like a girl.'

'This is the tuck shop,' Marcus said in his tour-guide voice, 'if you can afford it. My mum makes me bring lunch.'

'Me too,' Jack said. 'Maybe we could swap some time.'

'Is it wog food?'

'Nope,' Jack chuckled. 'Same boring Australian stuff you get, I reckon. I'm only a quarter Italian, you know. I mean Sicilian. My grandpa always corrects me. But I just got the wog genes is all.'

'You must hate school.'

'Not really,' Jack shrugged. 'Those bastards are just jealous of my good looks, I reckon. But I bet *you* must hate it?'

'Yeah. I just go to the library. Sometimes I wish I was...'

'What?'

They kept walking until they reached the library building where Marcus hid as often as he could. '... Somewhere else.'

'So I guess we're gonna be friends then, Marcus? Sounds like you could maybe do with one!'

'I don't need friends,' Marcus said abruptly. 'I don't need anyone at all.'

'Well, sounds like I'm gonna need a friend then,' he said, motioning to the kids behind them. 'So you ain't got no choice. Okay?'

'You like books?' Marcus tested him.

'Some,' Jack shrugged. 'My old man's got a few good ones,' he winked cheekily. 'You can come over this weekend if you like.'

'Nah, my mum won't let me stay over,' Marcus lied.

'Well I'll just stay at yours, then.'

That's just the way Jack was, and Marcus soon got used to it. He was forceful yet charming, outspoken but also a good listener. Jack was honest to a fault; he liked to call a dog by its name. Having been reserved for so long, it took Marcus some time to open up, but Jack brought out the best in him and it didn't take long for them to be inseparable, fending off aggressors and slurs, bonding in their mutual fight against the schoolyard bullies. To some extent there was strength in unity. At the least, it meant they were each teased for only half the time, because boys like Shane McHugh and Bully Bingham didn't like to pick on more than one kid at a time. The sight of the two school freaks laughing at them bewildered the bullies, making them think they were beginning to lose their touch.

Marcus and Jack spent just about every waking hour together, riding Jack's bike, inventing games (indoor Olympics, mostly) and swimming in Jack's pool – a rarity in the area and a highly sought-after venue in summer. But Jack never invited anyone else to play other than Marcus. They spent the majority of their time together at Marcus' house because Emile Catalano was unemployed and a solid drinker. Emile regularly vented his frustration on Jack and his brother Stefan, and Jack often came to school proudly displaying his latest bruises.

'See these?' he would say, pointing to the purple marks. 'They teach me to be tough. What these arseholes can dish out to me will never hurt half as much. If I can cope with the old man's fists, then Shane and Bully's words are a complete pushover.'

Marcus idolised Jack. He marvelled at Jack's honesty, his ability to trust others, his determination to speak whatever was on his mind. And, he couldn't deny it, he also idolised Jack for his beauty. Marcus wished he had fine skin and not the red hair and freckles he'd been born with. The boys spent so much time together that people began to talk. Marcus' oldest brother, Harold, made insinuations that Jack had become Marcus' girlfriend. Even Mabel started to worry, for although she couldn't recall seeing Marcus look so happy, she was concerned about what had suddenly caused him to come out of his shell – that strange Catalano boy. Marcus' brother George, and Shirley, one of his sisters, were the only ones to encourage it. Twins, and two years older than Marcus, they'd been so embarrassed of him at school, they avoided him as often as possible. They regarded him as nothing less than weird, and the fewer of the bullies who considered them fellow 'Apple Turnovers' the better. But with Jack's friendship, Marcus became a different person, and though he still got teased at school, at least he was less pathetic. The twins could go off to high school knowing Jack would help Marcus survive primary.

Stefan Catalano was four years older than Jack and he was even better looking than his brother. Stefan, however, was more masculine, his features already those of a man. Every once in a while, Stefan would join in on Jack and Marcus' fun – he never belittled their friendship, because he knew Jack needed an ally against the bullies at school and the one in their own home. He especially played with them in the pool, picking them up in his long arms and throwing them through the air. The boys made him feel manly and strong.

The longer they knew each other, the stronger the friendship between Jack and Marcus grew. They talked about why they were teased.

'If people call you a girl,' Marcus asked carefully, 'why don't you cut your hair short?'

'Haven't you ever read about Samson?'

'Who?'

'He's in the Bible. Haven't you ever read the Bible?'

'No.'

'My dad forced me to. He uses it to justify beating Stefan and me, and Mum. He says if we read the Bible we will understand.'

'And do you?'

'Nuh! It's all bullshit – there's lots of stuff about punishing people but I couldn't see much about beating your own kids.'

'Did Samson beat anyone?'

'No, silly. He had this great hair, and his strength was in the hair. Without it, he was weak.'

'I don't get it.'

'Well, it's like me, sorta. If I cut my hair it'll be because everyone thinks I look like a girl with it long. But that would make me weak, wouldn't it? To cut my hair just because some people think I should. I like long hair, and I guess being teased about it can only make me stronger.'

It didn't take long, however, for Jack to catch up with his brother and in two years he was the tallest in his class, had begun to shave and his thin frame had started developing muscles. On weekends he worked as a labourer down at the brickworks, just like his brother. The work turned him into a man, and he wasn't picked on by the kids in high school, not even Bully Bingham, who seemed to develop a newfound respect for Jack. Because Marcus was Jack's best friend, he was generally left alone too. All it took, one day playing Victorian Rules, was for Jack to punch Shane McHay in the face when he called Jack a nancy. Shane McHay fell to the grass and was out cold for several minutes. Jack was suspended from school for a week for his troubles, but the message was received loud and clear – Jack Catalano wouldn't let anyone tease him anymore. Even during the week of Jack's suspension, things were surprisingly quiet for Marcus. Not once in the five days did anyone say a negative thing to him and that, he was stunned to say, was the first such school week in memory. Five whole days without being picked on! He didn't know it at the time, but the day of Jack's suspension was the last day either he or Jack were taunted at school.

Overnight, Jack became a sort of school celebrity, especially among the female students. Because everyone knew Marcus was Jack's best friend, he got swept along for the ride too. Girls started talking to Marcus because they wanted to know all about Jack. To their surprise, however, in Marcus they discovered a sweet, polite and intelligent young man – it was hard to believe he was the boy who used to wet himself. People wanted to get to know Marcus for his gentleness and Jack for his looks – they made a popular duo. What surprised people most, however, was how loyal they remained to each other. Neither of them took the social turnaround too seriously, they enjoyed it but they knew to tread carefully through the minefield that was teenage idolisation.

Liz Catalano's decision to divorce Emile changed things for Jack. Emile was moving to Sydney and, despite the beatings, Stefan was to follow, determined to get away from small-town Daylesford. Stefan was disgusted at his mother's affair with the foreman at the brickworks and felt there was nothing else he could do. This was a man both he and Jack had been answering to in the scorching heat of the works for years, they had always detested him and his snide remarks about their 'pretty young mother', and now she was betraying them all by sharing his bed. There was no way in the world Stefan would answer to that pig in their home. While they couldn't blame their mother for wanting to leave the abusive Emile, they simply couldn't stand by her choice to be with Fat Frankie Foreman. Jack was devastated. At fourteen, the thought of changing schools terrified him! – he'd have to start all over again and work from scratch to gain the respect of his peers. He loathed Frank but also hated his own father. While he loved his brother and respected his opinions more than anyone else's, Stefan was practically a man and wouldn't be staying with Emile for long. It would only take Stefan a short time to find his feet in Sydney and then he'd be off on his own, leaving Jack as the only target for the pathetic old man's temper. Jack decided he loved his mother too much, he couldn't abandon her. There was also his friendship with Marcus to consider.

The evening of Stefan's departure was sadder and more momentous than even Jack could have predicted. Stefan was his ally and confidant for so many years, the very rock of his foundations. And while the common enemy was also leaving, it was undeniable that Stefan's mere presence served to protect

Jack from all the challenges life regularly threw in his face. Stefan was living proof that a member of the Catalano family could beat the bastards at their own game. With him gone, the odds of Jack's success continuing were questionable.

Jack was so distraught he couldn't even contemplate saying goodbye. When it was time for Stefan to leave, he took his bike and rode through town, circling it continually until he felt his legs could cycle no more. He found his way to Marcus' house and once in the sanctity of the small bedroom at the rear of the house, Jack fell into a useless, emotional heap. Marcus was wholly unaccustomed to such displays of emotion and had no idea how to react. What was expected of him in this sort of situation? Much to his own disgust, his first impulse was to laugh – this was the opposite of everything he knew of Jack, usually so dignified and restrained, now so vulnerable and emotional. At the same time, he was aroused by the sight of this vulnerability, aroused by the power he felt in this situation over someone he was usually in awe of. Marcus drank in this power and it centred him, gave him the energy to take control of the situation. He now possessed a strength which made him feel needed as a man.

Jack's sobs were loud and inconsolable. The tears rolled freely, snot dripped from the end of his nose, his voice was barely audible.

'Everything is gonna change now, I know it,' he said with a whimper. 'Stefan was more than just a brother. And I didn't even say goodbye. Marcus, I didn't even say goodbye...'

Marcus stroked Jack's back and occasionally made calming tones, hushes to soothe his one and only friend. The longer Jack sobbed, the stronger Marcus got, and he felt the stirrings of an erection in his shorts, so drunk was he on this power. He took Jack in his arms and held him tightly, rocking him back and forth lightly. Though he was desperate to dull Jack's pain, he could find no words to say. Instead, he stroked Jack's long hair as he had always wished his mother had done to his own head. He rubbed Jack's trembling body as he'd dreamed a thousand times his own mother had done to him when he was in pain. Then, feeling it was the natural thing to do, he took Jack's tear-streaked face in his hands and Marcus slowly kissed him. It was the paternal kiss both boys had been longing for since birth, the feeling of being loved and accepted by another man, fully embraced. It was a kiss without judgement, one without hesitation. For each of them it felt like something was being set free.

Marcus assumed that passion would be something forever denied him. He felt he would never be allowed the indulgence of loving something, or someone, completely. He had had no close contact with any person, no desire to hold someone closely. But there was something so incredibly relieving about this kiss that he sensed his entire life was leading to its fulfilment and only now would he be able to live like other men. He was now a man whose hunger to express passion outweighed the fear that what he desired would be denied. The night Jack's family was ripped apart was also a night which altered the relationship between Marcus and Jack, and it affected their futures as men.

Mabel's funeral wasn't an overly emotional event, as she would have wished. It was especially unemotional for Marcus. Over the years, he'd become estranged from his mother and the only communication they shared were phone calls for birthdays and Christmas. Two brothers had already died of heart disease and Shirley had committed suicide six years earlier, and the family had effectively ceased to exist. Mabel's death came as no shock; the knowledge that he would never see her again brought no regret. What challenged Marcus most was returning to Daylesford for the first time in eighteen years and that he'd have to persevere with his remaining two siblings' stream of questions. Daylesford was no longer real for him, it only served to remind him of the man he once was, a man he'd rather forget.

A life married to Maggie never quite delivered the happiness Marcus had longed for. He felt trapped by the mistakes of his past and coupled with his belief that he was a failure as a man and a father, Marcus chose instead to spend all of his time at work. He could hide behind his desire to keep providing for the family he now chose to distance himself from. He was so removed that he told Maggie he was travelling interstate for business, not to attend his own mother's burial. He knew he'd have to explain at Christmas why they had not received a call or a card but admitting that he was returning to Daylesford could be granting permission for Maggie to dig through his past. Dealing with the demons alone was far preferable to acknowledging a history they both ignored and he would deal with any argument around Christmas.

Maggie and Mabel never got along. Maggie saw her mother-in-law as a cold, controlling and manipulative woman. Mabel saw Maggie as the epitome of everything she feared for her son – a suburban marriage, trapped in a life she herself always regretted. What she wanted for her son was for him to see the world, to live unrestrained and to use his intelligence to get away from menial labour. Mabel hadn't spoken openly with Maggie from the day she had entered her son's life. The only time the women did speak was when Maggie answered the phone. Then, banal niceties would be exchanged about the health of the children before Mabel would ask to speak to her son. The fact that Maggie had fallen pregnant by accident was something Mabel could never forgive. She blamed Maggie for forcing her son into a life he was never meant to have. Marcus was still living at home when it occurred. He had achieved remarkably at school, deciding to study Economics at university. He was the first Apperton to get accepted to any institute of higher education and, given her own, long-buried aspirations, Mabel wanted him to succeed more than anything else in life. Marcus and Jack worked part-time throughout their final years of school, Jack abandoning the brickworks so they could both develop their passion for food. Their pipedream was to open their own restaurant in Melbourne. What neither of them realised was that Jack had always been the brawn, Marcus the brains, and this difference would make being together extremely testing.

They caught the bus into Melbourne together every weekday and parted ways at Flinders Street Station. Jack, having barely scraped through school, headed off to his cooking apprenticeship each day. Marcus was beginning to enjoy the student life. He thrived on the intellectual stimulation it provided him, a stimulation he now realised had been sorely lacking in his life, especially in his relationship with Jack. Marcus thought they still behaved like boys. What they shared really had no place in the adult world and he feared what would happen when they left that little town. Would they share as much, would their love for each other remain as strong?

Maggie wandered into Marcus' life at the height of his fears for the future and perhaps it was no coincidence, the gods conspiring to provide a radically different path for him in the face of his indecision. Ordinarily, he wouldn't have thought twice about her. That evening, as he played barman to the bonfire's guests, however, he was in the privileged position of overhearing what everyone said as they waited for their drinks. It was mostly a university crowd, they were slightly pretentious but he had grown accustomed to it and had even begun to embrace its flaws.

Jack felt uncomfortable from the moment he arrived, not knowing many people or how to break into their conversations, and he kept pestering Marcus to move away from the makeshift bar, knowing Marcus was committed to staying there. The more conspicuous Jack felt, the more he sulked and the more he drank. He knew these people represented Marcus' new life and were a threat to everything they shared. Before long Jack disappeared into the crowd but Marcus occasionally caught sight of him making a complete fool of himself, slurring his way into other people's discussions and dismissing their pseudo-intellectualism with a brush of the hand. He was the topic of many jibes at the bar and Marcus couldn't help but overhear. Most people wanted to know who the hell Jack was, why he was there and why he was behaving so erratically. Marcus knew he should have leapt to Jack's defence, or make an effort to rescue him from the spotlight. But he remained silent and, as the whispers spread through the crowd, he was transported back to those painful years of primary school. It made him feel sick and angry and he turned those emotions directly against Jack.

The more he heard, the more determined Marcus was to place some distance between himself and Jack. Marcus had come too far from the schoolyard to be dragged back there by Jack behaving in such an undignified way. Jack never read, never wanted to see films, never wanted to do anything in fact, except be with Marcus. Marcus' new friends were sceptical of Jack, the way he made little effort to join in with their conversations, and always tried to drag Marcus away. They started questioning Marcus about the true nature of their friendship, why he still hung around with Jack when they clearly had so little in common. Marcus explained it was a debt of gratitude for Jack's actions in the past and left it at that, but he was so petrified of being picked on again or rejected by these new friends, he could see only one solution and set about putting that in motion.

Maggie was sweet. A smart, fragile and beautiful girl with a magnetic smile. Her long dark hair smelled like honey and her small fingers were perfect. When she approached the makeshift bar at the party, Marcus decided to charm her. If he was to advance through life he had to start acting like a man. They began courting two weeks after the party, an innocent friendship beginning to blossom. While Marcus had his doubts about the longevity of a relationship with Maggie, it felt the correct thing to do, to be with her and protect her. He was lying to Jack about having to spend nights in the city, sometimes simply not showing up to meet him for the return bus home. After walking Maggie to the small apartment she shared with her mother, having missed the last bus home Marcus strolled the streets for hours, occasionally spending a night at a friend's house, other times sleeping in a park.

It took four months for them to make love and it was an awkward, clumsy affair. Maggie's mother could have come home from work at any moment; Marcus had drunk several beers and was having difficulty. Being Maggie's first time, tears began to stream down her cheeks and though he didn't know why, this excited Marcus the most. Her tears made him feel masculine and virile, just as Jack's had done years before. It was over in a matter of minutes – Marcus, in his confusion, had forgotten to withdraw. The intensity of the moment culminated in the two of them crying together in bed. Marcus on his back, one hand behind his head, the other cradling Maggie's back as he made out each disc of her spine. He knew he should never see her again, he knew the mistake he was making.

He avoided her calls for five weeks but when she finally cornered him, he would hear no talk of termination. Marcus' relationship with Jack had deteriorated even further and he wanted to be a father, to offer a child the paternal love he had been denied. They discussed it for hours and decided it was best for them to get married as soon as possible. Marcus knew he wasn't in love with Maggie but the confusion he felt made him believe that with time he could learn to love her and embrace what she could represent in his life. He had begun speaking to a priest at a church near the university, a young man he confided in and though he refused to pray for salvation, Marcus thought the chats with the priest were beginning to be effective. Marcus could never imagine being able to, or wanting to, share similar feelings for another man. Jack was special, their bond had been formed in childhood and it was completely innocent to begin with. Perhaps it was just a single, forgivable slip-up, just as the priest had suggested.

Jack hadn't even been told of Maggie's existence until the evening Marcus told him of the impending marriage.

'I've got this girl into some trouble,' Marcus said, teary-eyed. 'She's very sweet, and I need to do the honourable thing by her – I've asked her to marry me.'

'But that's ridiculous,' Jack said. 'You don't love her!'

'I'm not sure, Jack. I'm confused. I got her into this mess and I can't see her life ruined. That's not fair.'

'How long have you known her?'

'Six months, maybe more.'

'Jesus! You haven't even told *me* about her. Yeah, you must really love someone whose existence you don't even acknowledge...'

The look on Marcus' face confirmed Jack's fears in an instant. It was Jack's existence Marcus no longer acknowledged to the outside world. Jack knew it was all over but he couldn't believe it would end like this. Surely not, surely after all that had brought them together, all the adversity they had faced together... Jack moved to kiss him.

'Jack, stop! You're behaving like you did when we were fourteen. I'm nearly nineteen now, things have changed. *I've* changed. I don't think I'm the same as you, Jack. And that's okay, but I just can't . . . I don't think I feel the same way about life that you do. You need to start acting more like a man, you're not a boy anymore. It's not acceptable behaviour for a man.'

'You want me to start acting more like what? Like you? Right. I'm gonna go fuck some girl and be a man. You're an idiot, Marcus, you're going to be miserable.'

'I won't. I'm not! I want children. I'm happy and I want you to be happy for me too.'

'I don't know that I can. I don't know that I can look her in the face without feeling hate.'

'We want you to be the best man. People are beginning to talk about you and me . . .'

Jack could see little sense in trying to talk Marcus round. He knew about the girl, how could he not? He had followed Marcus for weeks, had seen he was visiting a priest, and seen Marcus with the girl. He always thought Marcus would realise the mistake he was making, but now he saw they *were* different; Jack believed in what they shared and Marcus wouldn't allow himself to.

'Okay, Marcus, okay. I understand what you're doing, you don't have to say anything else. You're fucking weak, you know that? You're much weaker than I thought you were, you've never stopped being the pathetic weakling you were when I first met you. But I'll be your best man because that's what you want, because that's what you think will make you happy. I know you're wrong and you're making a stupid mistake but I deserve better than this. I'll be your best man, but I never wanna see you again after that.'

'Jack?' Marcus pleaded.

'You're a coward, Marcus. I'll pose for your wedding photos just as you'll be posing. But that's it, that's the end of me and you.'

Though she was unable to express it, Mabel was sensitive to her son's needs and knew him better than Marcus thought. Mabel regretted the choices she had made in life and it nearly ruined her to know that her youngest would be making the same mistake. She refused her invitation to the wedding, labelling it a sham and ill-judged. She made a visit to Melbourne to see Maggie, to plead with the girl to think twice about proceeding with the ceremony. Mabel said she would even raise the funds for an abortion if the girl agreed. This was a modern time and women had a choice in these matters.

'You're a bright girl, Maggie, I can see that. Marcus isn't the one for you, he doesn't love you. I beg of you, as much for your own sake as my son's – don't make this mistake, don't choose to be miserable. It might not be bad the first year, or the fifth, but a mother *knows* these things. This is not right for either of you.'

Hearing of the visit, Marcus flew into a rage and collected his things from the house. He never returned to Daylesford while his mother was alive. Despite the opposition, despite his own deep-seated reservations, the marriage went ahead, as did the birth of the child. Marcus' repeated calls for reconciliation between him and Jack were ignored and eventually Jack's mother refused to pass on the messages Marcus left.

Returning to Daylesford for Mabel's funeral was therefore more sombre for this other history, rather than the passing of her life. It wasn't a history he cared to think of often. He hadn't seen his mother for nearly twenty years, and though the freeze between them had thawed slightly, there was no real desire for either to see the other face to face. Marcus couldn't stand it that she knew more about his past than anyone other than Jack. Rumours swept through town about Marcus' shotgun marriage to Maggie, but he'd managed to protect her from wagging tongues by first settling with her in Melbourne and then moving to Sydney two years later. He'd abandoned his studies so he could support his young family and as it turned out, on the job training proved more valuable to him than years studying for a degree. The moment he peered into his firstborn's eyes, the past seemed to trickle away. Maggie and the child were his future and a transfer to Sydney rewarded him with a career he had only ever dreamed of.

Deciding not to tell Maggie about the funeral was also a way of keeping that long-forgotten past buried. He would attend the funeral, he owed his mother that much, but he would go back to Sydney the same day and Maggie need never know that he had gone to Daylesford. His plan would have worked perfectly had it not been for the tall man who approached him after the burial.

'Hello, Marcus.'

Marcus stared at him for close to a minute without being able to speak. 'You look almost exactly the same as you did when I last saw you, Jack.'

'Well, marriage has aged you, old man,' Jack said and chuckled. 'I'm sorry, your brother and sister didn't think you would come, given everything… I would have…'

'Why *are* you here?' Marcus asked, silently accusing Jack of an ulterior motive.

'Daylesford is a small town, Marcus, have you forgotten? I always respected your mother and I got to know her pretty well over the past few years.'

'She never mentioned you to me.'

'Why would she? She was a shrewd woman, your mother. She knew more about the goings on in this town than anyone else. She only ever wanted the best for you.'

'Thanks, but I doubt that.'

'She told me everything she knew about your life. I've managed to keep in touch without you even knowing it.'

'I'm sorry, Jack. I'm just ... I've not seen you in so long and it's all a distant memory. I think I managed to forget – until now, that is ...'

'Sorry you saw me here today. I didn't want to interrupt you and your thoughts. I was going to leave without ... But, I dunno. Sorry. It was good to see you, Marcus.' With that, Jack turned to walk away, a slight hunch about his shoulders.

Though it made him sick to the stomach with fear, Marcus couldn't help but ask: 'Would dinner be out of the question?'

That evening, Jack made one of the best meals of his life. A rich bouillabaisse with fresh, homemade bread, followed by white chocolate mousse. Marcus called Maggie to explain he was stuck in Melbourne and would stay overnight. It was probably the second lie he had told her during their whole married life. It was nothing out of the ordinary for him to stay away from home, but had she been even slightly suspicious of her husband, she would have detected nervousness when he spoke, not to mention how quickly he wanted to get off the phone.

The two men talked mostly about Jack. He had lived the more adventurous life of the two, and frequently grew excited as he spoke about the places he had seen, and the lovers he had known and lost. This was a performance of sorts for him, subtly trying to make Marcus jealous of the course he had chosen for his life, as opposed to that chosen by Marcus. Jack knew the major events of Marcus' life thanks to the long conversations he had had with Mabel and Marcus was quite content to ask questions and listen. Hours passed and they still hadn't eaten, too absorbed in catching up on a life Jack once thought they would be sharing. As the wine flowed, Marcus began to grow envious of Jack's history, of the people and places he had known. Though Marcus had settled into his life, he had always wanted to travel but never had the opportunity. Jack's tales excited Marcus and made him feel like going out into the world to discover some of these things for himself. For the first time in his adult life, Marcus began to feel a void – a longing for male company, real friendship, someone who understood his past and someone with excitement to share. He supposed he had actually grown to love Maggie, but not as a sexual partner, not as a best friend – he loved her as the mother of his children. Though they shared a history of twenty years together, the fact she knew nothing of the traumas of his childhood depressed him. Jack not only knew about Marcus' sense of guilt over the death of Alfred, he had been the victim of the same bullying at school. They were similar in so many ways, sharing an understanding so deep it rarely required explanation. Maggie, on the other hand, never asked him a thing about his upbringing and showed no interest in getting to know what made him the man he was today. In all, she simply took him for granted and Mabel's disapproval of their marriage made Maggie pretend there was no pre-married past; Marcus began to exist the day she had met him.

Now that he sat again with Jack, Marcus remembered what it was to feel like a boy. How ironic that his desire to grow up so quickly was the impetus for pushing Jack away. Was Marcus ready to hit his midlife crisis? Is this what it was, this rekindled fascination for Jack's sense of adventure? Or was it merely that Jack's lifestyle, though foreign to him, reminded Marcus of how interesting he had once promised to be? It made Marcus feel remorseful... of so many choices he had made.

The evening gave Marcus renewed hope, and a desire to reconnect with the boy who had made the man, to begin searching for a genuine happiness and to show Jack gratitude for being his one true friend. Marcus never wanted them to stop communicating and he saw no harm in keeping in touch now.

Questions

Grief wasn't enough to protect Patrick from the barrage of questions he'd been fearing from the roomful of strangers. As he looked around the room at the uncle and aunt he'd never known, at the dozen business associates of his father, at friends of his mother, it only served to make him feel more alone than ever. Patrick knew nothing about the restaurant supply business and wouldn't hazard a guess what his father did for pleasure. What had he and Marcus talked about all these years? In Patrick's visits to see Leroy, the banalities exchanged between him and his father usually revolved around the latest books and movies. Marcus loved the classics but had gained knowledge of modern films too. While his mother was happy to rabbit on about her ladies' club, Isabel's latest letters or Leroy's new tricks, Marcus rarely talked about everyday events.

Questions

As he accepted condolences from strange faces, Patrick dutifully answered questions about his job, his marital status and where he lived. These people didn't care about the answers, they were just filling their own uncomfortable silences. Had Marcus told each of them about Patrick's life? At the very least, he could see Marcus was proud of his children. How sad that Patrick only came to appreciate this at his father's wake. He looked over at Isabel and watched her talking to other strangers. She spoke so eloquently, holding herself almost regally, her pale skin positively glowing. Marcus had had every right to be proud of her – she had established herself in another country, was studying for her PhD, was a well-respected journalist. They would have bonded over their mutual love of films as well, giving them so much to discuss.

Isabel suddenly met Patrick's gaze and he winked at her, mouthing 'sorry'. She smiled in return, and he felt utterly relieved. This small exchange marked the calling of a truce. They each found their stand-offs exhausting and yet they happened almost every time they spoke, as if by habit.

Patrick turned to see Simon Harlen approaching, looking handsome and polished in a black shirt and suit.

'Simon! It's nice to see you, thanks for coming. You really didn't have to...'

'I'm sorry about your father, Patrick. Is there anything I can do?'

It shocked Patrick that Simon would be nice to him when all Patrick had ever shown him in the past was indifference. Perhaps he had been wrong about Simon, maybe there was more to him than the confused boy he had seen on the surface.

'Thanks, Simon. We'll be okay. Thanks again for going to Brisbane for me, you're a lifesaver. I owe you one.'

'Don't even mention it,' he said and casually patted Patrick on the shoulder.

'No, honestly, I reckon you saved me from getting fired. Or maybe I would've resigned, I dunno. But I feel as though I owe you a favour or two.'

'Nonsense. You would've done the same for me, I'm sure.'

'I've been pretty horrible to you in the past –'

'Well, I wouldn't –'

'No, I have. I know I have. There's no excuse for it either. See I . . .' Patrick stopped to censor himself, but, staring into Simon's eyes, he continued as intended, '. . . if I'm being honest, I got a bit scared. I'm not very good in those sorts of situations. It was unfair of me to do a runner. I'm such an arse and I just hope you can forgive me.'

'Apology accepted.' Simon's dimple finally revealed itself. 'You've got a lot going for you, nothing to be scared of. Not with me, at least. So,' he said, changing the topic, 'which one of these arrangements did our illustrious leader send?'

'Yeah, right. I think the bitch managed to send a leave form for me to sign.'

'That sounds about right! Look, I should be at Newcastle Uni right now, I can't stay. Are you sure there's nothing I can do for you? Here, or at work?'

'No, thank you. And thanks again for coming, you didn't have to, but I appreciate it.'

'No problem. Would you pass my condolences on to your mother and sister? I don't feel comf –'

'Oh, of course. Yeah, I will.'

'Well, I'll probably see you at work next week, then.'

'Yeah, I suppose so. Thanks again.' How many times could he say thank you to one person without sounding like a broken record? But what else could he say, what else would anyone be expecting? Patrick knew this was his opportunity to start making amends for his past behaviour, which had ultimately left him dissatisfied with his present situation. He bit his top lip lightly, swallowed audibly and said, 'I've been so horrible to you, Simon, you're a better person than me to show forgiveness. My father's death is teaching me a lot about myself and I want to apologise to you, and make it up to you.'

Simon shook his hand and leaned in to give Patrick a half hug. At the same time as feeling awkward, there was an underlying tenderness which surprised Patrick.

'I'll buy you d-dinner or something next week,' Patrick offered. 'For being nicer to me than I deserve.'

'So long as you don't do a back-doorer.'

Patrick watched him walk away and regretted letting him leave so quickly; he felt deflated to be alone again in a room full of strangers.

Isabel was trapped in a corner of the patio with Norma. Norma was insisting Maggie had talked to Isabel about her son Hal, but Isabel had only a vague recollection of it.

'Do you ever get to London, dear?'

'No, not often. Every once in a while for work, but it's always very hectic.'

'Perhaps you could go visit Hal one weekend, then? I know he'd love to show you around London.'

I bet, thought Isabel. 'Well, I have to study on weekends . . .'

'Surely you can take *some* time off?' Norma decided to try a trump card. 'He's incredibly successful, my son. He's a merchant banker, owns a nice big apartment overlooking the Thames. He's also got a house in the country somewhere near Bath.'

'Oh, that sounds lovely, Norma, but even if I wanted to, I'm afraid I'm budgeting at the moment.'

'Anyway, why don't you think about it? I brought his contact details in case you wanted them.'

'Well, thank you, Norma. I'll look him up some time.'

Norma placed Hal's contact details in Isabel's hand. They were written on the reverse of a piece of photographic paper and as Isabel turned it over she saw a picture of a smiling man – he wore a red cravat, had round cheeks and was balding. Isabel looked closely and saw he was wearing mascara. This might explain why he wasn't married – he reminded Isabel of Liberace.

'You must ignore her,' someone said in French. 'Her son, we have been told, likes ballet, interior decorating and model trains. It is quite strange that some mothers refuse to accept even the most obvious truth.'

'I am tempted to meet up with him just to see if he is as gay as he looks.'

'I am Brigette,' the woman said and politely shook Isabel's hand. 'I am a friend of your mother's.'

'I'm Isabel . . . obviously.'

'Your mother talks about you often at our lunches.'

'Really?'

'Oh, yes. She's been known to read aloud from your letters. I find it lovely that you take the time to put pen to paper.'

'I like to write to Mum on paper because she's not very good with e-mail. I'm sorry that she bores you all!' Isabel said with a self-deprecating chuckle.

'Not at all. I've not been back to Paris in twenty years or more. Hearing familiar placenames reminds me of home. I'm a little ashamed to say that I have been living vicariously through your words. I'm often asking your mother to read from your letters.'

'I find it strange you all know so much about me. I don't know very much about any of you, just that you like to lunch. My mother's letters are three-quarters filled with lunch anecdotes but I can never remember who said what. I think the lunches have been good for her, though. I think she's got a better chance of dealing with this because you're all around.'

'Yes, we are all here for her. I was sorry to hear about Marcus, we were all at lunch when Kathy answered the phonecall. I have never learnt to deal with death, it took my son away from me many years ago and I still cry for him often. I was not going to come today because, as you probably saw, grief can take a strong hold of me.'

'I know it means a lot to my mother, so thank you.'

'Are you returning to Paris?'

'Yes, quite soon.'

'You have someone important to return to?'

'Just my job and my studies, my apartment. Paris is home now, I couldn't ever imagine coming back to Australia.'

'Home for me was always with my family. Now that I have none, I feel less grounded. I am transient.' Brigette paused to look for any sign of empathy in Isabel's face. Seeing none, she continued. 'How do you cope having your family so far away?'

'We've never...' Isabel decided this was probably not the best place to air her dirty laundry. 'Well, it's hard. I try to stay in touch as often as I can.'

'I am thinking of returning to Paris, I miss it so. Now more than ever. The only things keeping me here in Australia are the ladies, and memories of my son's life. If I return, do you think you and I could occasionally have lunch?'

'Yes. I think that would be lovely,' Isabel said. 'I have a wonderful friend, Nicolette. We brunch every Sunday. I think you'd like her.'

'You have no idea how pleased I am to finally meet you, Isabel. I feel like a proud aunty you've never known.'

'I'll have to go through all of my mother's letters and piece together more about you.'

'Or else we can just do that over wine.'

'Once I've –' Isabel motioned to her stomach before realising it was still a secret. 'Oh, yes. A nice long lunch would be lovely.'

'If you have time, Isabel, you must join us for a lunch in Sydney next Friday. Will you still be here?'

'I think so.' Isabel still hadn't decided how long she was going to stay. It all depended on how Maggie was coping, or how Isabel was coping with Maggie.

'Try to make it. We want to take Maggie out, to keep her mind occupied.'

Questions

Maggie was still at the table talking to Graeme, who managed Marcus' business. Graeme was a slight, pale Dutchman with deep acne scars on his cheeks. He had a habit of staring at the top of people's heads when he spoke to them, rather than into their eyes. This was just one of the reasons Maggie felt she couldn't trust him, though she appreciated the loyalty he had shown to Marcus over the years. Graeme had been with the company since its inception. He and Marcus first managed a group of restaurants owned by a wealthy Pole, working slavishly for Mr Kazimierz and seeing precious little for their efforts. Three of the six restaurants won several awards for excellence and Kazimierz took all the credit when, in reality, he'd only provided the start-up funds. All the vision had been Marcus' – the restaurant names, decor, location, chefs... Marcus made all those crucial decisions and Graeme was responsible for the equipment. Marcus' disillusionment with Kazimierz reached its peak at the time of Maggie's mother's death.

It was the sort of death you heard stories about, the long slow battle as cancer grew to invade her entire body. Watching her mother slowly fade to death was gut-wrenching but there was little the doctors could do to save her, dosing her up on morphine as often as possible. Maggie still sometimes woke at night to the sound of her mother desperately drawing each breath, the harsh rasp filling Maggie's dreams several times a year. Marcus' death was the first she'd dealt with since then and Maggie knew that dealing with yet another lost life wouldn't mean the anguish was any less.

Her mother never had a career to speak of, but was a shrewd saver and intelligent investor and bequeathed Maggie and Marcus a modest sum. Maggie hadn't thought twice about what to do with the money. She was tired of Marcus being overlooked for his role in Kazimierz's success and having his knowledge of the hospitality industry taken for granted. There was also selfish motivation as she was bored with his constant complaints about work, every moment he was home from it.

Maggie's inheritance formed the basis for Marcus' new business loan and he knew with Graeme's skills and contacts he'd be able to corner a large part of the restaurant market with relative ease. His was one of the first restaurant supply businesses in Australia and though it took a number of years, as exclusive restaurants began to crop up all over the country, so Marcus' business boomed.

Maggie accepted that Marcus' success owed a considerable debt to Graeme, but it was Marcus who had spent sleepless nights worrying about the business and it was the Appertons who had taken out a second mortgage on their home when its future was in doubt. Graeme helped to keep things successful, but Marcus guaranteed they were profitable. Over the past few days, Maggie had thought little about the business. She had been so consumed with planning the wake, and trying to regain hold of her own sanity that it hadn't occurred to her to be concerned about finances, about Marcus' assets or whether the business would be able to continue without him. She'd also avoided acknowledging that certain life decisions of her own would be just around the corner. Maggie shouldn't have been surprised when Graeme turned their conversation from sympathy to profit and loss.

'Everyone in the office was so shocked, Maggie. We're all deeply sorry and want you to know we'll do anything you want. Whatever you need . . .'

'Thank you, Graeme. Your loyalty has meant a lot to us over the years,' she said to his chin.

'Did Marcus involve you much in the decision making of the business?'

'Oh, not really. In the beginning he did because it was my mother's money, as you know, which got it off the ground . . . but ever since I retired I've just been receiving director's fees as I was quite confident in Marcus' business skills.'

'Have you thought what you'll do now?' His accent was thick and grating, turning the last word to 'nar', and there it was, his first step in assessing her intentions, and the possibilities for his future.

'Not really, Graeme, no. It hasn't exactly been the first thing on my mind.' She forced a complicit smile.

'No, Maggie, of course it hasn't.' He swallowed hard and ran his fingers over the scars on his face. 'I want you to know I'm happy to keep running it for you, until you decide. You have nothing to worry about when it comes to the business.'

Maggie began to feel guilty for doubting him. This was a difficult time for anyone who knew Marcus, she had to keep reminding herself of that. It must have been especially difficult for Graeme, someone who saw more of him than even she did. Marcus never gave Maggie any cause to doubt Graeme; she couldn't quite put her finger on why she was so negative toward him. Now she felt inadequate, unsure what more she could say.

'When you're ready to decide,' Graeme continued, oblivious to Maggie's interior monologue though proving it correct, 'I'm prepared to buy you out. I just want you to know that's an option.'

'Of course it is, Graeme. Of course it is,' she mumbled, before excusing herself.

Maggie went to lie down in order to avoid talking to Marcus' brother and sister, and to miss the empty offers of help as the mourners began to disband. Aside from herself, and perhaps Brigette (who didn't really count), Maggie couldn't see any visible signs of mourning, though. There'd been no tears, no outcries against the injustice, no solemn head-shaking and sighs of 'What a shame'. It was because these people were assembled together through a sense of duty, they knew nothing of each other or their tenuous ties to the dead man and, more to the point, knew very little of the dead man himself. As she sank into the familiar smell of her bed and felt the beginnings of a migraine, she saw little difference between the mourners and herself. She had cried a few times over the past week but Marcus wasn't close to her, just as he wasn't close to anyone in life. How could she expect those at the wake to show anything more than a vague sort of sympathy? This was what made her sad: a regret that forty-odd years of being with Marcus hadn't brought her any closer to understanding him, or herself.

Isabel took on the role of host when she noticed Maggie's disappearance. It was a predominantly passive role, smiling silently at people and offering some of the largely untouched food to unhungry guests. At the three-hour point, Isabel had had enough of accepting condolences from people she didn't know and, following Maggie's earlier cue, she began walking around the small house thanking people for coming and enquiring as to whether anyone needed her to call them a taxi.

In many respects, Maggie was quite surprised and rather touched to hear her children were more than capable to close the wake on her behalf, especially given that Isabel felt uncomfortable in most social situations and Patrick had done more than enough already. As she lay in the darkness of her room massaging her aching temples, Maggie overheard the pleasant manner in which Isabel spoke and she felt a sudden bloom of hope in her heart, the faintest possibility that perhaps Isabel's attitude toward her was beginning to thaw, just as Patrick's seemed to be doing. This was one thing she clung to in the confusion of facing up to Marcus' death: please let it bring me closer to my children, she thought, let it be cathartic for us all.

The feeling of being unwanted in the Apperton house swept through the party until it was down to just the last few. It hadn't escaped Isabel's attention that Patrick had been missing for some time and it annoyed her he could be so flippant and selfish. She could see his silhouette out on the jetty, Leroy sitting close by, simply ignoring where they ought to be.

'Is that Patrick out there?' a smooth-shaven man asked Isabel.

'Of course,' she replied with a hint of bitterness, 'he usually escapes when there's work to be done.'

The handsome man ignored the attack on her brother and made her feel childish. 'I'm Stephen Roth, your father's lawyer. You must be Isabel.'

'Yes.' She nodded her head at him, expecting another bout of post-death small-talk.

'Well, I just needed to talk to Patrick for a moment. Does the . . . is the dog dangerous?'

'Patrick's dog? Hardly! You'll be fine.' It was typical that he would want to talk to Patrick instead of her.

'I'm just a little wary of dogs,' he said and forced a laugh. 'Please, ah, accept my sincerest condolences and pass them on to Maggie. I'll be in touch with her in a few days to finalise your father's estate.'

'Thank you, Mr Roth.' Isabel shook his hand.

As he walked away from her, Isabel silently questioned what he could want with Patrick. Perhaps he just wanted to offer Patrick condolences, it was a lawyerly thing to do, after all. Somehow she expected it was more serious than that, though, and it intrigued her so much she began creating a number of scenarios in her mind. Marcus was leaving him an inheritance and not her. Yes, that must be it.

'I'll help you clean up,' Kathy whispered in her ear. It was uncanny that she managed to appear at exactly the right moment.

'Patrick?'

The man's voice scared him so much that his left hand inadvertently shook Leroy awake. Leroy half-heartedly snapped at him in return.

'Sorry, I didn't mean to startle you. I'm Stephen Roth,' he extended his hand, 'your father's lawyer.' Roth stared at the dog, unsettled by the show of teeth.

'Hi.' Patrick looked up at him and shook his hand without standing. He found him attractive, just his type. Patrick eyed him over – perfect skin, nice lips, broad shoulders, tall, a nice package by the looks of it, big, strong hands... and a stupid wedding ring! It was always the way, most of the men Patrick was instantly attracted to were married.

'I wonder if I could have a few words with you?'

'Sure. Here?'

'Yes, I suppose so. Mind if I take a seat next to you?'

'That'd be fine.' Patrick smiled, more to himself than Roth. That would be fine indeed. If there were gods, Patrick expected he would not live out the hour. Being so attracted to his dead father's lawyer at the wake. Surely that was punishable by immediate death.

'I was hoping you'd stay on up here until at least tomorrow. I need you to come see me in my office in Gosford.'

'What about?'

'It's to do with your father's estate.'

'I know he died without a will, Mum told me about that. I guess that means she receives everything, but she deserves it. Isn't it her you should be talking to?'

'No, not at the moment. You're not entirely correct, Patrick.'

'What do you mean?' Patrick shuffled uncomfortably.

'Are you able to come to my office? Tomorrow is fine, I don't mind coming in on a Saturday.'

'Maybe you can tell me what's going on. I don't want to toss and turn in bed thinking about it all night. Besides, I intended to return to Sydney this afternoon,' he lied.

'Very well. Your father did instruct me to leave a portion of his estate to you. I have his will in relation to this property only.'

Patrick frowned. He wasn't expecting this, and it made him feel excited but guilty that Marcus would single him out.

'I know it's frustrating, Patrick, but I really can't discuss it with you here. I have all the necessary documents at my office and I'll be able to tell you more there.' Roth smiled apologetically. 'I was terribly saddened to hear of Marcus' death, I'm sorry for your family.' He sighed as if in acknowledgement of saying the obvious. 'Your father was a fine, fine man, Patrick, you must know that. As well as a client, I considered him a close friend.'

'Thanks,' Patrick said, not knowing the polite way to address him.

'You can call me Stephen,' he said in response. 'Your mother will be fine financially, Patrick. Marcus was well insured and there's quite a lot of capital. You needn't worry.'

'Can I ask, though, is it legal for my father to leave something to me alone?'

'Of course. Absolutely everything your father owned was jointly owned with your mother. Both names are on this house, the business, bank accounts ... everything. There was another cottage up north, however, which belonged solely to your father. I believe it was purchased with some money left to him by his mother and while your mother could contest it, I doubt it would ever come to that. That's one of the reasons he kept it a secret all these years, I believe. I strongly doubt that Maggie knows a thing about it.'

'Well, thanks, I guess,' Patrick stuttered. 'Thanks for telling me now.'

'How does ten o'clock sound? I can answer any more questions tomorrow.' He reached into his jacket pocket. 'Here's my card with the office address. See you then and sorry again for your loss.'

Patrick couldn't decide whether it was the news of the inheritance or a secret longing for Roth that had him more excited. It shocked him that Marcus would have kept any secrets at all from Maggie, but then he supposed he and Isabel must have inherited their own secretiveness from someone. Why the secrecy? Could there be something in the cottage to solve some of the mystery of his father? Why did the people at the wake speak so kindly to him when he had expected none of them to even recognise him? The intrigue flowed through his veins as he sensed the possibility of a kinship with Marcus which extended beyond the grave. But what part of them was similar? It dawned on him now more than ever – Maggie could prove to be the vital link between the past and the present. Whatever the cottage told him about the present would lack one seminal ingredient... what of the past made all four of them who they were today? He resolved in that one instant to tell his mother about the cottage. Remaining secretive would only cement his isolation. He wanted to stop feeling incomplete and frustrated that not knowing himself meant he was unable to trust or love others. The older he got, loneliness was becoming frightening and he wanted to avoid dying alone.

Feeling invigorated, he took off his shoes and socks, stripped down to his boxer shorts, nudged the dozing Leroy awake and then did something he hadn't done since school – he ran. Together, he and his galumphing mongrel ran along the waterfront, burning in the blazing sun, running for no reason and refusing to stop until they were gasping for breath and it felt their legs could take them no further.

By the time Patrick returned to the jetty to retrieve his shirt, the sun was beginning to set behind the eucalypt-covered mountain which overshadowed the Appertons' street. It wasn't joy that filled him, but intrigue, as though his father's decision to bequeath him the cottage was recognition that he had always been loved and accepted. Neither of them had acted on that while Marcus was alive; there was a niggling sense of mistrust and fear Patrick couldn't ignore, something about his father which had forced him to stay at arm's length.

Patrick stopped outside the back door of the house when he heard yelling. Years ago, it had happened all the time, the two women of the house screaming at each other, the teenager refusing to comply with her mother's demands. It had been so long since Patrick heard them fighting, he stood frozen and disoriented, thinking he must be hearing things, wondering whether he'd somehow stumbled into the wrong yard or maybe the last twenty years were just a dream. Leroy went cowering around to the side of the house where his piece of foam bedding lay – he had never heard Maggie's voice so outraged and he reacted with a look of fear. Patrick's next impulse was to turn and run again, but it was getting darker now and curiosity was also getting the better of him. He felt a sudden pang of guilt that Maggie should have to face a typically selfish and abusive Isabel on the day she buried her husband and at the same time he had a strong urge to eavesdrop.

'What have I ever done to make you hate me this much?' The anguish in Maggie's voice was clear. 'What did I do to make you turn away from us and run to the other side of the world?'

'Oh, please, Maggie . . . where would I begin?' Isabel dismissed her with a condescending tone.

'Answer me, goddammit!' Maggie refused to be ignored. 'If I'm such a monster at least have the decency to call me one to my face, because I'm tired, Isabel, so very tired of this distance between us.'

'You're upset, Maggie. Now's not the time to be having this argument. I came here to help you, not fight.'

'Isabel, you're my daughter and I love you and I want you to forgive me for whatever it is I've done. But please, I beg you, tell me why you hate me so much?' Tears fell from Maggie's lashes to her pale cheeks.

'I never said I hated you, Maggie, we're just polar opposites. I don't understand what makes you tick and I have trouble understanding the decisions you've made in life. Let's not go there now, please, it's been a hard week and we'll try to address this when . . . in a few months or so.'

Isabel couldn't look Maggie in the eye, preferring instead to busy herself with scraping plates and rinsing dishes. She didn't see Patrick lurking in the background.

Maggie sighed. 'You just don't get it, do you, Isabel?'

'Get what?'

Maggie spoke to her in gentle tones, not wanting the conversation to get heated again but needing her voice to be heard. 'You're so absorbed in yourself, you're too blind to know when you're being selfish. You were like this even as a child...' Maggie shook her head thinking back on those years. 'You just didn't understand the concept of sharing. And now that you're in Paris, now that everything you do is about self-fulfilment, you've become Isabel, isolated from the world. When are you going to open your arms to embrace life?'

'What would you know about *my* life?' Isabel's cleaning was becoming more frantic.

'That's just it!' Maggie said almost excitedly, 'I only know what you tell me in letters but they're not about you, Isabel, they're about Paris. I pity you, and your determination to be lonely. I pity your inability to love and more than *anything*, I worry what you'll be like as a mother. It's never easy, Isabel, and sometimes it's downright terrifying. I'm scared for you because I don't think you have anyone to turn to and it saddens me so very much...' her voice was tremulous '...that you won't even consider turning to me.'

Isabel took a firm grasp of a thick crystal wineglass and hurled it forcefully onto the ground just in front of Maggie. Isabel was crying now, the colour of anger rising in her neck. She noticed Patrick, standing there mute and statue-like, staying out of any argument between them, as usual. 'Shut up now, Maggie,' Isabel said calmly, the glass explosion saving her from raising her voice. 'Why is it me? Why am I always the villain here? Maybe, just maybe, you know exactly how you drove me away. Open up to you because I'm pregnant?' she

216

shrugged, searching for the right words. 'That's completely foreign to me. When have you ever, ever felt or expressed anything like support for me? Giving birth isn't the last of it, you know, a mother is supposed to show her children love, maybe hug them every once in a while. I'm not sure I can turn to you because I have such little faith in *your* ability to love.'

Isabel motioned to Patrick, hoping to gain an ally, but he just stood with his mouth slightly agape, looking like a fool.

'I can –' Maggie blubbered.

'Let me finish!' Isabel snapped, her hands still soaking in the soapy water, searching around for another piece of cutlery to clean. 'You may well pity me but you don't have any right to speak about what I'll need as a mother. You show that goddamned dog more love than you've ever shown Patrick or me. Why do you find it so difficult to express love to your own flesh and blood? You can say anything you want about me, but the truth of the matter is, *you* know deep down what's in that closed heart of yours, beneath your facade of contentedness and hiding beneath your lies. You've never forgiven yourself for what happened to you as a mother, for lying over and over – not just to us, but to yourself. So you want us to be friends, to make up because Marcus is dead? For each of our sakes, so do I. Believe it or not, I don't want to keep running, but this was never going to be easy on any of us. So let's begin by talking about Jack.'

'You don't . . . you . . . I . . .' The look of sadness in Maggie's eyes was replaced by fear.

'Don't even bother,' Isabel closed her eyes, her voice more level now. 'No more denial, Mother. I remember him.'

'You?'

'I. Remember. Him.' Isabel announced each word to hit her mother hard with realisation. She removed her hand from the soapy water and saw that it was bleeding. She'd been gripping a knife beneath the suds and hadn't noticed the pain until now. She walked over to her mother, a woman who had always looked as though she was expecting a fright, and she stood staring into those eyes with determination. 'I remember him,' Isabel repeated. 'How can we talk honestly if we don't start with him?' Isabel methodically wiped her bloody hand on a tea towel.

'Think long and hard about whether you're prepared for all of this,' she continued, 'I know you have your reasons for lying, but if you want me to open up to this family, we need to focus on what this family once was, not what it's become.' Isabel crunched though the broken glass and didn't turn back to see her mother sink to her knees.

'Ask her who I'm talking about,' Isabel said sternly to her brother as she passed him, 'before you say a word, ask our mother to explain.'

Patrick was still trying to make sense of the exchange, feeling like a child who had interrupted an adult argument he was incapable of understanding. He knew he should have broken up the fight but something made him stay out of it. These words needed to be said.

Maggie sat crouching on the kitchen floor amid the broken glass, crying, feeling utterly drained, too weak to stand on her own. Jack. Her John. The name hadn't been mentioned by the family in over thirty years. In some ways, it was almost a relief for her now, to hear his name said aloud, to have the veil of his banishment finally lifted. The pain in her chest was so heavy it weighed her to the floor and she feared getting up now would be such an effort, her heart might stop beating. She felt a firm arm behind her back and was startled by the intimacy of the touch. Maggie turned to see Patrick crouching by her, the tears welling in his eyes as he tried to brush away broken glass with his foot.

'Do you think you're strong enough to walk with me?' he whispered gently.

This tenderness caused her to cry even harder, the thought that she had pushed Patrick away from the family. Patrick was so gentle, less confrontational than his sister. Maggie looked into his eyes but couldn't speak, her lips formed to make the words but no sound came out.

'It's okay, you don't have to say anything. Let's get you up off the floor and into bed.' Patrick couldn't bear to see his mother this weak because he feared it was a preview of his own future.

She was surprised by the strength with which he lifted her. She had never needed her son like this and it made her feel helpless to be so reliant on him now. It struck her then – her own mortality, life slowly slipping through her fingers as he was rising to the vigour of it. Her son, her baby, was now truly a man and there was a sense that now *he* would be the male figure in her life, the man she would rely on to help protect her from the harshness of the world. Maggie wanted to stop crying but couldn't.

Patrick guided her down the hall towards her bedroom. He helped her climb back into the unmade bed and placed the covers over her. She turned her face away from him, embarrassed to be so emotionally raw in front of him, so exposed to his judgement.

Finally, she found the strength to speak. Her voice was weak but Maggie persevered. 'I'm sorry to be like this in front of you, Patrick. I never intended for you to see me like this.'

'It's okay, you don't have to apologise to me.'

'It must be a shock for you...'

'It's okay to let go now, Mum, you're better off opening yourself up to the pain, it will help you get better in the end. Can I do anything now? What can I do to help you?'

'I... I'm really not sure. Do you hate me too, Patrick?'

'I've never hated you a day in my life. I never will.'

At those words Maggie let out an unrestrained sob and buried her face deeper into the pillow. She loosened the covers to free her hand and waved Patrick away.

He understood. It was her time now and he shut the door softly behind him.

Patrick found Isabel sitting in a small dinghy dry-docked on a patch of grass a few hundred metres from their house.

'I don't want any company at the moment,' she said without malice.

'But I came to see how you are,' he said in response.

Isabel half-smiled and Patrick took this as an invitation to join her. Leroy made a clumsy attempt to jump into the dinghy as well, but sensibly decided otherwise at the first sign of rocking.

The siblings sat in silence for some time, facing each other. Isabel was looking at the light reflected on the other side of the Broadwater. In the bright moonlight, Patrick studied her face. It had been so long since he had actually looked at his sister, he didn't recognise her features well. The crowsfeet forming at the corners of her eyes, her strong, almost masculine, nose, the bruised colouring of her lips. He didn't think they looked like brother and sister – Patrick had darker skin, his eyes were blue, hers were hazel, his nose was slight, hers strong. Her skin, her very manner, was becoming more European. Isabel felt his gaze and met it.

'You can't stand Maggie, can you?' he asked bluntly.

'I think that might be simplifying it a bit,' she sighed. 'It's not that I can't stand her. No ... she's our mother. I suppose I can't understand why she behaves the way she does. I suppose I just ...' Her voice faded as she continued staring out at the water.

'Just what?'

'We've been through the same shit, maybe we should be able to talk about it together?'

'Do you really think Mum and Dad have been that bad?'

'I don't think you know everything. But that could be a good thing, Patrick, I'm not sure you'd want to know.'

'Being in Paris is you running away, isn't it? Living in Paris isn't about having a different life – it's about trying to forget this one.'

'Yes, Patrick. I have run away. I am still running away.'

'From what?'

Isabel looked at her brother. She felt much older than she actually was, somehow more maternal. When had her youth disappeared? Here she was, thirty-seven years old and yet it felt like she was still twelve, and Patrick a boy of seven. 'Oh, God.' She sighed again. 'I don't think I can do this. It's funny, I feel like I need to protect you from the truth.'

'Let's take this boat out,' Patrick said impulsively. 'Let's act like kids again!'

'We can't, it's stealing!'

'We won't get caught. Anyway, none of the neighbours would call the police, have you noticed how polite everyone is around here?'

'But it's dangerous. What if another boat comes along, we don't have any lights.'

'What other boats? Stop being such a killjoy, we'll be fine.' He jumped up, excitedly. 'Come on Leroy,' he urged the dozing dog.

'Patrick!' Isabel protested, but by now he was heaving the wary Leroy into the dinghy, securing the oars and pushing the boat down the incline towards the water. Isabel held on to the sides of the boat to steady herself.

'We'll be alright.'

Within minutes he was rowing them out towards the centre of the Broadwater. Leroy suddenly found his confidence and was their mascot, his two front paws up on the bow. The sound of the water as it swirled beneath the slicing of the oars soothed Isabel. The moonlight was beautifully reflected in the black water. Patrick rowed strongly, building up momentum as he went.

They could be anywhere in the world right now, thought Isabel.

'I'm pregnant,' she announced, just loud enough to be heard.

Patrick stopped rowing. The oars dripped black water and the boat continued to glide along at the same speed. 'Is that good news?' he asked cautiously.

Isabel hesitated, choking back tears. 'Well, yes. I think it is. I mean, I'm scared as all hell and I never thought I'd be a mother, but, yeah, I'm happy about it.'

'Congratulations.' Patrick leaned over awkwardly and planted a kiss on her cheek. 'I'm happy for you too then. Did Maggie guess you're pregnant? Is that what the fight was about?'

'I didn't even know whether I was going to tell her but she guessed it and then when I told her about how it happened, or with whom I should say, she rolled her eyes so dismissively it just made me so mad. It wasn't just that, she questioned whether I was prepared for it and it bothered me she'd use this as an excuse for her to get close to me. After thirty years of barely talking, I fall pregnant and *now* she wants to be there for me? I dunno, I just don't think I can wake up one day and say "Now I'll let you into the life you never wanted to know anything about".'

'But she's so desperate, Isabel, surely you can see that?' He locked the oars into the rowlocks so they could drift in silence.

The wind no longer in his fur, Leroy grew tired of standing and finally settled on the seat next to Patrick.

'Of course I can see her desperation but she's a stranger to me, Patrick, and there's a lot of ground we need to cover before things even get close to being normal.'

'She's not a stranger like Dad was. I've always thought Maggie was quite predictable really, haven't you? I mean, name one thing she's ever done that's surprised you. Dad was the one I could never work out.'

'If she's not a stranger, then she's an outsider. I know she's right in some ways; I've got used to being on my own, not answering to anyone. If Maggie could just admit certain things about the past, that's what I need. Then perhaps we can start again with my baby. I only just found out, Patrick. It scares me half to death and I couldn't think about much else on the plane. If I'm being totally honest with myself, I still haven't decided whether it's best to keep it.'

'So who's the father? What does he say?'

'Well, aside from the fact that he's really the only man I've been with . . . he's also married and has three other kids. Legitimate children. And he's my boss.'

'Fuck me! You don't do things by halves, do you? And I thought *I* fell for the wrong men!'

'He's not the wrong man, though,' Isabel shrugged. 'It's good – I have my independence, he's there when I need him and he doesn't demand much in return. But it's still very much a secret. Only one other person knows about it, and now you and Maggie. So he's the right man for *me* . . .'

'But not necessarily the right man to have as the father of your kid?'

'Exactly. I don't think he's overly impressed or excited by the whole prospect. It was totally unexpected – I certainly wasn't taking risks. At least, I thought I wasn't.'

'So . . .'

'So . . .' she mimicked. 'This isn't exactly how I expected my life to turn out.'

'And Maggie says you should turn to her for support?'

'She's convinced I'm not good mother material. But then I'm convinced she's not grandmother material, so we had a bit of a fight about it.'

'But it was more than that.'

'Yeah, it was.'

'You have to tell me, Isabel. You can't keep avoiding the issue.' The hurt echoed in his voice. He was tired of feeling as though everyone in the family knew a big secret, except him.

'I've said some pretty horrible things to you over the past few days, Patrick. Actually, make that the past few years. I've been awful.'

'I thought that's what siblings did,' he said jokingly. 'Annoyed the hell out of each other and made the other one feel bad.'

'You know,' she began, leaning over the edge of the dinghy to run her fingers through the water, 'when you came to Paris I really didn't want you to be there. You were cramping my style. I was, you know, finding myself and all that crap. I was busy forging new friendships and trying to be an impressive Australian. And then you burst into that life – a bright, infectious person and everyone loved you for being so open to things. Every one of my friends at the time thought you were fantastic, even Vincente. You reminded me of something I wasn't, of the things I wanted to leave behind.'

'But why do you hate your past so much? I don't really get it. It wasn't great, but it wasn't hell on earth either.'

'I'm getting to that,' she chided him jokingly. 'Be patient, little brother.'

'Sorry,' he mumbled, sounding like a nine year old.

'And then you met Jean-Marc... To see you two together, it hurt so much. I mean, I knew he was gay but that didn't change a damned thing. Seeing you so happy made me angry. Why were you allowed to be happy? What had I done to deserve such misery? Blah, blah, blah. All that shit. I was so confronted by your ability to love someone else that I resented you for it. I wanted you to be miserable just like me. So, yeah, I admit I hinted to Mum and Dad that you might be gay. In a way, I wanted them to make you miserable, as I thought they'd done to me. Then all those letters you and I started writing to each other – when you thought we were getting closer – I just thought we were drifting further apart. I used you to get closer to Jean-Marc because he asked about you all the time, not that I told you he did. He really loved you, Patrick, whatever you think of that time now, you should know it was genuine. He was going to go to Australia and then, well, he met the American and left Paris. I started hating him instead of you. I was so bitter, so selfish. Then he got sick and nothing mattered anymore. He came back to Paris alone and though I didn't see him very often, it was enough to know none of it mattered. I stopped writing to you because I felt such guilt for the way I'd been treating you. I had behaved like Maggie and it made me never want to see this family again.'

'But you still talked to Mum and Dad, you came back...'

'Yes, I did. It was Dad. When he came to Paris for business he was a changed man, you could see it in his eyes, the way he talked, the way he walked. Everything about him was different. We talked a lot and I began to see that if I could start forgiving him, at least, then maybe I'd be able to stop feeling so bitter about everything. So I wrote to Mum and I spoke to them on the phone pretending everything was okay again. In some respects, meeting Alain took my mind off other things. But coming home has made me feel bitter again and I really hate it. I hate feeling like this. That's why I'm going back to Paris as soon as possible. I want you to drive me to Sydney tonight so I can call the airline first thing in the morning.'

'Tonight? You should stay just –'

'Patrick, I have to leave now. I have to get away from here. I'm being honest with you and I've told you all this to help you understand why I hate it here so much. I'm sorry I hurt you in the past, that's a side of me I'm not very proud of. But then Maggie, to have her questioning me as a mother...'

'Were you abused, Isabel? Is that what this is?'

'What?' she stared at her brother blankly.

'Did someone abuse you? Is that it?' It required an enormous amount of bravery for him to ask the question. He was unsure if he'd be able to cope with the answer.

'No. Not sexually. No, I wasn't abused. I...we...we had a brother, Patrick.'

'What?' he shook his head in disbelief and his hand instinctively moved to stroke Leroy's fur.

'We had a brother. John. We called him Jack. He was six years older than me.'

'Jesus...' Patrick mumbled. It made no sense but it was the only word he could form.

'He died when you were one, he was only thirteen. He was hit by a car. I don't remember the accident clearly but I was there. I remember Jack, though. I remember his smile and the way he seemed to hold the family together. He had such a way about him and he made Mum and Dad so happy.' She was crying now so Patrick moved Leroy and went to sit next to his sister, placing an arm around her shoulders as she sobbed.

'What happened to him?'

'He ran onto the road and got hit. He died instantly. And then they pretended nothing happened, that he never existed. Mum went around and collected every trace of him. Every game, every piece of clothing, every photo with Jack in it. She took everything away and we never spoke about it. I was five or so, I was asking where Jack was, why my brother couldn't play anymore, but Mum and Dad always hushed me and told me to stop asking about him. There was no grieving, no acknowledgement of loss. For years I blamed myself for sending him away – I wet the bed, I threw tantrums, I couldn't sleep and, instead of getting me help, Mum and Dad ignored it. I was in trouble and they took the easy option. How miserable I was, I am, because they couldn't deal with their loss and understand I was in pain too.

'You won't remember much, but I barely spoke at home. I was too scared to say anything because I thought *they* would take me away like they took my brother away. When I grew up and realised none of this was my fault, that I had nothing to feel guilty about, I just shut down. I was too scared to feel a thing.'

Patrick strengthened his hold and pulled her into him. They felt like kids again. 'Isabel, I'm sorry you felt like that. Sorry I didn't know about any of this.'

'I wanted to come here and forgive her but I don't know if I can. You think I'm happy?'

'I honestly don't know.'

'I'll tell you that I'm coping, as well as I know how. I've cried myself to sleep so many nights and now I just wonder how I would've turned out if our parents had handled things differently. I can't blame them for everything in my life, but I find it very hard to let go.'

'But now that you're going to be a mother –'

'If I have this child I couldn't imagine losing it. I can't believe what Maggie went through, it must have destroyed her. But you know what? You just can't afford to let your other kids go, she should've been stronger for us. I'm not asking her to let go of Jack, but she had us too and by removing Jack's presence from her life it felt as though she wanted us removed too. How many times I've sat with her and she's simply not been able to say a word, no connection to pick up on, not even to chat about the weather, for god's sake. I felt so unwanted by her.'

'What about Dad?'

'He was different. He was always at work and in a way we got used to that. But he did make the effort, even if it was just small-talk. We knew he was proud of us, but Maggie, she's just so cold.'

'But we were cold right back, can't you see? When we were kids you used to rouse on me for being nice to her.'

'Did I?'

'All the time! You made up games for how we could ignore her and you'd punish me if I caved in.'

'I don't remember that.'

'I just think we all need to work on this, Isabel. Do we even need to assign blame? My life's pretty screwed up too but I can't keep being angry with her, because it's turning me into a miserable old man. I need to grow up and I think you do too.'

'I need to go home. I need to stay away from here, I'm not strong like you.'

'If that's what you wanna do, then do it, but I'm staying here to confront my past and ask Maggie to help me get over it. If you go, I don't know how you're gonna get any stronger. It's different for me, Isabel, I don't remember our brother and I'm not going to pretend that my situation is the same as yours. But if you go without talking to her properly...'

They sat for close to an hour, the boat drifting slowly but not going far. When Patrick started to feel sleepy he stood up and made his way back to the middle seat. He lifted the oars from the rowlocks. 'Come on,' he said tenderly. 'If you want to go tomorrow, we should get some sleep.'

As the boat turned around and the warm night breeze blew against them, Leroy once again took up his position over the bow, lifting his head toward the moon.

Answers

Maggie sat on the edge of her bed in the darkness of the room she had once shared with Marcus, listening to her children sneak about the house as though she would not be able to realise what they were doing. The events of the day told her the process of reconciliation was going to be a long battle and wasn't something she could force.

It wasn't within her to confront Isabel again. She felt so empty, so drained of energy; she couldn't have done it even if she had wanted to. Her children had been running from her their whole lives and they would probably continue to do so until she died, perhaps even still. All cried out, she was even too empty for tears. It wasn't just losing Marcus, and the loneliness she knew she'd have to endure, it was also Isabel's accusations, the cruel way she spoke to her with little regard for how it would make Maggie feel. Though she felt she ought to, Maggie couldn't be angry, she couldn't blame Isabel for her feelings. Each one of them was equally guilty of failing to make their family work as a unit – secrecy was just the surface stain of the Appertons. Deceit, denial, desire – these were the uglier faults of them all.

It surprised Maggie to hear Patrick knock on her door to announce they were leaving.

'Sorry to bother you again,' he said as he crept into the room.

'Oh, don't be,' she said and smiled. 'I suspected you both might want to sneak off.'

'It's Isabel, Mum. I tried talking to her but she's scared. There's so much bitterness in her I don't think she's capable of facing this just yet.'

'Is there anything we can do to make her stay?'

'I'll try again in Sydney, maybe she'll feel differently then, but she's so confused and I think this will take a lot longer than you'd hoped.'

'I'm trying, Patrick, can you see that?'

'Yes. I can, and I know Isabel will come round, but in her own time.'

'I hope you're right. And us? Patrick, can you tell me? Are things getting better between you and me?'

'Isabel's explained some things to me and I need to think a bit. There's so much going around my head I just don't know where to start. But I do know that you and I need to just listen a bit more to each other, ask the questions we need answers to.'

'Yes, that's true.'

'Can I get you a cup of tea before I go?'

'No, I'll be fine. You just work on Isabel for me, I want her . . . both of you to be happy. That's all I want in life now.'

'I'll come back to see you again tomorrow.'

After she heard the car start, Maggie sat thinking. How could Isabel possibly think Maggie was in denial? There was barely a single morning of the past thirty-two years that Maggie hadn't woken to think of her lost son, hadn't longed for things to be otherwise and wished the pain would disappear. How could Isabel possibly comprehend what it meant for a mother to be denied her firstborn and then to be denied her right to grieve? She heard Isabel's defiant steps on the footpath outside her window and considered running after them, begging her to reconsider. But Isabel was the type of woman who couldn't be cajoled – each decision had to be on her own terms. A skilful strategy was required to convince Isabel of anything and Maggie knew there and then it would have to take place on Isabel's territory.

If John were alive today, how different would their family be? She insisted on calling him John, not by his nickname Jack. Maggie imagined dealing with Marcus' death with her eldest son there and knew it would have been easier having him by her side. He would be handsome like his father at that age, married to a loving wife and there would be two or three grown children. Maggie wouldn't be so afraid of children then, if she hadn't lost her John. They would call her grandma and she would spoil them with treats and take them for walks with Leroy. Isabel wouldn't have run away to Paris, she would be living in Sydney and maybe she wouldn't be so lonely. She might have found herself a nice husband rather than be in some adulterous affair with her boss. Best of all, mother and daughter could have been friends. John would have run the family business for them and Patrick would . . . Of all of them, Patrick would probably be the same person. Hadn't he just said there wasn't really an issue between them? He was the one she could rely on now, not a son she could never have back. Patrick was her godsend – how glaringly obvious it should have been all along.

The drive back to Sydney was silent, save for the humming of the car's engine and the occasional click of the air-conditioner. A sad mood filled the space between them, each lost in their own thoughts. The thought of becoming an uncle was surprisingly appealing for Patrick. Bringing a new generation of Appertons into the world could cause his dissatisfaction with the present to melt away. Perhaps the future would be something to get excited by? Having Isabel open up to him for the first time in years made him want to stay close to her, attempt to salvage some of the unity he thought they had after his Paris trip. With his life so empty, so void of promise, family was the one constant he would be able to rely on. Bridging the gap between Maggie and Isabel would probably make his life easier in the long run, give it some meaning. And yet, a part of him knew he could just as easily continue without Isabel; when she returned to Paris he would not long for her company. Their brother's existence helped to explain some of the vagaries of what it meant to be an Apperton but Patrick knew there were still many unanswered questions about how they had got to where they were. Part of him hoped his father's cottage would hold some of the answers, but he knew not to expect too much from Marcus' legacy. The cottage could prove to be little more than an annexe to the empty shell that had housed them as children.

Damn Isabel for being so impulsive. In the dinghy, Patrick was tempted to tell Isabel about Marcus' cottage but he didn't think it would help her in any positive way. It was best to wait to tell her about it after he had seen it for himself and maybe the lawyer would be able to explain more in the morning. Ah, the lawyer.

Perhaps Patrick could use the cottage as a hook to make Isabel stay. Isabel was so stubborn, he knew nothing else could convince her to stay. And yet, part of him wanted to see the cottage alone, this was his chance to understand Marcus. With Isabel by his side, she would undoubtedly cloud any discoveries he made, casting her own view over things and affecting his judgement just as she had done with their mother over the years. He wanted the lawyer to himself too, however pathetic that would sound if he said it out loud. If Marcus wanted to trust him with the knowledge of the cottage then surely this was his first step in getting to know his father better – and gaining a better understanding of himself.

Whenever he returned from a visit to his parents' house, he only began to relax when he saw the city's skyline, the dark steel of the Harbour Bridge and the lights of the skyscrapers reflected in the water. It bothered him Isabel wasn't awake to see these things, she showed no interest in Sydney and all it had to offer. How much of what she had revealed tonight could be blamed for the distance she placed between herself and everyone she knew? What weight did she need to offload before she would be able to feel whole again? They should attempt to resolve some of these issues before Isabel disappeared again to her cocoon on the other side of the planet.

He knew it was totally beyond his control to change Isabel's mind about her flight. She'd called the airline as soon as they got in the car. Isabel had to be at the airport by midday on Sunday and insisted on taking a cab to a hotel the next morning so that Patrick could sleep in. They stayed awake a while longer watching television but not paying any attention to it and sipping a herbal tea. Isabel had dark circles under her eyes, her skin was pale and blotchy.

'You feeling okay?' he asked, more by way of making conversation than through any specific concern.

'I feel like shit, actually,' she said. 'Emotional outpourings have never been my strongest point and I haven't slept much since coming here. I think I'm still suffering from jetlag.'

'I don't think you should spend tomorrow night in a hotel and are you sure you want to fly out Sunday? You're pregnant, remember, maybe you should rest up some more.'

'I really don't know,' she played with the tea strainer in her mug. 'I know I have to get away again before I go too far, I think it's best for Maggie *and* me.'

'Tell me what you really want to say to her.'

'No, I won't do that. Sorry. I . . . I reckon I just need to get back home and sort through my thoughts. And then if you're okay with it, I might write you a letter about all of this.'

It struck him as an archaic thing to do, to send someone an actual letter, especially as she now had the chance to speak to him face to face, but she was a writer after all. He mumbled, 'Okay.'

'I know that's probably the coward's way out but I don't think I'm brave enough to say it all to you in person. If I write it in a letter hopefully I'll be able to order my thoughts a bit better. I've always been better on paper than to someone's face.'

'Can I just ask you one thing though?'

She nodded, prepared for the worst.

'Were you ever tempted to tell me about Jack before today?'

'Oh, God. Of course. Countless times.'

'Then why –?'

'I couldn't. I was protecting no one but myself. I just wasn't ready to dredge up all the shit I've struggled with. I'm still not ready... I suppose that's why I have to get back to Paris. I'm still "on the run".' Her cheeks reddened at the term, or perhaps it was the heat of the tea. She got up slowly, patted him on the shoulder and went to rinse her mug. On the way through to his bedroom she stopped. 'I'll try to talk to Maggie eventually, but at the moment...' She paused. 'Maybe not right away, but soon.

'I was thinking, Patrick, I want you to know I respect you for who you are and we'll both sort ourselves out, I'll make up with Maggie eventually.'

'For what it's worth, I do think you're making the wrong decision. In Paris you'll fall back into your familiar routine and Maggie will barely enter your thoughts.'

'Maybe, but if I have this baby, I think coming to terms with our relationship will be part of being the best mother I can be.

'If Maggie had just said she believed in me, and supported me, that's all I needed to hear. Just because I'm doing this my way instead of hers doesn't mean it's the wrong way. I came here with good intentions, honestly I did, and I saw glimpses of Maggie thawing but then she lost me all over by saying I couldn't, that I wasn't capable of being a good mother.

'And if you don't keep the baby?'

Isabel thought for a moment and realised she couldn't consider termination any longer. 'I'm going to be a mother.'

'Why don't you stay and have it here?' he asked, knowing how futile the suggestion was.

'I suppose I'm worried that if I'm not on that flight on Sunday, the simple truth is I don't know what I would end up doing to myself. Do you understand? I have to go now, whatever that means for my future, and I need time alone in a hotel before I go.'

Patrick nodded.

''Night, Patrick.'

'Bye,' he said softly into his empty mug.

She tried getting some sleep but it proved to be pointless. She disliked the unfamiliarity of Patrick's bed, being immersed in its foreign, masculine smells. Isabel thought of the comfort of her bed in Paris, the crisp freshness of the sheets she changed weekly, the smell of her shampoo on the pillow cases, the comfort of her duvet. She couldn't wait to get to the hotel.

Isabel thought of her future with Alain, of how much she missed his touch. Would he play a role in their child's life, or would this mean he returned to his normal existence with his wife and children? Or could this be the impetus for him to leave the wife behind to be with Isabel permanently, for them to forge an existence of togetherness? Isabel cursed the course of her mind; she hated to entertain fantasies that would never eventuate. Was it fair to bring a child into a single-parent world? Isabel rubbed her belly which, though no different in size or shape, felt significantly altered, somehow already beginning to evolve. To say there was a right or wrong family structure was ludicrous. If Isabel had learnt from the pitfalls of her own upbringing, then surely this would provide a good basis for her own child's happiness. Alain was merely a bystander in this development. A catalyst, certainly, but if he chose to leave her now then Isabel knew she would survive because her unborn child could provide the love she had always craved.

Patrick got up early by his standards and tidied up the apartment before heading to Roth's offices in Gosford. Roth told him again that Marcus intended to keep the existence of the property a secret from everyone else in the family. The cottage now belonged to Patrick and Roth instructed him that he was to do with the house and the contents as he wished. What could the contents possibly be? The idea of keeping a secret excited him but he knew he would be telling Maggie about everything because this was his new resolve – to sustain Marcus' secret life was to remain buried beneath the weight he so desperately wanted to shift. The meeting lasted no more than twenty minutes before Roth handed over the solitary brass key and some poor directions, etched in his father's unmistakably messy scrawl.

The letterbox announcing number sixty-five was unimposing – a simple red tin box on top of a twisted stem of white metal. How often did Marcus come here, often enough to get mail delivered? The otherness of a life Patrick was only now beginning to know intrigued him. What had gone on in the cottage and what escape had it provided Marcus from his regular life? He was afraid as he turned up the drive. Would Marcus' ghost inhabit the cottage and continue to keep his son at a distance? Or worse, perhaps the cottage would reveal no secrets at all, answering none of his questions.

The cracked concrete driveway was steep, either side of it was unruly bush, coastal vegetation that could grow well anywhere, even on rock. Was all this land now his? His car struggled up the steep incline and Patrick pushed it on cautiously, unsure whether to expect a sudden turn or dramatic end. But the path soon levelled out and turned right, revealing a small dishevelled weatherboard cottage. He parked his car in a clearing in the shade, and heard it sigh as he shut off the engine. Patrick took a deep breath and shivers ran down his spine. He felt like an intruder.

He was met with the smell of dry Australian bush. He felt the crunch of leaves underfoot and a chorus of birds and insects greeted him, reminding Patrick of his childhood, when Marcus had taken the family on frustrating, fight-filled holidays.

'Marcus,' he said aloud, 'why did you bring me here?'

Three steps led up to the cracked wooden verandah which, he now saw, wrapped itself around the entire cottage like a belt. A hammock was strung between two of the verandah's supporting posts and he guessed it would receive the afternoon sun. Patrick fumbled in his pocket for the key Roth had given him. Just one key, he thought, what a luxury, comparing its simplicity to the five he was forced to keep for himself.

The layout of the cottage was simple. To the left was the first bedroom, a guest room rarely used, by the look of things. In its centre was an ornate four-poster bed, with a trunk at its base. There were two doors leading onto the verandah, with no curtains. A small chest of drawers stood against one wall and a bedside table matched it. The room smelled of pot pourri and two towels, a face washer and a small cake of hotel soap were arranged delicately at the end of the bed. He had been expecting someone. Did this guest, the one from Marcus' secret life, know he had died?

The room across the hall was clearly Marcus'. The enormous bed in the centre had the eerie appearance of being recently slept in. Patrick could almost make out the shape of his father in the curves of the mattress. He was drawn into this room. He opened the wardrobe and peered inside. Perfectly hung clothes, neatly arranged shoes and a set of shelves holding crisply folded t-shirts and underwear. Patrick put his hand to his mouth and took another deep breath, hearing the heavy pounding of his heart for the first time.

On the wall above the bed there hung Gerome's 'The Bath', an enormous framed print stretching almost to the ceiling. Patrick knew the image – he had seen the original at an exhibition in London and had sent his parents a postcard of it. He couldn't remember why it appealed to him so much at the time. In it there was a naked, fleshy white woman carefully being washed by an African maid. The woman was sitting on an uncomfortable looking bamboo crate in an oversized bathroom ornately tiled in jade green. He had never found out what the Arabic on the walls meant. The white woman seemed almost to be ashamed, unable to look the maid in the eyes, but the maid was tender-faced, as if she had been asked to wash away the white woman's shame. Perhaps that is what had appealed to Patrick, the reversal of vulnerability. Why Marcus had invested in such an unsubtle, huge print of it would never be known.

This room smelled of a deep, musky cologne unfamiliar to Patrick. He couldn't remember ever smelling cologne on Marcus. A book rested on the bedside table, open and face down, a sepia photograph of a young man on the cover. The thought of moving the book irked him, disturbing the page that was left so deliberately marked by his father. This felt like it was somebody else's house, for surely if it belonged to a man he had known for thirty years it would reveal something of Patrick's understanding of him. If Marcus made this a home then it was finally confirmation that father and son were strangers and this upset Patrick more than he thought it would.

The long hallway was lined with shelves bowing under the weight of countless books. One wall, he saw, was brimming with paperback novels, each one with a broken spine and tattered corners, each one read by Marcus. Patrick ran his finger along the shelf. In the collection he recognised many of his own favourite authors, copies of the very titles he had taken to his parents' house in order to fill some of Maggie's silences. It must be mere coincidence so many titles were the same as the ones he had read. How unrealistic was it to suppose Marcus made a mental note of any of the books Patrick read so he could purchase his own copies? Was this how the father understood his son? These books were his now, everything he saw in this cottage was his to do with as he pleased.

On the other wall every book was related to film – biographies of stars and directors, books dedicated to specific film eras and genres, critiques, reference books and magazines. This is how Marcus gained such impressive knowledge of current film trends and now Patrick could appreciate that he did all of his reading here, in his own world. Why hadn't he felt comfortable reading in front of Maggie? Patrick was excited to be the new owner of all these books. His relatively nomadic existence from one small apartment to the next prevented him from keeping a library of his own and, uncannily, this was exactly the kind he had longed for. On one side of the hallway the books were *about* him, and on the other side they were Marcus' way of getting to know Isabel.

At the end of the hall was a bathroom looking out of place in a cottage built at least fifty years ago. It was almost kitsch in its modern design – a feature wall covered in small red tiles and a skylight overhead. There was a large white spa with gold fittings, and a slate-floored shower. One of the taps was dripping so Patrick leaned in to turn it off tightly. He looked at his reflection in the mirror, seeing again his resemblance to Marcus and wondering whether he would be able to fool the cottage into thinking the new master of the house was in fact the same as the previous one.

The lounge was deceptively large. It too was filled with bookcases but these were stacked with DVDs, videos and CDs. There must have been thousands of them, all alphabetically arranged, he noticed. Two glass doors led to the verandah and facing the wall backing on to Marcus' room was a deep three-seater couch. It was positioned in front of a large plasma-screen television mounted on the wall. It, in turn, was surrounded by a high-tech home-theatre system that would cause even the most discerning twenty-something yuppie's mouth to water. Patrick chuckled to himself – this was obviously his father's oasis. It was a place for him to indulge in his own success, far away from the restrictive influences of Maggie. Maggie constantly complained about 'senseless spending'. The technology in their home was mid-eighties, at best. He remembered how she had fixed Patrick with a completely stunned gaze at his suggestions that it was time for his parents to upgrade to DVD. Had he seen, out of the corner of his eye, Marcus smiling to himself?

The back of the cottage was devoted to the preparation and consumption of food. The open-plan kitchen, thanks no doubt to Marcus' many industry contacts, was stocked with the very best, latest appliances. Patrick had assumed Marcus didn't like cooking, but when did Maggie ever give him the chance? She had an annoying habit of beginning the meal hours before they were ready to eat. The meat would be dry and overcooked, the vegetables bland and mushy. She had done the same for Marcus' wake and the pastries absorbed too much moisture from their fillings, the cakes were too dry. It was her way of keeping busy, of keeping anyone from beating her to the task at hand.

A large dining table looked through the glass doors at the rear of the cottage, over dense bush towards glimpses of the ocean. The back verandah was deeper than the front and sides, and another large dining table was placed in its centre. Did Marcus entertain here? And if so, who? Patrick started imagining the *other* Marcus, well read, well cultured, cooking meals for his guests as they dined in this tranquil setting. This Marcus was lively, knowledgeable and chatty. And this Marcus would have been flamboyant, unashamed to show off his success and share it with his friends. Patrick pushed this image of his father out of his mind. Had he entertained it any longer, he would have questioned why he had been refused a part in it – to say nothing of Maggie.

He opened up the glass doors and was met with the sounds of summer; the bell sound of a teardrop bird and the distant thunder of Pacific waves crashing on golden sand. Patrick took a deep breath and a feeling overwhelmed him – he felt peaceful for the first time in months. Perhaps he would be able to seduce Simon with this new life of his?

He turned back into the cottage wondering where to explore next. A wall of neatly framed photographs caught his attention. He approached them cautiously, half expecting to see Marcus guiltily smiling with another wife and children, signs of Marcus' other life that would only add more confusion to his already hazy understanding of the situation. There were a lot of photographs of Patrick – mostly of him as a boy, but also a few of him more recently, photos he could barely remember being taken. There were photos of Isabel the girl and Isabel the Parisienne. A photo of her and Marcus at the base of the Eiffel Tower, both looking a little awkward. There were photos, too, of Isabel the girl with an older boy beside her and a baby in her arms. This older boy had unmistakably Apperton features and a cheeky boyish smile. This was his brother! This was Jack. Patrick's pulse quickened as tears welled in his eyes. There was such excitement in this discovery of photos of a brother he had never known, of photos that were supposedly lost.

The photos hadn't been destroyed after all. How confusing it must have been for both his parents, to suddenly have their firstborn taken away and then to try to wipe him from memory. But the mind has its own pictures and the existence of a mere photograph, or its removal, wasn't strong enough to alter the images of the mind. How could Marcus have kept these from Maggie all these years?

There were others: photos of Jack as a baby, of Jack as a toddler, on his first day of school. The photo that sent his heart plummeting, however, was one of the Appertons as a complete family. The Appertons as he'd never known them and could never know them. He saw a proud, beaming Marcus looking like Patrick today, a laughing Maggie with a new baby in her arms. Maggie, laughing! There was also the innocent, beautiful Isabel crossing her eyes as a thin, tanned, shirtless Jack pulled her pigtails straight up from her head.

Scattered throughout the wall of photos were images of another man. He was very tall and classically handsome. Where had Patrick seen his face before? There were photos of the same man looking older, weathered. Photos of him and Marcus as

246

older men, the taller one always staring straight into the camera. Patrick remembered looking at his parents' wedding photos while Maggie showered. He recalled seeing the photo of the tall man and Marcus, both wearing their cheap suits, laughing as they shared some private joke. Patrick had forgotten to ask Maggie about him.

Patrick thought he heard the sound of tyres struggling up the steep drive. As though he had been caught doing something he knew he shouldn't, his face was scarlet and he hastily wiped tears from his eyes. Patrick walked around the verandah expecting nothing, thinking he had imagined the sound, but he found a strange car parked next to his, making the distinct clicking sounds of an engine recently shut down. He thought this might be someone to tell him this was a mistake, the cottage wasn't his after all. He was, in fact, trespassing on someone else's property, someone else's life.

The man struggled to get out of his car, slowly unfolding his lanky and ageing frame. He was impossibly tall but slightly hunched, as though expecting to hit his head against something at any moment. He looked like someone emerging from a helicopter, cautiously avoiding its blades. Here was the man from Marcus' pictures, suddenly brought to life.

'Hello?' Patrick called out, hating the timbre of his voice as he tried to sound authoritative.

'You must be Patrick –' the man said with a half-smile.

'Who are you?' Patrick's voice revealed a hint of confrontation.

'I'm Jack. Jack Catalano,' he announced, as though it should ring some bells with Patrick. The old man extended his hand to shake Patrick's. 'I've heard so much about you; it's so great to finally meet you.'

He shook Jack's hand but couldn't look in his eye.

'I'm sorry about your dad,' Jack hesitated. 'He'll be missed. I hope you know that.'

Patrick objected to hearing these words come from a complete stranger. 'So how do you know my father?'

'Oh, Patrick,' Jack sighed a little too familiarly, 'there's so much to tell.'

'Would you mind telling me what's going on? If another stranger tells me my father was a wonderful man I'm going to scream. So if you can explain some of this to me then come inside, but if not . . .' Patrick looked into the man's eyes for the first time and saw that he was unsuccessfully attempting to hide a deep sadness. Patrick decided to soften his tone in hope of getting some answers. 'You look like you could do with a cup of tea. I've never used the kitchen before but come in and I'll make you one.'

Almost sheepishly, Jack said, 'I know where everything's kept,' and this came as no surprise to Patrick.

Patrick sat at the dining table watching Jack make his way around the kitchen with a deftness that showed he knew it well. The tall man was surprisingly nimble, and it was clear that moving around a kitchen was second nature to him, as though his size allowed him to move from one side to the other without actually moving his feet. Patrick studied him carefully, trying to imagine his place in Marcus' life. Marcus who had apparently never had a male friend but whose secrets were so close to unravelling that Patrick could almost taste them.

It was Patrick who decided to break the silence between them. He had no idea how to begin the conversation so he decided to get the hardest part of it over with first.

'So, just how close were you and my father?'

'Well,' Jack said and almost chuckled before realising it would be inappropriate, 'I suppose you could say your father and I were best friends, we shared everything. I guess you might want to punch me or something –'

'I didn't ask for the commentary.'

'No. No, you didn't. It's unfair of me to make assumptions about you, Patrick. I suppose I'm just concerned you'll be so angry with me that you won't give me a chance to explain things properly. You'll probably stay loyal to your mother.'

'Loyal?' he rubbed his forehead. 'I don't know a damn thing about family loyalties any more, I don't think I ever did. All I know is my family is so full of secrets, we could hardly be called a family. Lies are the only things keeping us together. If we all started telling the truth now I reckon we might all go our separate ways. Either that or we would end up killing each other.'

'You can't hate your father for this, you know. It hurt him so much to be deceptive, but he felt he was protecting you all from unnecessary pain.'

'It wouldn't take a genius to work that one out,' he looked at Jack questioningly, 'but sometimes it's a bit easier to hide behind lies than tell the truth. You still haven't answered my question, Jack.'

'Your father and I were about as close as we could get.'

Even though he had suspected this was the case, Patrick was utterly floored to hear the statement. He felt so rejected by his father, so mistrusted, that it began to make sense to him why he'd chosen to push his family away. Maybe he always subconsciously knew about Marcus. How many times had he noted the lack of affection between his parents? Even as a teenager while his father went off on business trips, Patrick had convinced himself that Marcus would never return, that each trip would be the one to see Marcus join his other family for good.

Now this confirmation from Jack left a pit of anxiety in his stomach. He and Marcus were so similar – distant, secretive, deceptive – and yet even Marcus had managed to find someone he truly wanted to be with. It made Patrick feel hopeless, to have been denied this knowledge, to have been lied to all these years by a father who refused to acknowledge they had so much in common. No wonder his mother had similarly rejected Patrick. Though he often ridiculed her naivety, of course she would have known this about her husband. To watch Patrick follow the same path must have rubbed her face in the disappointment that she'd been trapped into living Marcus' lie.

'I'm sorry you lost him but I'm just astounded that you both felt you couldn't trust me with the truth. You can't be expecting me to jump up and down about this and hug you as my new best mate or anything. Marcus never ever stood up for me, never once made me think he respected me for being gay. And now you come along, a photo from my parents' sham marriage long ago, to tell me, "Hang on a second, your father wasn't the man he said he was". Well that's great, what a relief! And all this time I thought *I* was the screwed-up one. Now I know Dad's little secret everything can be better. Sorry, but I just can't buy into that.'

'Your father didn't have . . . He wasn't proud of the deception, Patrick, of his treatment of Maggie or you and Isabel. Deep down he knew marrying Maggie was the wrong thing to do and more often than not he was too racked with guilt to show anyone true love. You turned out to be everything he should've been but he could never show you how proud he was of you . . . and that almost destroyed him. He couldn't deny that he envied you.'

'That's ludicrous.' Patrick rolled his eyes.

'Is it?' Jack smiled, his voice remaining steady. 'Your mother had an incredible hold over Marcus. And you should know that he loved her very much. I don't think he would've survived long in this world without her, he wasn't strong enough to take the path you and I did. But at the same time, Maggie's inability to deal with you pushed Marcus away and it's the very reason they grew apart.'

'It's not like you're telling me anything new here, Jack. Forgive me, I mean, I've never seen my parents even close to intimate, and Dad wasn't exactly the most masculine man I knew, but it's dealing with the fact that he was leading a double life, *that's* the thing. Why couldn't he have just trusted me with who he was? And he never bothered trying to get to know me either –'

'He knew you better than you think he did. Have you seen those novels in there? He read everything you read; saw every movie you ever mentioned even *wanting* to see. He used to talk about you all the time, it drove me crazy! He cherished every tiny piece of information you shared about yourself. But he could never ask you to open up. He used to say to me that it would happen when you were ready to make it happen. How could he ask, or expect you, to open up when he was so closed himself?'

Outside, a brief shower turned the leaves a glistening gold and the animals were momentarily silenced. A wet earth smell crept inside and Patrick imagined spending his evenings alone here or perhaps with Leroy. Jack clearly saw the cottage as his too and Patrick felt an immediate dread that Jack was here to take it away from him. Why had Marcus chosen for Patrick to have it?

'But Maggie must've known about Dad and you,' Patrick said. 'How couldn't she, or at least suspected something was going on? Why stay trapped playing happy families?'

'I'm not one of Maggie's biggest fans. Sorry. But the decision to stay with her was definitely Marcus'. He felt a sense of obligation to be with her, to provide for her. Like paying for his sins, if you ask me. Now whether she suspected the truth? Well, you and I would ask how anyone could be with someone for forty years and *not* know, but it does happen, Patrick. People often don't want to know, so they just block it out. Either way, you can't blame Maggie for making him stay because, in most ways, he felt he needed to be there.'

'That doesn't really make much sense to me. What a sad man he must've been.' Patrick shook his head. 'What an arsehole to destroy so many lives because he couldn't deal with who he really was. *You* must hold one hell of a grudge.' There it was – Patrick's first sign of empathy, though he wanted to despise the man in front of him, he found he couldn't.

'Ah, no!' Jack said and smiled. 'I'm nearly seventy years old. Too old for grudges. I knew Marcus nearly sixty years and he could do very little wrong in my eyes, despite breaking my heart once or twice. I loved him like I've never loved anyone my whole life, but he was a complicated man and even I couldn't understand why he refused to be strong and tell the world who he was. I couldn't have married a woman, but that's me and although he broke my heart, it felt like only he could heal it again.'

'So you knew each other well before he met Maggie?' Patrick probed.

'Why do you ask?'

'I saw some wedding photos the other night and the one of you and Marcus got me wondering. I meant to ask Maggie about you but it slipped my mind with the funeral and everything. I wonder what she would've said, what new lies she would have told.'

'Yes. We were together before Maggie – in a schoolboy kind of way. Your father rebelled against it because he never wanted to be labelled. He used to tell me it was just experimentation, that all boys fooled around before settling down with a woman. It was never like that for me, of course, it was love and lust and then some. But things were very different for our generation and, of course, there was also your father's childhood –'

'I know nothing about that,' Patrick interrupted. 'He never spoke about it.'

'No, I know,' Jack placated him. 'He never even spoke of it to your mother, nor did she ever ask. Maggie's not big on details. Anyway, Marcus was an unhappy child for a lot of reasons and being with me, in some ways, brought back too much pain from his past. Maybe one day I'll tell you more, when you're ready.'

'Yeah, we'll see.' Patrick was surprised by how relaxed Jack made him feel when all he wanted was to show anger, to throw something against a wall, yell abuse, anything. But what would have been the point of that? What was the point in feeling anger at all? Marcus was a liar and so Patrick had never got to know him. It wasn't as if these revelations rewrote Patrick's history, what was done was done. 'How did you end up at the wedding? Weren't you miserable?'

'I went as a favour to your father. I was the best man. I meant it when I said I would've done anything for him. There were a lot of rumours about Marcus and me where we grew up. Appearing happy at the wedding was a way of silencing some of the whispers, it helped Marcus with the escape he dreamed of. I never totally understood the importance of the deception at the time, given that your father left town the day of the wedding and didn't return until his mother died many years later.'

'Jesus, that must have killed you, being best man.'

'It was the saddest day of my life, I think,' Jack said reflectively. 'But it also made me stronger. I suppose I thought Marcus was too good for me in those days and there was a certain romance to being jilted by a man I thought I would never have.' Jack went to look at the photographs on the wall, this odd collection of their separate and together lives.

'Jack, it feels like I'm supposed to hate you, but I don't see the point.' Patrick got up from the table and collected the empty mugs. 'Do you want another cuppa?'

'It wouldn't have surprised me if you hated me, it's a risk I've thought about. That's one of the reasons I didn't stay at the funeral, to confuse you on a day you deserved to have to yourself. But there comes a time when there are certain things children deserve to know about their parents. Deceit is a family legacy which has to end with someone. Let that be Marcus, let his death serve some sort of purpose. I wouldn't mind something a little bit stronger than tea, actually. How about a gin and tonic? Oh, come on,' he urged, 'just one.'

'Yeah, okay,' Patrick nodded. 'Why not?'

Jack got up from the table and got busy making the drinks. Strange that there was alcohol in the cottage given Marcus rarely touched the stuff. They took their drinks and went to sit at the table outside to watch the sun dry up the rain coating the eucalypts.

'It's a pleasure to meet you,' Jack raised his glass. 'I'm sorry it's under these circumstances though.'

'I dunno what to say, Jack. I didn't even know you existed before this week and now I find you're the key to unlocking everything I never knew about my father. Maybe I have no right to know?'

'Are you angry with me? It's okay if you are, I understand. Do you want me to leave?'

'No. No,' Patrick reassured him. 'It's all a bit overwhelming, that's all. You're welcome to stay here for a while,' he said, cautious not to extend too open an invitation. 'I'm going back to my apartment. I'm still a bit confused, and I need to clear my head.'

'That's understandable, I mean –'

'You know, I'm not really in mourning,' Patrick interrupted. 'I'm pretty emotional and I've burst into tears at strange moments, but it's not with grief, it's not about losing my father. I can't explain it. I can't mourn for someone I never knew and now that I'm finding out about him, I'm beginning to realise I will miss him. I just wish I'd felt like this while he was alive. I guess you've suffered a bigger loss than the rest of us.'

'Oh, that's not true. We're all going to miss him terribly, even you, you'll come to see. And Maggie relies on him day to day more than I ever did. I live in Victoria and come up here once a month or so I have my own life to lead. Your father was very much a part of it, but he wasn't my reason for being. Not like he used to be. Maggie, on the other hand, may suffer a loneliness that will make her a very unhappy woman. I tried to convince Isabel to stay but she wouldn't have a bar of it.'

'You spoke to *Isabel*?' Patrick asked.

'Yes,' Jack admitted softly. 'Just this morning.'

'She never –'

'I know, you can't be angry with her though. Your father swore her to secrecy and she promised him she'd never utter a word. I secretly went to Paris with your father, I was never going to meet Isabel but, in a city of however many million people, she ran into us by sheer coincidence. I suppose that was Fate's way. Your father tried to lie about me, naturally, but Isabel is one smart cookie and she screamed at him for long enough to get the truth. You know, I often blame myself for the distance between Maggie and Isabel. Your father said that once she knew the truth she treated your mother worse, blaming her for refusing to let Marcus go, just as you were inclined to do. I never quite understood why Isabel was prepared to accept your father's deceit but not your mother's.'

'I think it's because Isabel sees so much of herself in Maggie. Maggie stands for everything Isabel dislikes about herself. Marcus was always distant, Jack, he was quiet and unassuming most of the time, but our mother had very strong opinions and often voiced them. It's hard to explain, but I guess it all boils down to one simple fact: our mother never made either of us feel wanted whereas everything Dad did was for us. He made sure we got whatever we needed, he paid for our education, he sent us overseas –'

'That was your mother's money.'

'Maybe, but she never talked about those things. It was almost as if Dad paid for them without her knowing. It hurts to say this, but I can't tell you the amount of time my mother looked away when I tried to talk to her, how it was Dad who found the time to meet with our teachers, Dad who helped us find apartments . . . It was never Maggie. Often, when she spoke it was to tell us how strongly she disagreed with what we were doing. It was almost as if she wasn't interested in our lives because of the decisions we were making. Isabel took that hardest but I think I was able to understand why she couldn't talk about my life.'

A magpie landed at the end of the wooden table and looked at them suspiciously. Its yellow eyes darted between the two men as though it was trying to make sense of the conversation, its noble head contemplating whether a kamikaze attack or a simple escape would be most effective. Patrick pretended to rush at it, making it fly away in fright.

'Maggie and Isabel haven't exactly bonded during this visit...'

'Yes. Isabel wouldn't go into detail when she called from the hotel, she just said that she couldn't bear to stay. I've only met her twice and I was sorry to have missed her this time. Letters are a wonderful form of communication but they're not a pinch on being able to look someone in the eyes.'

'Running away is just Isabel's way. It's her thing.'

'It's mine too,' Jack said. 'I think she and I have quite a lot in common, those letters go back many years. I ran away for about twenty years of my life. Straight after your parents' wedding I sailed around the world like a floating nomad, never wanting to stay put, not getting close to anyone. They were wild days, Patrick, I was in a lot of pain, a lot of denial. I lived as though I was immortal; I was afraid of nothing and no one, except perhaps myself.'

'And the fingers?' Patrick motioned to the two stumps.

'Not self-mutilation or a barroom brawl, if that's what you're thinking. Something as mundane as chopping carrots on a boat in a storm, I'm afraid.'

'You should definitely invent a more glamorous story.'

'Oh, I have, over the years, never you mind! I thought you would prefer the truth.'

Patrick took a large gulp of his gin. The truth. 'So when did you forgive my father?'

'Oh, I always forgave him. Stupid, I know. I returned to Australia when my mother got sick. I'm convinced she faked it, just to get me to come home from France. The old trooper's still kicking and she's fitter than you or me, I reckon. I returned to Daylesford to be with her again and once I was there . . . It's such a small town, I got to know your uncles and aunts, and your grandmother. I think your grandmother always knew about Marcus and me, and she never forgave your father for choosing to marry Maggie. When she died in the seventies, I went to her funeral. None of us expected Marcus to be there, he hadn't returned to Daylesford in about twenty years. But he did come and I nearly died when I saw him again, he simply took my breath away.'

'You're beginning to sound like a romance novel.'

'Cheeky bugger!' he chuckled. 'But you're right – I can be a bit pathetic when it comes to love. So anyway, I'd been dashing off to sea every couple of years, going to as many ports as I could. I had no real reason to come home to Australia except for my mum and she knows half of Victoria, so she didn't need me. But then I saw Marcus again so I stayed.'

'What about the rest of your family?'

'My father drank himself to death and my brother, whom I loved very much, disowned me when I told him I was gay. Then he went and got himself killed in South America before we had a chance to make up.'

'I'm sorry,' Patrick said awkwardly.

'Me too.' Jack smiled again, a wise, knowing smile. They sat silently for a few moments.

'So you re-fell in love at the funeral?' Patrick broke the stalemate.

'I did, yes. But Marcus didn't, he was very hesitant at first. We became the best of friends without being...He'd never been unfaithful to Maggie. It took us years to get close to each other again and by then we were practically old men. It was very awkward, a lot of false starts. Your father would often leave in the middle of the night and not talk to me for weeks on end.'

'Why? Because he couldn't handle his own guilt?'

'No, I think it was because he felt so relieved and so excited he didn't know what to do with himself.' He said this in a matter of fact way. 'I think he realised that he'd lived an unhappy life, and denied himself so many things.'

'Did he begrudge having children?' Patrick asked the question despite already knowing the answer. The past few days showed him Marcus cared about him more than he ever said.

'Oh, God, no. He always said that the three of you were the best things he'd done in life.'

'Did Marcus talk to you about Jack?'

'Not all that long ago. It took him a long time to open up about him. I was the one who encouraged him to put the photos up on that wall in the kitchen. I'd never seen Marcus more upset than when he talked about losing his son. He loved that boy so much.'

'It's no coincidence he was your namesake?'

'Yes that's right, only I never knew him. He was killed before your father and I met again. It took Marcus many months to tell me the full story. Naturally, I knew about Jack from your grandmother, but I gave Marcus the time he needed.'

'Why the hell was that kept a secret, I wonder? Surely we would've found out about him sooner or later.' Patrick knew it was unfair to expect Jack to know the answers to all his questions, but questions were the only thing his mind could form and he'd be damned if he would stay quiet now, in the face of everything.

'It was just too painful for them. From what I know, Maggie blamed herself for his death and couldn't cope with the guilt. Marcus even considered getting her proper help.' Jack spoke the words cautiously, as though this in itself might cause Patrick to lose his cool. 'Neither of them knew how to mourn. Your grandmother Mabel taught Marcus some habits that make no sense to an outsider like me, but they were all Marcus knew. Did you know his father committed suicide?'

'No, I didn't.'

'Marcus discovered the body when he was just a boy. Mabel never talked to him or any of the kids about it, she just refused to acknowledge that he'd ever existed. Remember we're of a very different age, your parents and I, not to mention your grandparents. Not that I'm making excuses for how Jack's death was treated but you have to weigh up all the players, and the pasts each of them bring to the table.'

'Does Isabel know all this?'

'Jack wasn't my secret to tell and she never asked me about him. Our letters weren't particularly intimate and I'm not surprised she left without asking any questions. I think she used my letters as a way to understand Marcus better. I don't know your sister well but I think she is protected by the secrecy, to a large extent, I think she may not be as tough as she makes out. The truth does strange things to some people and, like your mother, perhaps Isabel is too fragile to accept it.'

Jack noticed Patrick's gaze had moved away from him and was now lingering off in the distance above the eucalypts. 'Patrick?'

'What?'

'You asked before whether Maggie ever suspected about Marcus and me? Well, if she did, and Marcus insisted their boy was called Jack even though it wasn't his name, then I could imagine letting go of my namesake might have helped Maggie wipe the memory-slate clean. If Maggie ever did know about Marcus and me, I can tell you now she's long since wiped it from her consciousness.'

'I completely disagree with you. I think you're under-estimating my mother. How could any mother wipe the slate clean after losing her son – the very reason she got married to a man she shouldn't have? I'm sure my mother knows a lot more than we all give her credit for. Put yourself in her shoes for just a moment, Jack. What a miserable life! It isn't self-protection that's kept her quiet all these years, it's probably depression. My father, now I think about it, wasn't the great provider after all. I'm sorry to say it, Jack, but he was selfish. Marrying my mother may have been a brave act for him in your eyes, but look what that did to our family. Look what his dishonesty has done to my poor, maligned mother.' Patrick raised his voice, something he had only begun doing since his father's death. He couldn't remember the last time he had felt such strong emotions and he longed to return to the calm Patrick, the one whose resolve was rarely affected by other people's intentions.

'I'm sorry.' Jack responded to his tone with calmness, always wary of igniting what he thought was Patrick's short fuse.

'It's not your fault, Jack. Well, maybe it is. I don't know ... It's not like I'm gonna take all this out on a complete stranger. I've been such a fool all along, the only member of the family to have no information and yet I jumped to my own conclusions. I can't believe Maggie's had to deal with all this on her own. You should've seen her, she was so weak yesterday she could barely walk. And what does Isabel do? She runs away again rather than stay to help her mother through. My father must have thought so poorly of Maggie, he's treated her like a plaything, taken her for an idiot.'

Jack got up from his side of the table and went to hug Patrick from behind. 'I know this is hard for you too, and I know I'm virtually a stranger to you, but I want you to know that I'm here for you, anytime. Any questions you have, anything you want to know, you can call me, okay? I want you to understand Marcus.'

Patrick got up awkwardly from Jack's embrace and couldn't look at him. 'Thanks,' he mumbled unconvincingly. 'Thanks for being honest with me. At least someone around here can manage a bit of truth. I need to be with my Mum now –'

'Are you sure that's –?'

'Yeah, I have to. While it's all fresh in my mind, I wanna try to make sense of things. And I need to do it now because if I don't, then I know I'm gonna think about it too much and

I'll just end up running away like Isabel. I don't want to do that. While I've got some courage to talk to Maggie about all of this, I'm gonna make sure things don't go back to being exactly as they were before.'

'Marcus is gone, Isabel's in Paris. You can't actually change anything, you know. You can just take all that I've told you and keep it for yourself.'

'I don't want to keep it to myself. I see you come from the Marcus school of thought but again, you're wrong, Jack. I *can* change things, I can show my mother I'm there for her and perhaps, for the first time in her life, I can tell her that someone finally understands what she's been through. After I speak with her I might call you, or I might never call you. I just don't know.'

Jack nodded and shook his hand, sensing that hugs were, at this stage, out of the question. 'It's your decision, Patrick, and I'll respect that.'

'One other thing, Jack. My father trusted me with the knowledge of this place. Even if you hadn't come here, the pictures on that wall were all I needed. Have you considered that perhaps my father trusted me for the very reason he knew I would be there for Maggie, he knew I could be the one to help set her free from this depression?'

'I don't know what your father was thinking.'

'You can stay here, like I said.' Patrick dismissed him and looked about for his keys. 'But you also have to appreciate that my father left the cottage to me. It's not yours anymore. Can I have your number?'

Jack wrote his number on a Post-it note and Patrick folded it in half before shoving it into his jeans pocket. Patrick took several of the photographs from the wall and looked Jack in the face.

'I hope I've done the right thing by being honest with you.'

'You and Dad *both* should've done it while he was alive. Things might've been different. People might, in the long run, have been a hell of a lot happier.'

'Drive carefully, Patrick.'

Jack's words echoed around Patrick's otherwise empty head and he rebelled against them. Frustrated, he weaved in and out of traffic on the freeway and pushed his car faster than he had done before. He remembered what Jack said about being invincible and he felt it now, felt the power of not giving a damn. All the deception he had lived through made him feel hollow and he no longer cared what was to become of him. Life or death, a family or none to speak of, a lover or alone. The only thing he craved right now was to get Maggie through the lies to help her find a truth to hold onto and in the process he hoped to be able to change the course of his own life.

He glanced on the seat beside him at the pictures he had taken from the cottage. They were tokens of the last thirty years of deception they had all suffered and in his possession they could be an effective antidote to Maggie's depression, allowing her to reconnect with the past, being the catalyst for her to finally grieve over the death of her little boy. Patrick felt more strongly than ever that this was his father's intention. He should be the one to walk Maggie through the minefield of her past. It was all coming together in his mind now – of course Maggie would rebel against Patrick's sexuality. Not my son as well, she would have thought. Not this curse that's trapped me into a life I never wanted. He must be a constant reminder of the mistakes she'd made and if he could only get her to express those feelings then they could be discussed in depth, deconstructed and dispatched. He wasn't so strange after all, his life wasn't so hopeless, everything was falling into place. He understood things now, he appreciated his position in the family and could finally begin to rights its wrongs. Time could only tell what this meant for his life, but he felt it was being resolved, just as his understanding of the past was being realised.

Patrick wasn't surprised to see Kathy's car in the driveway. Why would Kathy choose to have a woman like Maggie as her friend? How much more did she understand? He marched toward the house taking deep breaths and reminding himself to remain calm, not to rush into things. Maggie's response over the past few days was to go and lock herself in her room and refuse to come out. All he wanted was to tell her he understood. As he approached the front door, the house met him with its familiar smells – the air freshener, the wet-earth smell of a lawn that was perpetually soggy, and the lingering odour of the previous week's meals.

He didn't bother knocking and, as was his custom, he ignored the groans of an excitable Leroy who jumped at the front gate like a canine possessed.

'Patrick!' Kathy greeted him from her position at the head of the dining table, as though this were her house and he her son. 'What a wonderful surprise, we were just –'

There was something about the look on Maggie's face that reassured Patrick he was doing the right thing. He had been rehearsing his opening line for most of the drive but when he looked into his mother's eyes he knew there was no need for rehearsal, the more things could flow naturally, the easier it would be to get at the truth. Maggie looked charged, a woman ready to take on the world. He juggled the stack of framed photographs and beamed, hoping Maggie would be as thrilled with them as he was.

'Hi, Kathy,' he spoke calmly. 'No surprise, really. I came up because I really need to talk to Mum about a few things.'

'We were just talking about you, Patrick.' Maggie smiled, 'you've saved me a trunk call.'

Only she would call it a trunk call in this day and age, he thought.

'Kathy was asking whether I wanted to sell the house and I want your opinion.'

It wasn't the news Patrick was expecting to hear but it pleased him to know she was exploring her options. In many respects, leaving the family home could be the perfect first step to shattering the facade of the Apperton family. 'Sell?' he asked. 'If you think you're ready for such a big move, then I'd say it's a great idea.'

'Oh well, we haven't got as far as that yet,' she said. 'I might move in with Kathy for a while and then see what happens, see where my mood takes me.'

Patrick bit the bullet. 'Actually, Maggie, I wanted to talk to you about a few things.'

'Shall I put the kettle on?' Kathy got up from the table.

'Well, I, ah, I wanted to talk to Mum alone if that's okay?'
Patrick looked at Kathy, unrealistically hoping she might get
the hint that this was family business.

'It's okay, Kathy,' Maggie reassured her. 'Some things need
to be for family only.'

'That's fine, I can take a hint.' Kathy gathered up her things,
kissed Maggie goodbye and told her she'd call her later in the
day.

As the front door closed behind Kathy, Maggie motioned
to the pictures in Patrick's arms. 'What have you got there?'

He hesitated before answering. 'It's a very long story but
I've got something for you. Maggie ... Mum ... this might be
hard for you but –'

'What is it, Patrick?' she hurried him.

'I brought you these pictures.'

He placed the first photo of the whole family delicately in
front of Maggie and then studied her face, watching for
recognition.

Maggie picked the frame up and brought it closer to her
eyes. She squinted slightly and her hands began to tremble.
Maggie looked her son in the eyes and she smiled. 'Patrick,
where on earth –' Maggie burst into tears. 'That's my baby
boy,' she said between sobs. 'Oh my god, Patrick, that's my
John, my baby. I thought I'd lost him twice but these photos ...
Patrick, how?'

'Dad left them to me. They're for us, Mum, they're for you.'
Patrick laid the other photos in front of her. 'Are you alright?'
he asked with a waver in his voice.

'Yes, I'll be okay.' Maggie was drawing shallow breaths, her hands shaking as they reached for each picture.

Patrick pulled a chair up next to his mother and he sat with his knee touching her leg.

'Maggie?' he whispered. 'Mum? I want you to know I understand. And I'm, I'm so sorry for what you've suffered.'

'Oh, Patrick, I don't know what to say.' Maggie had no control over her emotions and was unsure whether she would laugh or cry. Her heart was filled with such warmth. She felt more alive, more whole than she had felt for longer than she could remember.

'You don't have to say anything, you just need to know I understand, Mum. I'm sorry and I'm here for you.'

'Do you know how long I've been waiting for someone to say those words to me? Can you ever understand just how much they mean to me?' Maggie wiped tears away.

'I can imagine,' he said.

Maggie was too choked to say anything else so she sat with her eyes closed, her mind replaying the days on which these photos were taken. It felt as though they didn't belong to her, that happiness was another woman's, so foreign to her was the feeling now.

'Dad had these at a cottage he owns,' Patrick began by way of explanation. 'Isabel told me about our brother after your argument with her. When I saw these photos, though, I just thought they might help you, Mum, help you deal with what's happened.'

'Yes. Yes, they will. I'm so sad but so happy. I've lost my husband and you know I loved him in my own way but I'm ashamed to say I can't help feeling that somehow . . . Well, a burden is being lifted and it's starting to feel like I can be myself for the first time since I was a girl.'

'How did we end up like this, Mum? How did we ever make it through?' He gathered up the photos and stood to make them a cup of tea.

'The truth is,' she heaved herself up from the table with difficulty, 'I honestly don't know how I managed. Other people have had it far worse than me and I suppose I just clung to that fact. I would tell myself over and over, "Well, it's not as bad as this," or, "At least I don't have that". Your father's cottage –'

'Did you know about it?'

'I suspected, but I never asked him. I never asked your father to explain anything because I didn't feel that was my place. He ignored my pain and I didn't ask about his.'

'Was the truth that painful?'

'The truth hurt, but it hurt less when we tried to ignore it. I guess we thought we were also protecting you and Isabel, trying to spare you from some of the pain we felt. But I know that didn't work, so I hated myself even more. The number of times I wanted to talk to both of you, to sit down and explain it all.

'I fell pregnant with your brother not long after I met your father. We'd never talked of marriage and I never expected that we'd stay together. Marcus insisted we get married, so we did, even though I knew it was a mistake. Do you know what that's like, Patrick? To enter into a lifelong mistake willingly?'

Patrick looked at her blankly.

'It happened before I could even blink twice. John was born in 1959 and your father insisted on calling him Jack even though I hated that name. I was not much more than a girl myself, I wasn't strong enough to argue. When he was thirteen, just after you were born, I took you all shopping. John and I had fought about something as insignificant as a new football, or some new game. I was suffering from depression, post-natal depression, only no one really spoke of it then and it barely had a name. We were crossing a road. I had Isabel...' she faltered for just a moment but regained her momentum to continue talking. 'I had you in a baby carrier on my chest, Isabel's hand in my right hand and shopping bags in my left. We were crossing the road and as he always, always did, John tried to help with the shopping bags. And I shook him off. I was so angry about his tantrum in the store that I screamed at him. "Just go on home ahead of us, John, I don't want you around, right now," I said. I wanted to punish him, to show him he couldn't be mean to me and get away with it. But he was shocked to hear what I'd said and he started running. He jumped out onto the road and I watched him get hit by a car. I watched the whole sickening thing, I heard the sounds – the squeal of brakes, the skidding tyres, and I literally heard him get crushed to death. Your father suggested we clear everything from the house – the photos, games, clothes, everything. I wasn't allowed to grieve; we were never to speak of him. We pretended it never happened because I would have killed myself if I'd been allowed to dwell on it and perhaps your father knew that.'

'I can't imagine how horrible it must have been. What you must have put yourself through.'

They walked to the back verandah with their cups of tea and sat facing the water.

'I simply don't know how I did it. I don't understand how I managed when there were days I thought I was going insane. I had such guilt, I felt entirely responsible. I wanted to, I *needed* to talk about it, but Marcus refused. Your father changed overnight, Patrick. He used to be talkative, affectionate to you kids, a genuinely fascinating man and then, boom! It all stopped. He'd made a decision to keep everything to himself. I blamed myself for that too. I don't care what any parent says – it's always the firstborn. Not that you love more, but they have a different place in your heart. John's birth was the greatest thing that ever happened to me and to lose him, to be responsible for your firstborn's death and to never, ever be able to speak of that pain... Could you possibly begin to understand that, Patrick?' Maggie was steely-eyed, retelling the tale as though she had not lived through it herself.

'That's not all. What else aren't you telling me? Can we talk about it now, Mum? Can you help me understand?'

'I blamed you.'

'Why?'

'I blamed you for my depression, my mood. I never wanted a third child, neither did Marcus. We had stopped making love, effectively, save for one of the rare nights your father had been drinking. And you were conceived and I didn't want you. The depression I had after giving birth was the worst thing, something only those who have experienced it can understand. So my yelling at John at the side of the road that day wasn't me, I loved him more than anything in the world. I'm sorry,

Patrick, for the way you and I have turned out but if I wasn't allowed to face my own blame –'

'I've always felt there's something you hate about me. I always thought it was because I'm gay but the last few years, I dunno. I don't think you're that much of a bigot. I started to realise it was just me you hated, maybe you just don't like the fact that I'm your son.'

'It's not hate. I could never hate you. I love you, believe that or not, it's the truth. But you more than Isabel, you served to remind me of that pain I hold deep inside. I haven't always been cold-hearted and I'm sorry if that's all you think I am. I suppose I have to admit I've been a spectacular failure as a mother and a wife. And when your life amounts to nothing but, it's a pretty sobering realisation. I'm trying to make amends, I really am trying. Isabel can't forgive me and I'm trying to start afresh with you. I hope you can try to forgive me.'

His heart melted to hear her so vulnerable, to understand how much pain she held inside. Whatever effect her words had on him was irrelevant for the moment. His only aim was to support her and to show her that admitting the truth would put both of them on the road to happiness.

'Of course I can forgive you,' he said. 'I've never hated you, I told you that. If only you'd trusted me to understand, to know you as a person, not just my interpretation of this character I call "Maggie".'

'Admitting failure, Patrick, is a virtue I don't have. I can acknowledge how negative an influence I've been on my children and both of you, you both seem so lonely to me. Your loneliness is palpable and every day I know I've helped to create that. I know this is, was, a family of four very unhappy people and John's death was the moment it all started going horribly wrong. If we could turn back the clock, if John was still here –'

'You don't call him Jack.'

'That was your father's name for him. It wasn't his real name and I never liked it.'

'Why not?' he pressed gently.

'I suppose you know about Jack Catalano, too?'

'Yeah, I met him today. So you knew about the two of them?' Patrick found this the hardest part, as though his own sexuality made him an accomplice to the adultery. He avoided Maggie's eyes, though he knew they were fixed on his face.

'Of course I did, Patrick. Marcus thought he was very adept at keeping that secret, constructing his intricate lies, but you can't be unfaithful for a lifetime and expect to get away with it.'

'How come you let it happen? Why did you let him lie to you, why didn't you leave him?'

'I told you we should never have got married in the first place. I knew that. Your father and I were good friends, great friends to begin with, but we never were good together in that sense. Marcus became my routine. There was raising you and Isabel to consider, the business, the house. You know I've never been alone my whole life, until now? I went straight from my mother to Marcus. Alone is the great unknown for me. We shared a dirty secret with John's death and in a way staying with Marcus protected me. We shared the blame as best we could and if I was alone I would've crumbled. I know it sounds silly coming from a grown woman but I was so scared of the world, scared of what I could do to myself. Marcus was my penance.'

'My father was a liar, full of deceit! How could he do that to you? How could he do that to us?'

'You can't blame him, Patrick, you mustn't. He was scared too, perhaps more than me. He loved you children so much and he shielded you from the truth to protect you from it, just like he did about John. I know he thought of leaving me, probably a million times, but he'd set up his double life and to be frank, that suited me just fine, on the whole.'

'But your husband was gay!' It was a word Patrick didn't like to say aloud very often.

'Don't say that!' she snapped at him. 'Not because I can't handle hearing it,' she added, 'but because I'm not sure that Marcus was, in the true sense of the word. I'm quite certain he never slept with another man his whole life. I never once saw your father look at another man longingly, never saw any evidence – videos, magazines – to suggest he was. I believe that he, well, I suppose he was in *love* with a person named Jack Catalano. I also believe your father found me physically unappealing, though to admit that makes me feel completely worthless. I indulged his other life because my life with him was all I knew and to contemplate one without him was, until now, beyond my comprehension.'

'You should have left the bastard!'

'I know, but guilt, loyalty, social pressures...When I fell pregnant, he made a commitment to me. I'm ashamed to say that even after forty years, I didn't know Marcus Apperton very well, nor did he know me. But I held on to that commitment of his and I pretended, as best I could, your father had no one before me, that I'd imagined the whole thing that happened before we got married. Jack Catalano always hated me and your grandmother forbade the marriage. I tried to ignore it, I tried to tell myself there were other reasons but I knew, deep down, I was your father's scapegoat. In those days, though, being a single mother, or having a procedure, well, I couldn't even contemplate those, so marrying Marcus felt like my best option. What other choice did I really have? You can't hate him because there wasn't a single day of my marriage I doubted how much he cared for me, for all of us.'

'So what about Isabel? Did you think she would learn to forgive you?'

'I'm really not sure.'

'But she knew all of this, all along. Why is she so pro-Marcus and unable to understand what you've been through?'

'I think she sees some of her own mistakes in mine. She can be a miserable girl and she lacks the strength to find out why. I'm her scapegoat too but I don't dislike her for that, I just give her the space she needs. I know she'll come round. Maybe it'll be long after I'm gone, but she'll work out I'm not the devil and, maybe, one day she'll even think of me with love. You might think that's impossible but I can tell you here and now that I've only ever wanted to see you both happy. I don't mind your lifestyle, I never have. Marcus was so envious of it, he was so proud of you, and I suppose that's what always upset me. I was an attractive young woman and no one ever made me feel it. I haven't wasted my life, but I failed it and now I'm not sure where to take it. It feels like sixty-odd years down the drain. You will both come to see, in time, that we're all victims of our past. The decisions I made in life, though rarely good, were made in less than ideal circumstances. What you do with your life is up to you, but it tears me apart to see you so lonely.'

'I'm not *that* lonely,' Patrick protested weakly.

'Yes, you are. If you can learn anything from me at all, that's it. No one should have to be as lonely as I made myself. You sit at Macmaster's Beach for hours on end, gazing out to sea –'

'How did you know about that?'

'I'm your mother.' Maggie tried to sound intuitive, but relented. 'Cheryl lives there and she recognised Leroy.'

'Oh right,' Patrick said to the ground.

'Yes, anyway . . . telling you all this isn't as cathartic as you might imagine it to be. I'm fairly damaged goods, as you kids might say. I'm not sure there's much that can change that. I've managed to remain calm telling you all of this, somehow. The only thing I hope is maybe you and I can start again. Things shouldn't go back to as they were before; we should never allow that to happen.' There was a hint of desperation in her voice suggesting there was more she should be telling him, but for now he allowed her to rest.

'I wish we'd had this conversation twenty years ago, Mum.'

Patrick got up from the chair and touched Maggie briefly on the shoulder. 'I'm gonna leave you the photos,' he said. 'I hope they can bring you some happiness. My whole heart is full of compassion for what you've been through and you know what?'

'What?'

'I think you're an amazing woman and you're going to be a brilliant grandmother. You have lessons to teach, Mum, and I want to know everything there is to know about you. Come on, let's take Leroy for a walk along the beach.'

Leroy

'He can sense something's going on, I just know it,' Maggie said to Brigette. Maggie was clearly nervous, sitting like a schoolgirl and biting her fingernails, frequently turning around to look at Leroy with compassion.

'You worry about that dog like he is human,' Brigette shook her head. 'Dogs don't have thoughts, they just *be*. They adapt to anything you throw at them, they are very simple animals.'

'Not Leroy,' Maggie argued. 'He's so perceptive. I suspect he knows exactly what's going on.'

'Darling, you have to stop worrying. The dog is fine. You are using him to vocalise your own fear, it is very plain to me.'

Brigette was right, of course. Maggie had never been so scared in all her life. Thank heavens Brigette was here to help her through. This was, for all intents and purposes, the first real journey of Maggie's life. This was the first time she would be leaving her flawed but comfortable existence to face a world she knew nothing of, and one which knew so very little of her.

'You do think I'm doing the right thing, don't you?' Maggie asked feebly. 'I mean, what if it's one huge disaster?'

'It can't be,' Brigette reassured her, sounding more French now that she was finally returning to her homeland. 'I know what I am doing, Maggie, and sometime you too will learn to trust in your instinct. You will regret none of this, I assure you. You are doing the best thing for you, and for your family.'

'It's just so unlike me,' Maggie said nervously. 'I never thought I would do something like this. I couldn't do it without you, you know that don't you, Brigette?'

'Nonsense! You are finding strengths you never knew you had, that is all.'

'It's funny where life takes you, how one day you think you understand it all, and your place in it. Then the next day it's all turned upside-down and you can barely remember your own name. We do adapt though, you're right about that. I think it's just human nature – you either sink or swim. I suppose I've found my swimming legs.'

'This thing called grief,' Brigette began, 'it eats away at you, at your capacity to love, and get on with your life. To lose your firstborn son, well, you know, Maggie – it changes you. It's as if your son has taken a piece of you and when he dies, so does that part of you. It is a light you passed on to someone else to carry, never expecting that light to fade before your own. That is never the way it is meant to be. So what choice do you have? It has taken us both so long to acknowledge that we are changed women. What I'm saying is that we need to embrace change in order to survive.'

'I still haven't cried for him. John, I mean. My son. I've not properly dealt with it.'

'But Maggie, you *are* dealing with it. You talk of him now. When you telephoned me that night, and talked to me about him, I knew you were beginning to deal with it then. And just to have that connection with you, to know that you have felt my same pain, I think you have made it better for me. I have always been able to cry about Andre, but now I can think of him without the tears. And *that* is the difference you have made.'

'Oh, Brigette,' Maggie began to cry.

'Look at the two of us!' Brigette wiped tears from her eyes. 'Couple of old ducks on their first trip together. We promised to make this fun, not morbid. You have so much to look forward to, I have so much to show you, Maggie. Did you ever think that life would suddenly become so exciting? That life would be full of so many surprises in your sixties?'

'No,' Maggie smiled through her tears. 'I honestly thought that was impossible.'

Leroy's insistence on standing the whole way made the journey that much more demanding. It was sweltering in the back of the car and he began panting heavily, having long ago knocked over his waterbowl by accident. All he knew was he was a long way from home, trips in this car always ended in discomfort, in a place where he was poked and prodded, and worst of all, sometimes made to stay the night. He planned his escape for when the car began to slow down, but the car was stopping and starting so frequently, he began to fear the journey would never end.

The car eventually turned into a very steep driveway and the wheels squealed as it struggled up the path. Leroy, still standing, was thrown mercilessly against the back window and yelped, not so much in pain, but in fright and indignation. How very unpleasant this whole thing was. Finally, the car stopped.

'Alright, Leroy,' Maggie said with a compassionate sigh, struggling to get out of the car.

Leroy began to wag his tail. If she thought he was about to go into this place calmly, then she had another think coming. He bounded around and faced the back of the car, waiting for her to appear before him. There she was. She was reaching for the handle. A rush of air and direct sunlight, a gap, and Leroy bolted.

'Leroy!' Maggie called with futility, 'Leroy!'

He didn't care where he was going, just away from people. He bolted into the bush and bounded over the scrub. He liked this place. So many new smells, new sounds, new places to explore. Almost immediately, he forgot what he was running from.

Back at the car, Brigette slammed the hatch closed and calmed Maggie. 'He will be back, don't worry. He must be parched. He will be back for water in a matter of minutes, you will see.'

'Ladies,' Patrick emerged from the verandah looking at the scene with amusement.

'Oh, Patrick! Leroy! He –'

'It's okay, Mum, I was watching. You know, this place is fenced all around and he won't go down the driveway, it's too steep. He's not going anywhere; I'll go find him later. I told you I should've picked him up.'

'He was okay in the car until the end . . .'

'He'll be fine here,' Patrick reassured her and leaned in to give her a kiss hello but Maggie hesitated for a split-second and the timing threw Patrick. It ended with a kiss near her ear. Brigette kissed Patrick on the cheek, marking it with lipstick.

'You have it looking beautiful,' Brigette said of the cottage.

Along the whole length of the verandah were perfectly manicured gardens. Bright, luscious native plants surrounded the cottage, making it look less like four walls plonked in the middle of nowhere, and more like a home.

'I've hardly lifted a finger,' Patrick said with embarrassment. 'A friend of mine has done pretty much everything.'

'A friend?' Maggie cooed. 'Anyone I know? Is anyone else here?'

'No, Maggie, and don't worry, you won't have to make small-talk with anyone, there's no one here.'

'It's not that, I just need to use the bathroom and –'

'Well, you know where it is,' he motioned toward the front door.

Maggie dashed off through the cottage.

'How's she been?' Patrick asked Brigette. 'Nervous?'

'As you would expect,' she smiled. 'I do not think she has any fingernails left! She has been talking a lot, also. Almost endlessly. You know how she does that –'

'When she's shit-scared? Yeah, I know!' Patrick chuckled.

'She bought tapes, you know? She has been practising her French with me. I have to say, for a beginner, she is actually quite good.'

'You're kidding?' Patrick shook his head.

'You would have no idea. She has read about one thousand books in the last six weeks – everything from French cuisine and history to how to be a good grandmother.'

'I hope you know what you're letting yourself in for, Brigette!'

'But Patrick, I think Maggie is fabulous. This change in her, she has been reborn and she seems to be taking everyone she knows along on her journey. Seeing Isabel is important and it will be great for both of them, but Maggie needs to go on this journey for many other reasons. It's given her something to live for.' Brigette was blushing, as though she had said too much or given some secret away.

'She's more energetic than I've seen her in ages, I'll give you that much. Come in for a cuppa before you go to the airport.'

Over tea, the mood was relaxed and jovial. Patrick couldn't remember the last time he had seen his mother so talkative or found her more interesting, if ever before. The change in her was overwhelming and at times he questioned whether it was contrived, or whether someone so set in their ways could genuinely change for the positive. She now had more money and freedom to do as she wished, having sold the business to Graeme, but her turnaround had also come through letting go of the skeletons in her closet, of facing the pain she'd kept hidden for so long. She was slowly beginning to accept that, though life hadn't been what she'd hoped for, there was still some time to make amends.

Things between Maggie and Patrick were better than ever. For the first time in her life, Maggie sent her son a long letter. In it, she talked about John and her marriage to Marcus, and how if she could live her life over again, yes, of course she would do things differently. Patrick read the letter through ten times or more, and then got into his car and drove to be with her. He had spent more nights with her than in his own apartment recently. A genuine friendship was beginning to form between them. They were both still hesitant at times and wine helped lubricate their conversations with honesty, but getting to know his mother was helping Patrick change his outlook on life. He had reignited his communications with several acquaintances, who had all remarked that the new Patrick Apperton was so much more approachable, so genuine.

'Now, it's the herbs I'm most worried about,' Maggie was saying. 'They always seem to be thirsty, and no matter how often I water them, they always feel dry.'

'I promise I'll check the garden every week. You've got Brett to do the lawns and watering too, it'll be fine. I still think you're mad, though, letting a fifteen year old spend every weekend in your house.'

'It's all about trust, Patrick.' Maggie smiled at him. 'Brett knows if he can do this, he'll have proved something to his mother and me. It's his first real step towards adulthood.'

'That's the new Maggie for you,' Patrick teased. 'Encouraging teenage drug-fuelled orgies.'

They sat in silence sipping their teas and admiring the bush beyond the back garden. It was gradually taking shape after many weekends' work. The area right at the back of the cottage had become a petite Japanese garden in the midst of unruly native bush. It had been Simon's idea and he had slaved long and hard to make it look just right. Patrick spent countless hours watching Simon without his shirt on, hard at work as the heat of the sun made sweat trickle down his strong back. There had, or so Patrick thought, been hints of a relationship igniting between them but Patrick was resisting his mind's lust, for now. Patrick promised himself that he would never lie to Simon, would never take advantage of him. Until Patrick was certain about making a definite commitment to him, he wouldn't complicate matters with intimacy. A month after Marcus' funeral, Patrick apologised to Simon by way of an expensive meal. He had admitted to being an arsehole repeatedly, and told Simon he had every right never to talk to him again. Most of all, though, Patrick spoke about the journey he was on and the lessons he was learning along the way. The question remained, though, was Patrick ready to become vulnerable enough to show love?

Somewhere in the distance, Leroy shot off a rapid succession of enthusiastic barks.

'He's probably found a brown snake,' Patrick joked, getting chuckles only from Brigette.

Maggie patted her chest. 'Don't joke about things like that, Patrick. Are you sure he's going to be okay out ... out *here*?'

'Yes, Mother. He's never going to want to go back with you.'

'Over my dead body,' she said bluntly. 'Maybe I should have left Leroy at the kennel after all?'

'There's no way I'd make him go to some dodgy kennel. You're only gone for four weeks and I'm a man of leisure now, Leroy can keep me company.'

'Well, Brigette, we've got a plane to catch.' Maggie changed the subject.

'Are you sure you don't want me to drive you?'

'No, it's fine,' Brigette said. 'Kathy will take us.'

'That's good,' Patrick said with relief. 'We've nearly finished the garden. If I work hard I should get it finished today. When you return, I hope we'll be celebrating the success of my magnificent water feature.'

'Have you got that present for Jacques?' Maggie asked Patrick.

'Yes. And you're not French *yet*, Mum. You can call him Jack, you know.'

'Your nephew's name is Jacques, Patrick. I'll call him by the name he was given at birth.' She pronounced it 'Zharkus'.

He watched her pause momentarily in front of the wall of photographs. She had returned the ones he'd presented to her, insisting he hang them back where they belonged, knowing he'd keep them safe. Maggie lingered longer than he thought was healthy, so he walked to the front room where he slept. He still referred to it as the front room rather than his own and, aside from the gardens, the cottage was still mostly untouched. Maggie followed him instinctively while Brigette got Leroy's things from the back of the car.

'I got him some Australian clothes,' Patrick explained to Maggie. 'To remind Isabel of his heritage more than anything.' He'd folded the small green singlet emblazoned with a beer logo in a way which hid it from Maggie so she wouldn't refuse to take it. It'd be too large for a newborn but Jacques could grow into it. 'And there's a letter and some biscuits for Isabel in here,' he handed her another package. 'They used to be her favourites when we were kids. I always hated the coconut, maybe she still likes it.'

'I am doing the right thing by going to Paris, aren't I, Patrick?'

'I think you are, yes. Isabel's getting better at this Mum, she's dealing with things. She won't leave Paris now because of the baby and if her therapist says seeing you is healthy, then she'll definitely make the most of it. It'll be great, just you wait and see. Just don't . . .'

'Just don't what?'

'You know, just don't –'

'Smother her?' It was the first time he could recall his mother accurately finishing one of his sentences. His silence was consent. 'I won't. I've nothing to gain by doing that, and I have everything to lose.'

They looked at each other in silence for a moment, thinking of everything that had happened since Marcus' death.

'He hasn't returned my call yet,' Maggie said.

'Jack senior?' They'd christened him with the name almost as soon as Isabel had given birth to her own Jack, as though it was inevitable that Jack senior would remain in their lives. Maggie nodded. 'He will; he said he would, didn't he? He just wants to make sure you're ready to see him, to hear all he has to say. I think he's probably still psyching himself up for it. You both loved the same man, and he doesn't want to do anything to jeopardise things, that's all.'

'I understand. Just tell him I'm ready, if you happen to talk to him? If he calls you, tell him *you* believe I'm ready.'

'I will, and I do think you're ready to talk to him. Now you go and have a good time and don't rush things with her.'

Maggie tenderly took his face in her hands and kissed him firmly on the forehead.

Patrick stood at the top of the steep driveway to wave them off and surprised himself by calling, 'Phone me when you get there,' to the back of Maggie's head.

Almost immediately, there was a loud rustling to his right and Leroy came to jump and slobber all over him. It filled Patrick with joy, this unashamed ritual of mutual unconditional love. Leroy moaned and whimpered with delight.

'Hey, fella! Hey, my boy! What have you been finding in the bush? What you been doing in there, eh?' Patrick petted his dog enthusiastically before calming him down with some soft strokes to the top of the head. 'Welcome to your new home, Leroy Brown, at least for a month or so. You've been dumped, old boy, we both have. She's got a grandson now.'

Leroy looked up at him and wagged his tail briskly, panting with excitement, happiness and thirst.

'Now come around the back, we've got a hell of a lot of perving to do today. Simon'll be here any minute and he's bringing my redundancy cheque with him.'

An hour later, Simon was in the garden fiddling with the water feature and doing his best impression of a Greek god.

'Did they get off alright?' he asked without looking up, his mind on the task of connecting hoses.

'Yep,' Patrick said. 'Now, what can I do to help?'

'Dig a few holes if you like.'

'Great, just what I felt like. Why the hell not? Nothin' else to do.'

Leroy walked cautiously towards Simon and began to lick his feet.

'Simon, this is Leroy,' Patrick introduced them.

'I know,' Simon laughed. 'You told me all about him on our date that time.'

They worked solidly in the garden until the sun began to set behind the tin roof of the cottage. The only thing left to be done was water in the new plants. Patrick sent Simon to have the first shower and remained in the calm golden light to finish the job. It was a stunning moment: the sound of running water, the sight of fresh glistening leaves and the sense that tomorrow would bring more beautiful things.

Maggie

Being in the presence of her son always rejuvenated Isabel and she found she craved his touch, to cradle his sweet-smelling head beneath her chin and to drink in his existence. She believed he was an old soul, his eyes revealing a depth of knowledge and a boundless curiosity hinting that he understood all he saw. Isabel could stand and watch him for hours at a time, utterly engrossed by all he did. Every day there was something new to observe and she appreciated he was the very reason she existed; her life had finally been given meaning.

Nicolette remarked that Jacques was one of those one in a million children whose eyes held you captive, one who'd hold the world in the palm of his hand when he got older. She noticed the change in Isabel toward the end of her pregnancy, a mellowing of sorts.

The pregnancy was a hellish rollercoaster ride of emotion for Isabel, sending her plummeting to the depths of depression some mornings, only to be riding the highest of highs the next, but the moment the nurse placed Jacques in her arms, Isabel knew she was a different woman. The sense of fulfilment she felt was a complete surprise.

Isabel lay in bed watching her son sleep on his first birthday. His little breaths were tinged with the last effects of a cold and she noticed in the corner of his right eye a tiny tear forming to roll down his cheek. He woke as he always did, with a bright smile to greet her. He giggled to realise he was sleeping in his mother's bed and he rose to his knees to crawl over to her, lifting her nightshirt so he could nuzzle her still swollen breast.

'Happy birthday, my darling son,' she said in English and he looked up at her and nodded, letting her nipple fall from his mouth as he let out an audible, satisfied sigh.

Isabel stroked his soft dark hair as he continued drinking her milk, one hand resting gently against her breast, the other placed nonchalantly against the pillow near her head.

'What were you dreaming, angel one?' she asked, this time in French. 'What brought a tear to your eye?'

She could have stayed like this for hours, just having him lie across her chest and looking up at her with unquestioning love. Isabel thought of her mother often in these days of motherhood. Maggie was a new person those weeks in Paris, teaching Isabel things about parenting no book had bothered mentioning. How bizarre it was to see Maggie touch her grandson with utter devotion.

'Today I thought we could go to the Jardin du Luxembourg,' she spoke soothingly. 'We'll take some food and cake and sing you happy birthday. Nicolette will bring you a ridiculously expensive present you'll have to grow into, and Jack senior will bring you treats he knows I don't like you eating.'

Jacques finished his morning ritual and laughed at his mother. He crawled toward the end of the bed knowing it was a naughty thing to do.

'And where do you think you're going, cheeky monkey?' She grabbed him under the arms. 'Trying to run away and get into mischief? Come on,' she stood him up, 'let's get you changed and bathed for your big day.'

Bathtime was his favourite part of the day. He loved the sound of running water, and how it splashed. The tub was a zoo of toy animals living permanently on its ledge, one always managing to find its way into her hair when she soaked at night while Jacques was asleep. It was funny the way routine became so unquestioned. Isabel still feared she was getting motherhood wrong, a final test to prove she was incapable of emotions most people took for granted. Often she wished Maggie was around to talk to and it was in those moments her heart filled with regret. But she adapted well enough to being a single mother and while there'd been some unexpected lessons along the way, it was now second nature to her.

As she was towelling dry her baby's tiny body, wondering what to dress him in for his special day, the telephone trilled on the floor next to her. It was another sound Jacques loved. Isabel quickly grabbed some of the sponge animals to keep Jacques occupied and answered the phone on its fifth ring.

'*Oui?*'

'*Bonjour, ma sœur.* What does the little tiger think of his first birthday?'

'That it's just the same as any other day, I think. But I haven't given him any of his presents yet and I'm sure he'll love all that wrapping paper!'

'I sent something over with Jack senior, is he there yet?'

'No, it's still quite early here, I'm just getting him bathed and dressed.'

In the background, Patrick heard his nephew let out a delighted squeal.

'Tell him his uncle said "hello" and "happy birthday".'

'Uncle Patrick says "happy birthday" Jacques,' she cooed at him. 'And he's sorry he can't be here to celebrate like he said he would.'

'I know, I know,' he moaned. 'Stupid me for going and starting my own company instead of continuing as a man of leisure. I'll get there for the next one.'

'Is that a promise?' she teased him.

'It's a promise to Jacques, yes. How are you, Isabel?'

'Yeah, I'm pretty good actually. I'm a bit tired trying to juggle everything but I'm okay. I was watching him this morning and I just feel so lucky to have him, you know? He brings something to my life I never thought I'd have and all the fatigue and the changes to my life – they mean nothing because I have this precious angel here in front of me. Anyway, how are you? How's Simon?'

'He's well. He's been preparing the cottage for the auction and we've been hunting around for apartments but I'm scared about the whole living together thing.'

'He's the one who should be scared! Come on, it's about time you settled down with someone, what's there to be scared of?'

'Me, I guess.' They both chuckled. 'I dreamed about her again last night –'

'And?'

'I miss her, Isabel. I miss the friend she'd become to me.'

'I enjoyed getting to know her, too. Having Jacques changed everything for me and I loathed myself for the way I treated her. I knew so little, I was such a fool. And then just as things were getting better . . . Do you think she knew all along?'

'That she was dying?'

'Yeah.'

'Maybe. She definitely started behaving weirdly and did all these things she'd never have done before. I mean, she ran off to Paris, for Christ's sake, who'd have ever thought she'd do that?'

'I just wonder if she knew before Marcus died. I wonder if she would've told us everything anyway, while Marcus was still alive.'

'I reckon she did know. I think she wanted forgiveness from us without it being tied to sympathy. I just can't believe how strong she was.'

'Are you okay?'

'I have my good and bad days, to be honest. I think to myself "I'm an orphan" and it kind of alters my reality a bit. I miss her existence more than I ever thought possible.'

'Now that I'm a mother myself, Patrick, I want Jacques to be my best friend, I want him to know everything about me and I trust in him that he'll still love me unconditionally. She taught me that, you know, and it's the best thing anyone's ever said to me.'

'Of course he'll love you unconditionally,' Patrick said with conviction.

'I know in a strange little way Mum is watching over Jacques, I think she'd just want him to have a better life than we had.'

'She's still a part of us,' Patrick said. 'And Jacques will come to know her through us, and through photos.'

Isabel looked at the photo she'd placed in the hallway. Three generations of Appertons, her mother looking content.

'For sure,' she agreed with her brother.

'Make sure you give Jacques a huge hug and kiss from me, okay?'

'I will. Thanks for calling, Patrick. It's sweet of you to remember.'

'Take care and have a great day with him.'

''Bye.'

'See ya.' They hung up at the same time.

Isabel walked into Jacques' room and watched him crawling to follow her. She got a fresh nappy from the top drawer and turned Jacques onto his back. She marvelled at the tiny birthmark near his navel and she leaned down to blow a loud raspberry on his belly. Jacques giggled with glee.

For his birthday outfit, Isabel chose something bright. Nicolette had brought him blue overalls he still hadn't worn. She slid his little legs into the pants and pulled his bottom up to slide the material underneath. From the third drawer she took a tie-dyed t-shirt she thought was cute and placed it carefully over his head before buttoning the straps of the overalls in place. She knew Jack senior would approve of the look.

'Yes, very cool,' she said softly to her son. 'You're my handsome man.'

Todd Alexander was born in Sydney in 1973 and has travelled to most corners of the globe. He has degrees in Modern Literature and Law and has been writing for as long as he can remember. *Pictures of Us* was inspired by various conversations with his mother. As they learned to relate to each other as people, rather than as 'mother' and 'son', new characters formed in Todd's mind. Maggie, Patrick, Isabel and Marcus were born to explore what makes a family work, or fail. Though this is Todd's first novel, his work has been published in several magazines and poetry publications. After six years in the book industry he now works as a marketing manager and writes in his spare time.